DARK TIGER

ALSO BY WILLIAM G. TAPPLY

The Brady Coyne Novels   *Hell Bent*
One-Way Ticket
Out Cold
Nervous Water
Shadow of Death
A Fine Line
Past Tense
Scar Tissue
Muscle Memory
Cutter's Run
Close to the Bone
The Seventh Enemy
The Snake Eater
Tight Lines
The Spotted Cats
Client Privilege
Dead Winter
A Void in Hearts
The Vulgar Boatman
Dead Meat
The Marine Corpse
Follow the Sharks
The Dutch Blue Error
Death at Charity's Point

The Stoney Calhoun Novels *Bitch Creek*
Gray Ghost

Other Fiction *Third Strike* (with Philip R. Craig)
Second Sight (with Philip R. Craig)
First Light (with Philip R. Craig)
Thicker Than Water (with Linda Barlow)

Nonfiction *Trout Eyes*
Gone Fishin'
Pocket Water
Upland Days
The Fly Casters—1946–1996
Bass Bug Fishing
A Fly-Fishing Life
The Elements of Mystery Fiction
Sportsman's Legacy
Home Water
Opening Day and Other Neuroses
Those Hours Spent Outdoors

DARK TIGER

WILLIAM
G. TAPPLY

Minotaur Books ✹ New York

This is a work of fiction. All of the characters, organizations, and events portrayed in this novel are either products of the author's imagination or are used fictitiously.

www.minotaurbooks.com

Library of Congress Cataloging-in-Publication Data

Tapply, William G.
    Dark tiger : a Stoney Calhoun novel / William G. Tapply.—1st ed.
       p. cm.
    ISBN 978-0-312-37978-0
    1. Calhoun, Stoney (Fictitious character)—Fiction.   2. Government investigators—Crimes against—Fiction.   3. Fishing guides—Fiction.
4. Amnesia—Fiction.   5. Maine—Fiction.   I. Title.

    PS3570.A568D37 2009
    813'.54—dc22

                                                        2009016570

First Edition: October 2009

10   9   8   7   6   5   4   3   2   1

For John and Kim Brady

ACKNOWLEDGMENTS

Sometimes it's about more than just writing a book. The kinds of help and support and encouragement and care that I've received over the past two years have enabled me to keep writing, and sometimes to write stuff that pleases me, at least. But it's about more than writing. It's deeper, more heartfelt, more, well, supportive. It's taken the form of visits, of cakes and pies and casseroles, of dump trips and supermarket trips, of animal-sitting and driveway plowing, of phone conversations and e-mails and funny cards.

So I need to thank the following people for their help and support, for their good wishes, for their karma, and, incidentally, for helping me to keep working on this book:

Vicki, my dear wife, Superwoman, who did it all, and is still doing it;

Our amazing kids, near and far—Mike, Melissa, Blake, Sarah, and Ben;

Our Hancock, New Hampshire, friends and neighbors, and especially Cindy's Knitters, and my Friday-night poker crew, and Kim and John Brady, and Chris and Diane and Katie Streeter, and Sy Montgomery;

Dr. Steven Larmon and Dr. Marc Gautier and Susan Brighton; also Ursula, Krystal, Sue and Jay; Anna Schaal;

My colleagues at Clark University, especially SunHee Kim Gertz and Ginger Vaughan;

My students at Clark;

My mother, Muriel, and my sister, Martha;

My cherished friends, including my college roommates from way back then; my very oldest pals from high school days; my Boston fly-fishing, head-shrinking, poker-playing buddies; and, all the guides and writers and editors and fellow fanatics from our happy world of fly fishing;

And my editor, Keith Kahla, and Fred Morris, my agent, whose flexibility and support and caring have made all the difference.

Chickadee Farm
Hancock, New Hampshire
April 2009

DARK TIGER

Stonewall Jackson Calhoun was sweeping the floor around the display of chest waders and hip boots when the bell dinged over the door, signaling that somebody had come into Kate's Bait, Tackle, and Woolly Buggers shop. Calhoun glanced at the clock on the wall. It was nearly two o'clock on this drizzly-gray Tuesday afternoon in the middle of May.

He looked toward the front of the store, where he expected to see Kate shaking the rain out of her hair. She'd told him she'd be back by noon at the latest from her monthly meeting with the people at the rehab place in Scarborough, where Walter, her husband, was living. Dying, actually.

Turned out it was Noah Moulton, not Kate Balaban, standing inside the doorway. Noah was a veritable flower garden of color in his blue Portland Sea Dogs cap, maroon corduroy pants, green cotton shirt, black rubber boots, and yellow rain slicker. He was pretending to study the rack of fly rods against the wall next to the counter.

Calhoun continued to sweep the scarred pine-plank floor. He happened to know that Noah Moulton disapproved of what he called the "blood sports"—fishing and hunting, never mind trapping—so it was unlikely he'd come into the shop to buy anything. Nor was Noah more than passing friendly with either Kate Balaban or Stoney Calhoun, who co-owned the shop, so this probably wasn't some kind of social visit.

So unless he'd just stepped in to get out of the rain, that left a business reason. Noah was the real estate broker who had arranged Kate's and Calhoun's rental of this space for their shop. Their lease was up at the end of July. Calhoun guessed that their landlord, a man from Augusta named Eldon Camby who'd made his fortune on an empire of Burger King franchises, intended to jack up their rent again, and Noah, who profited from the commission, had been delegated to deliver the news.

"Be with you in a minute, Noah," called Calhoun. "I gotta finish up what I'm doing here. You should take a look at those new Loomis rods. The nine-foot six-weight is particularly sweet."

Noah waved his hand without turning around. "Take your time, Stoney."

Calhoun swept the pile of dust and dried mud and rooster feathers and dog hair and bits of tinsel into a dustpan and dumped it into a wastebasket. He leaned his broom in the corner and went to the front of the shop, where Noah Moulton was standing with his hands clasped behind his back, gazing out the side window toward the parking area.

"Kinda pissy out there," said Calhoun.

"May used to be my favorite month," Noah said without turning around. "Flowers, sunshine, baby birds. Those were the good old days. Lately, I don't know, climate change, global warming, whatever it is, you can get thunderstorms, nor'easters in May. Snow, sleet, hail. You never know. Remember a couple years ago we had that blizzard on Mother's Day, dumped a foot of snow on folks' newly planted tomato vines?"

Calhoun nodded. He wondered what was really on Noah's mind. He guessed it wasn't the weather.

"So you're sweeping your own floors, huh?" said Noah.

Calhoun shrugged. "It ain't hard work, and I seem to be pretty good at it." He laid on the Downeast accent, which always seemed to annoy native Mainers like Noah Moulton. Calhoun guessed they thought he was mocking them. The truth was, talking like a Mainer came naturally to him, even if, as he'd been told, he did grow up in South Carolina. He didn't mind annoying men like Noah Moulton, either.

"I was hoping to catch you and Kate together," said Noah. He continued to look out the window, and if Calhoun had irritated him, he didn't show it. The shop's parking lot was empty except for Calhoun's battered Ford pickup and a new-looking pewter-colored four-door sedan, which Calhoun figured belonged to Noah. It looked solid and uncontroversial—the kind of vehicle a real estate man would drive.

"How about some coffee?" said Calhoun.

Noah turned and looked at him. "I wouldn't mind. Just black would be good."

"Pot's in the back. Why'n't you come on, we can sit and talk back there. Or were you interested in buying a fly rod?"

"I got all the fly rods I can use," said Noah.

Which, Calhoun guessed, was none.

Calhoun led the way to the back office, where he and Kate each had a desk, and Ralph, Calhoun's Brittany, had his dog bed and water dish. A computer sat on Kate's desk, along with a printer and a telephone and a fax machine. Otherwise, Kate kept her desktop clear and neat.

Besides his own computer, which he hardly ever used, and a telephone, Calhoun's desk was piled with catalogs and magazines and plastic boxes of flies and fly-rod tips and broken reels and snarls of fly line and hackle necks and dyed buck-tails.

When Calhoun and Noah Moulton walked into the office, Ralph lifted his head, looked at the two men, yawned and sighed, tucked his nose back under his stubby tail, and resumed sleeping.

Calhoun poured two mugs of coffee from the stainless-steel urn in the corner and put them on his desk. He pointed Noah at one of the spare wooden chairs, then sat in his own desk chair.

Noah shrugged out of his yellow slicker. He folded it a couple of times, then pulled a chair over to the side of Calhoun's desk and sat on it. He laid his folded-up slicker on his lap, set his baseball cap on his knee, and combed his fingers through his thick white hair. He opened his mouth as if he were about to say something important. Then he closed it. He reached for his coffee mug, lifted it to his lips with both hands, and took a sip. He swallowed, put the mug back on the desk, glanced at his watch, cleared his throat, looked up at Calhoun. Smiled and shrugged.

Noah Moulton was narrow in the chest and wide in the hips. Shaped like a lightbulb.

"So who died?" said Calhoun.

Noah shook his head quickly. "Far as I know," he said, "nobody we know has died lately. It isn't good news, though, Stoney. Seems like I should be telling you and Kate together, but I got an appointment in twenty minutes."

"Sounds like some kind of real estate news," said Calhoun.

Noah Moulton nodded. "Yes, sir. It is. Seems that Mr. Camby, who owns this place, as you know, he's got somebody wants to buy it."

"So you came here to see if Kate and I want to put in a bid for the place? Give us first refusal? That it?"

"Not even," said Noah. "It looks like a done deal, Stoney. You and all your inventory's gotta be out of here at the end of your lease."

Calhoun shook his head. "You aren't serious."

Noah nodded. "Afraid I am."

Calhoun shook his head. "That just ain't right. We've been here—hell, Kate started renting this place about ten years ago. You can't just . . ." He flapped his hand in the air. "It's not right, that's all."

Noah shrugged. "It's spelled out right there in your lease. Mr. Camby's obliged to give you two months' notice. Your lease is up the end of July, and here we are, just the middle of May."

"It still ain't right." Calhoun glared at Noah Moulton. "Whose side're you on, anyway?"

"Sometimes I find myself on both sides," Noah said.

"I expect it can get damned awkward for you," said Calhoun.

Noah looked up and smiled quickly, indicating that he had caught the sarcasm. He picked up his mug of coffee, then put it down. "Don't shoot the messenger, Stoney." He twisted his baseball cap back onto his head, then stood up and shrugged into his rain slicker. "You'll tell Kate, then?"

"Supposing we talked with Mr. Camby?" said Calhoun.

"Mr. Camby wouldn't take kindly to being threatened," said Noah, "if that's what you've got in mind."

"I thought we could appeal to his good nature," said Calhoun. "Kate and I, we might like to buy the place ourselves, since it's up for sale."

"You can try, I guess," said Noah. "On the assumption that Mr. Eldon Camby has a good nature to appeal to. Or you could convey an offer through me, if you want, since that's more or less my job and what I'm good at. But I'm pretty sure that Mr.

Camby's not going to be receptive to offers, any more than he would be to threats." Noah shook his head sadly. "He's already shaken hands and signed papers on a deal." He reached down and touched Calhoun's shoulder. "I'm sorry as hell about this, Stoney. You want, I'll keep an eye out for another place for you. Who knows? This might turn out to be a good thing. Find you a bigger shop, better location, more agreeable landlord?"

Calhoun looked at him for a minute. Then he stood and headed for the front of the store, leaving Noah Moulton no choice but to follow along. When they got to the door, Calhoun turned and held out his hand.

Noah hesitated, then shook Calhoun's hand. "You want me to start looking around for you, then?" he said.

"Can't stop you from looking," said Calhoun, "but I gotta talk to Kate, see what she wants to do and who she wants to deal with from here on."

Noah shook his head. "This isn't my fault, Stoney."

Calhoun patted Noah's shoulder. "Don't worry about it. Things'll work out. Thanks for dropping by." He reached for the knob and pushed the door open.

After Noah Moulton left, Calhoun gave Ralph a whistle, and the two of them went out to the front porch of the shop. Calhoun stayed under the roof and out of the rain, which had started in the morning as a steady wind-driven downpour but now, in the afternoon, had turned into a soft, misty drizzle, though it was still damp and chilly and unpleasant. He kept looking up and down the street, wondering where the hell Kate was.

Ralph wandered over to the side parking area. He gave all the shrubs a leisurely sniff and a quick squirt and decided there were no partridges or quail out there, so he trotted back up onto the porch and poked his nose at the front door.

They went inside. Calhoun went back to his office and

checked his phone to see if Kate had called while he was outside, but there were no messages.

He wasn't exactly looking forward to telling her that their lease had been terminated by Mr. Burger King, but he was a little concerned that she still hadn't returned from her meeting at Walter's rehab place. It wasn't like Kate not to call if something came up.

CHAPTER TWO

It was a little after four thirty when Calhoun heard Kate's Toyota truck pull into the side lot. He recognized the distinctive voice of the Toyota's engine. To him, the sounds that engines made were just as individual and distinct as people's voices. Calhoun guessed that back in the time before a lightning bolt slammed into the back of his shoulder and obliterated his memory, he'd been trained to identify vehicles by the sounds of their engines. He wasn't sure how much good this talent would do him now, but it did enable him to know when Kate had arrived without having to look out the window.

Ten thousand volts of electricity had wiped out Stoney Calhoun's memories of his entire previous life, which, he figured, was a mixed blessing, at least. As well as he could tell, though, getting zapped by lightning hadn't affected his talents and abilities. The last seven years—his new life, and the only one he knew—had turned out to be a great adventure in self-discovery. He'd learned that he could cast a fly and speak French, repair an outboard motor and shoot a jump shot. He could recite several Robert Frost poems and sing the entire

Revolver album and cook venison chili without a recipe, and he understood, without thinking about it, how to kiss and touch a woman—Kate Balaban, to be specific—in ways that seemed to give her as much pleasure as him.

That bolt of lightning had left him deaf in one ear and absolutely intolerant of alcohol, neither of which had proved to be much of handicap.

A couple of minutes after the sound of the Toyota's engine fell silent, the bell over the door dinged, and then Kate came in, stomping mud off her boots.

Calhoun, who was sitting at the fly-tying bench toward the rear of the shop turning out a batch of Dark Edson Tiger bucktails, watched her and smiled. All these years they'd been together, and he still had to swallow hard whenever he first saw Kate Balaban after not seeing her for a while. She was tall and broad-shouldered and slim-hipped, with the regal nose and high cheekbones and strong jaw that betrayed her half-Penobscot-Indian genes. She had long black hair, which she usually wore in pigtails or a braid, but today, because of her meeting with the doctors and nurses and therapists at Walter's rehab facility, she'd pulled it back and pinned it up in a kind of bun that somehow emphasized those amazing cheekbones and gave her an elegant, more formal appearance. Downright glamorous, in Calhoun's opinion.

Today she'd dressed for the occasion—tailored gray pin-striped slacks and matching jacket over a bone-colored silk blouse, thin gold chain at her throat, black high-heeled boots. Calhoun's breath caught in his chest. He liked best of all the way she looked in a pair of fish-slimed cutoffs and a ratty old Grateful Dead T-shirt and the pink fishing cap with her braid sticking out the back, but it was always a surprise how good she could look when she went for elegance, too.

He tried not to think about Kate lying naked and asleep in his bed with her hair loose and splashed over the pillow and the sheet only half-covering her.

Stonewall Jackson Calhoun and Katherine Balaban were business partners, best friends, and off-and-on lovers. Lately, the loving had been mostly off. Kate had pretty much stopped coming to Calhoun's cabin for steaks and sleepovers. Even so, there was no doubt that they continued to love each other.

Walter, Kate's husband, was the issue. Or, more accurately, the issue was the guilt that both Kate and Calhoun felt about him. Walter knew about their relationship and insisted that he was all for it, but now that his multiple sclerosis had advanced to this new, more ominous stage, they didn't feel right about enjoying the pleasures their own healthy bodies gave each other.

It seemed to Calhoun that they were waiting for Walter to die, but he and Kate never talked about it that way.

She hung her jacket on the peg by the door, unpinned her hair and shook the dampness out, and then came over to the bench where Calhoun was tying flies. She stood behind him, and he could smell the clean, flower-and-rain scent of her hair. She touched the back of his neck and gave his shoulder a quick squeeze. "Nice flies," she said. "Remind me what they're called?"

"These are Dark Edson Tigers, honey," he said without looking up at her. "Invented by Mr. William Edson, who lived right here in Portland, back in 1929. He invented the Light Tiger, too, but I much prefer the dark version. Dark Tigers imitate smelt. Good on the lakes for both salmon and trout right after the ice goes out."

She leaned over Calhoun so that her breast pressed against the back of his shoulder and took one of the Dark Tigers from the batch that he'd tied. "It's quite pretty," she said, "but it doesn't look much like a smelt to me."

"What it looks like to you don't really count," said Calhoun, "inasmuch as last time I checked, you weren't a landlocked salmon. Your pectoral fins ain't the right shape, thank God."

Kate laughed softly, put the fly back, then went around and sat on the stool on the other side of the bench from where Calhoun was sitting.

He looked up at her and caught something in her eyes that suggested it might not be a good time to tell her about Noah Moulton's visit. "Everything okay, honey?" he said.

She shook her head. "You want to know the truth, I'm so mad I could spit."

"What's going on?" he said. "What can I do?"

She gave him a small, unconvincing smile. "It's not your problem, Stoney."

"Walter, huh?"

Kate shrugged.

"Don't tell me it's not my problem," he said. "That just hurts my feelings. You and I are way past that. You got a problem, it means I got a problem. That's what loving each other is all about."

She smiled. "That's not the only thing it's about."

"You better tell me what's going on with Walter."

Kate blew out a breath. "It's not Walter. Not that he's exactly getting better. That's not going to happen." She shook her head. "It's his damn insurance, Stoney. Instead of getting my usual update from the doctors and therapists and caregivers this morning, I ended up in a conference room with folks wearing suits and neckties, some of 'em people I never even met before, including the damn COO of the place, a slick fellow named Gibson who runs a whole string of these facilities, got one of those smooth pink faces looks like he sandpapers off his beard and a sly smile that never shows his upper teeth? Anyway, they're all giving me this double-talk bullshit, and near as I can figure out, they're trying to tell me that if Walter isn't showing improvement from the rehab, after a while the insurance for it gets cut off, which is ridiculous, since MS is a progressive disease that nobody gets better from, and everybody's known that from the beginning. Anyway, if the insurance money dries up, they're explaining to me, as apparently it's about to do, it means Walter can't stay there at this nice facility any longer unless I can pay for it myself. Which I can't, of course, over five hundred dollars a day."

She glared across the fly-tying bench at Calhoun, and he saw the dampness in her eyes. Knowing Kate, he guessed they were tears of anger and frustration, not sadness, and certainly not self-pity.

"They must have had some suggestions for you," he said.

"Oh, sure." She gave him a big phony smile. "We got options, all right. I could bring Walter home and hire nurses. Or quit my work and stay with him myself. He pretty much needs someone with him round the clock now. Or there are places the government will help you pay for where you can dump a terminal person like Walter for the purpose of letting him get on with dying, if you don't mind the smell and the dirt and the crappy food and the lack of trained staff, not even to think about what it does to the spirit of the person you call your loved one. Or your own spirit, for that matter."

Calhoun wanted to get up and walk around the bench and give Kate a hug, but he could tell that hugs weren't going to help her right now. "What can I do?" he said.

She narrowed her eyes at him. "You?" She shook her head. "Nothing, Stoney. There's not a damn thing you can do. I got another meeting next week to go over my options with some of the people at the place, and meanwhile I thought I'd give Annie

Cass a call, see if she's got any brilliant ideas." She looked at her wristwatch. "Maybe I can catch her at her desk. I'm gonna try Annie right now, okay?"

Calhoun shrugged and nodded, and Kate stood up and headed for her office in the back.

Annie Cass was Kate's lawyer. Calhoun supposed they should talk with Annie about the termination of the shop's lease, too. He'd suggest it when he told Kate about Noah Moulton's visit. He didn't think this was a good time to dump more bad news on her.

He hadn't thought of any other suggestions. He felt a powerful urge to help, to do something to make Kate feel better, to get their problems solved, to get their lives smoothed out, but he didn't know what to do. Not knowing what to do was always worse than having a plan, even if the plan was dumb and bound to fail—and right now, Calhoun didn't even have a bad plan. It just felt like he and Kate had been pig-piled by the gods of bad luck on this gray drizzly Tuesday in May.

A half hour later, Calhoun was at the counter at the front of the shop talking on the phone with the Patagonia sales rep when Kate emerged from her office. She came over, leaned her forearms on the counter, looked Calhoun in the eye, and held up one finger.

"Hang on, there, Johnny," Calhoun said to the man on the other end of the phone line. "I gotta put you on hold for just a minute." He clicked the HOLD button, then put the phone on the counter. "What's up, honey?" he said to Kate.

"I'm meeting Annie at the Sea Urchin in fifteen minutes," she said. "We're gonna drink some beer."

"Annie gonna help you get this thing with Walter straightened out?"

"I don't know about that," said Kate. "Mainly, we're going to drink beer." She leaned across the counter and kissed Calhoun on the mouth. "I'll let you know if Annie comes up with something," she said.

He nodded. "Be sure to get some food in your stomach while you're at it. Try the fish chowder. That's the Urchin's specialty."

Kate ruffled Calhoun's hair. "Their specialty, as you know, is their selection of New England microbrews. Annie and I figure on sampling several of them." She kissed his cheek and headed for the door.

Calhoun watched her go. He still hadn't told her about Noah Moulton's visit and the bad news about the lease on the shop. Kate was preoccupied with her problem with Walter, and the opportunity to talk about the future of their business just hadn't come up.

He'd have to do it. He didn't look forward to it.

CHAPTER THREE

By the time Calhoun had locked up the shop and he and Ralph had climbed into his truck to head home to his cabin in the woods, the wind had shifted and the sky had cleared, and suddenly it was a pretty late afternoon in the middle of May. Through the open window, the wet earth smelled fresh and fertile, and in the slanting sunlight, the young leaves on the maples and poplars and birches washed the hillsides in muted pastel shades of mint and blush and lemon.

As he drove, Calhoun tried to figure out what to do about the lease on the shop. Noah Moulton hadn't held out much hope that Mr. Eldon Camby would change his mind about selling the building, and the thought of trying to find a new place and moving all their stuff was close to overwhelming. If that wasn't bad enough, there was Walter, apparently having his insurance cut off and getting kicked out of his rehab facility, and with no place to go.

When problems came, Calhoun thought, they came in bunches, and he wasn't exactly bubbling with inspirational solutions.

"You got any thoughts?" he said to Ralph, who was riding shotgun with his nose sticking out of the half-open side window.

Ralph turned to look at Calhoun, and the way his tongue lolled from his mouth, it was pretty clear that as usual, the only significant thoughts the dog was having concerned food.

Well, maybe Annie Cass would have some useful advice for Kate. Annie was a lawyer. Lawyers never seemed to be at a loss for ideas, such as, when in doubt, sue somebody.

Calhoun lived in a place he'd built himself, with help from his friend Lyle McMahan, in the township of Dublin a little over half an hour's ride by pickup truck due west of the shop in Portland. They'd erected it—it was more than a cabin, though less than a house—atop an old cellar hole that the Fire of '47 had leveled over sixty years earlier. It overlooked a little spring-fed stream named Bitch Creek, where native brook trout lived and reproduced.

Every time Calhoun pulled into his driveway, it reminded him of Lyle, who had cleared the roadway with a chain saw. Lyle had given Calhoun the Brittany pup he named Ralph, after Ralph Waldo Emerson, too. Lyle, just a kid in his twenties, had ended up murdered, facedown in a trout pond. Stoney Calhoun had found his body and then proceeded to track down his friend's killer.

The long dirt driveway wound through the woods and ended in a long gentle slope to the house. Calhoun turned off the road and proceeded no more than twenty feet before he stopped the truck. "Whoa," he said to Ralph. "Looks like we got company."

He turned off the ignition, got out, and squatted down to examine the fresh tire tracks in the wet driveway ruts. Judging by the tread and their depth and the distance between them, they'd been made by an automobile, not a wider, heavier vehicle like a truck. Their edges were sharp, and the dampness they'd squeezed from the compressed earth was pooling in them, which told Calhoun that they'd been made within the past hour or so. There was one set of tracks going in and none coming out. Whoever had driven down to Calhoun's house was still there.

Calhoun leaned into his truck, pulled his .30-30 Winchester deer rifle from behind the seat, cranked the lever to jack a cartridge into the chamber, and snapped his fingers at Ralph. "Let's go," he said. "You heel."

They slid into the woods and eased their way through the underbrush parallel to the driveway, Ralph trotting along behind Calhoun's left side, until they came to the crest of the slope that looked down on the house. In the open area in front was parked a new-looking Audi sedan.

Ralph growled in the back of his throat.

Calhoun touched the dog's forehead, and he stopped. "It's your old buddy," Calhoun whispered, "come to pay us a visit. Somehow, I ain't surprised."

He stepped into the driveway with the .30-30 tucked under his arm, and he and Ralph strolled down the driveway to the house.

The Man in the Suit was sitting in one of the wooden Adirondack chairs on the deck sipping from a can of Coke that, Calhoun assumed, he'd helped himself to from the refrigerator inside.

The Man in the Suit—all the times this man had come to the house to pick Calhoun's brain, he'd never mentioned his name—lifted his hand. "Welcome home, Stoney," he called. "Turned out to be a nice day after all, huh?"

Calhoun climbed up onto the deck and stood directly in

front of the man, who was, as usual, wearing a gray suit with a blue-and-red striped necktie. The Man in the Suit had first appeared shortly after Calhoun settled here in Maine after being released from the VA hospital in Virginia. He didn't trust the Man in the Suit. He didn't trust the government agency that the Man worked for.

Well, he'd been told repeatedly that paranoia was a common side effect of getting zapped by lightning, if it was lightning. He did have a big jagged scar on his shoulder and no other explanation for it, but even so, it did occur to him that important secrets might still reside in the inaccessible recesses of his brain—secrets important enough to kill to protect, or at least important enough to obliterate a man's memory to keep secret.

The Man in the Suit, who drove an Audi sedan and always wore a suit, kept showing up at unpredictable times to check on what memories Calhoun might have recovered. It was pretty clear that Calhoun had once known important secrets. It didn't take a genius to figure out that now, if he ever did happen to remember one of them, it would be prudent to pretend he didn't.

The Man in the Suit tried to bribe Calhoun with information about his past life. Calhoun pretended he didn't care about that. He was a lucky man, he said, getting to start over again with a clean slate.

There were times, though, when Stonewall Jackson Calhoun ached to know something about his parents, or if he'd been married, or, especially, if he had any children.

Calhoun looked down at the Man in the Suit. "It all makes sense now," he said. "Why're you doing these things to us? What the hell do you want?"

The Man in the Suit cocked his head and smiled. "What're you talking about, Stoney?"

Calhoun jacked the cartridge out of the .30-30 onto the deck, picked it up and stuck it in his pocket, and leaned the rifle against the wall. Then he sat in the other Adirondack chair. "Losing the lease on the shop," he said. "The rehab place saying they're going to kick Walter out. You didn't need to do that. You want something out of me, why don't you just ask?"

The Man in the Suit lifted his Coke can to his mouth. His throat clenched like a fist. Then he put the can on the table. "*Me* ask *you* for a favor?" he said. "You know the answer to that one."

"You might've tried before bringing all this bad luck into my life," said Calhoun, "and it ain't right, making Kate part of it."

The Man in the Suit shrugged. "I could've asked," he said, "and you, of course, would've told me to go to hell, and if I then proceeded to threaten you, you'd've just laughed at me, and so then I'd've had to show you that we were serious about needing your help, so time being of the essence here, we figured we'd streamline the process and show you we were serious before asking you." He gave Calhoun a quick flash of his gray, humorless smile. "So now you know how serious we are about this. You want to lose your shop, and you want Kate's husband out on the sidewalk in his wheelchair, all you've got to do is say no to me."

"What if I say yes?" said Calhoun.

"Mr. Eldon Camby's buyer changes his mind," said the Man in the Suit, "and the shop's lease comes up for renewal. Meanwhile, a vice president in the insurance company's corporate headquarters in New York overrules the folks in the Maine office, and Walter's place in that nice rehab facility in Scarborough is secured for the rest of his life."

"When?"

"Just as soon as I've got your word, Stoney. Tomorrow. This weekend at the latest. We haven't got a lot of time. It's up to you."

"I don't know what you want from me."

"No," said the Man in the Suit, "you don't, and you're not getting it from me. I don't have any details anyway, nor would I be authorized to share them with you if I did. I just need you to agree to do it. I guess you've got to trust me. All I can say is that it's something you're uniquely suited to do. In fact, there's nobody else we know of with the combination of skills and knowledge and personality required by this job. Only you. If there were somebody else, I probably wouldn't be here talking to a hostile man with no memory who doesn't like me. On the other hand, Stoney, we've been taking good care of you all these years because we figured the day would come when you'd want to say thank you, make things even, and I bet you've understood that all along."

"You saying I owe this to you?" said Calhoun.

The Man in the Suit nodded. "Absolutely. Well, not me personally. You might say, your country is calling you. It needs you, and here's your chance to pay back your country for all it's done for you. It'll take maybe a month—six weeks at the outside—of your life."

"Six weeks away from the shop," said Calhoun, "right at the height of the fishing season. Our busiest time."

"That's right. Too bad. Can't be helped." The Man in the Suit looked hard at Calhoun. "You must not tell Kate—or your friend the sheriff, or anybody else, for that matter—what you're doing or where you're going. Not even a hint. You understand that, right?"

Calhoun shrugged. "So if I agree to do this—before you even tell me what it is—you'll take care of the lease on the shop and guarantee that Walter will always have a spot in that rehab place?"

"You've got my word on it," said the Man in the Suit. "Tomorrow. If you agree to do this right now, I'll see that both matters are resolved tomorrow."

Calhoun cocked his head and smiled. "Your word."

"I've never lied to you, Stoney. I've always been absolutely straight with you. You might not like me or what I do, but you've got to admit, I've always been a man of my word."

"I was going to shoot you the first time you trespassed on my property," Calhoun said. "I still sometimes think it was a mistake not to."

"If not me," said the Man in the Suit, "it just would've been somebody else. No matter how deep in the Maine woods you go, we'll always have you in our sights."

"So okay," said Calhoun. "I obviously got no choice. So I'll do it, whatever it is. What happens next?"

"Next," said the Man in the Suit, "you'll get a call from a man who calls himself Mr. Brescia."

"Brescia," said Calhoun.

"He goes by Mister," he said. "*Mr.* Brescia. He'll give you the details."

"When?"

"Pretty soon, I'd expect," said the Man in the Suit. "We've got something pretty urgent going on, Stoney. Like I say, your country needs you."

CHAPTER FOUR

A little before noontime the next morning Calhoun was sitting in one of the wooden rocking chairs on the front porch of the shop sipping coffee with the Orvis sales rep, who said he wanted to talk about their new line of waders and wading boots, but who seemed even more interested in telling Calhoun about his recent bonefishing trip to the Bahamas.

Calhoun had never fished for bonefish. He had a lot of questions. He figured one of these winters he and Kate would shut down the shop for the month of February or March and go someplace equatorial and fish for tarpon and bonefish and permit and snook. Venezeula, maybe. Or Belize. As much as he loved the coming of springtime, Calhoun didn't think he'd ever get used to those damn New England winters.

The Orvis guy's name was Rumley, and everybody called him Rummie. He was a young guy—barely thirty, Calhoun guessed—and he seemed way more interested in fishing than in selling waders, although with all of his stories and his general enthusiasm for fishing, he was actually a very effective salesman. Calhoun was all set to stock some of the new Orvis stuff, just because he liked talking with Rummie and always looked forward to his visits.

He heard the phone ring inside the shop, and a minute later Kate, who'd been at the counter, poked her head out. She gave Rummie a quick smile, then looked at Calhoun. "I got an important call I want to take in my office," she said. "Could you watch the front of the store?"

He nodded. "Sure." He stood up. "You want to come in, talk some more, add to my discontent because I've never waded a bonefish flat?" he said to Rummie.

Rummie shook his head. "Miles to go before I sleep, Stoney. You got the catalog and my card. Give me a call."

"And if you don't hear from me," said Calhoun, "you'll call me, right?"

Rummie smiled. "We got the best waders and boots in the world. I wouldn't feel right if you and Kate didn't stock them. I'll call you."

They stood up and shook hands. Rummie headed for the parking area beside the shop. Calhoun went inside.

There were a few customers milling around, mumbling to each other and stirring their forefingers around in the fly bins. A couple of them, guys who often dropped in during their lunch hours, looked up at Stoney and nodded by way of saying hello. Calhoun nodded back at them.

He looked toward Kate's glassed-in office at the rear of the store. He could see her with both elbows on her desk leaning forward holding the telephone tight to her ear. Her hair was spilling over the side of her face so that Calhoun couldn't see her expression, but her neck and shoulders looked tense. He hoped to hell it wasn't more bad news.

Ten minutes later she opened her office door and came to the front of the shop. She was frowning and shaking her head.

"What's up, honey?" said Calhoun.

"Damned if I know," said Kate. "That was Mr. Gibson himself calling me. The bigwig from that big national string of rehab facilities? The man who smiles with no teeth, who just yesterday was telling me how they had to kick Walter out because the insurance had got cut off? Well, today Mr. Gibson is telling me how he personally got the Powers That Be—that's what he called 'em, Stoney, the Powers That Be, all caps, as if they were some big damned church mucky-mucks or something—how he personally got them to reverse their decision, and now Mr. Gibson himself is guaranteeing that Walter will always have a place there in his Scarborough facility."

"Well," said Calhoun. "That's great."

Kate was still frowning. "It is. I know."

"The best kind of news."

"Annie said she was going to make some calls," said Kate. "She said it wasn't right and she'd do her damnedest to get it straightened out, but I didn't believe it'd be that easy."

"What's right is right," said Calhoun. "This is right. Don't matter how it came to be, does it?"

Kate looked at him and smiled. "No, I guess it doesn't. It's a giant relief. I just don't understand what happened, that's all."

Thank the Man in the Suit, thought Calhoun. *He created the problem, just to show me that he could, and then he solved it. Damn him.*

Calhoun went over to Kate and touched her hand. "I'm glad about it," he said, "no matter why it happened. You have a good time with Annie last night?"

Kate gave his hand a quick a squeeze, then stepped away from him. She didn't like to show their relationship in the shop, especially when there were customers around. "We got good and drunk was about all," she said. "Gotta admit I'm feeling a little queasy today. Annie's a lot of fun, but I never honestly thought she was such a hot-shit lawyer. I gotta call her, tell her what's going on, thank her."

Calhoun smiled. "You should definitely do that."

Noah Moulton showed up around three that afternoon. Kate was behind the counter at the front of the store, and Calhoun was talking to a customer about the new line of Loomis fly rods. He watched as Noah glanced at Kate, then spotted Calhoun.

Calhoun quickly asked the customer to excuse him for a minute and went to the front of the store so he could intercept Noah. But it was too late. Noah had set his elbows on the counter. Kate was just turning to see what Noah Moulton had to say.

"Noah," said Calhoun, fixing the real estate guy with a hard look, "you need to talk to me?"

"I want to talk to both of you," he said. "Good news."

Calhoun went with it. "Good news, huh?" He glanced at Kate. She was frowning at Noah.

"Mr. Camby changed his mind," said Noah. "Decided not to sell after all. We're working up a renewal contract for you and wondered how you'd feel about five years, guaranteed no increase in rent, provided you folks spruce up your sign and continue to have somebody mow the grass and clip the shrubs and weed the gardens once in a while. How's that sound?"

Calhoun shook his head. "We can't guarantee you we'll stay here for another five years."

"No increase in rent?" said Kate.

"That's right," said Noah. "In return for normal mainte-nance."

"We need to have an out," said Calhoun. "You don't know what's going to happen in five years."

"It's a good deal, Stoney," said Kate. "Worst case, we might have to sublet it."

"We can work out the details another time," said Noah. "I just wanted to tell you first thing that you don't have to worry about getting evicted after all. Figured you'd want to know." He held out his hand to Kate, who shook it, and then to Calhoun, who shrugged and shook it, too.

Noah headed for the door, then stopped and turned back. "I'll talk to Mr. Camby about building some options into your lease," he said. "I don't see any problems."

Then, with a ding of the bell over the door, Noah Moulton was gone.

Calhoun gave Kate a smile, then went back to the customer who needed a new fly rod. Kate returned to her office.

After the customer left with an aluminum tube containing one of the new Loomis four-weights under his arm, Calhoun went to Kate's office and tapped his knuckle on the glass.

Kate looked up, frowned, and jerked her head for Calhoun to come in.

He went in and sat in the straight-backed wooden chair beside her desk.

Kate glared at him. "So what the hell was that?" she said.

"What?"

"Noah Moulton. Evicting us? Was I supposed to know what he was talking about?"

Calhoun shrugged. "He came in yesterday while you were in Scarborough. I was going to tell you, but you were so upset about Walter I figured I'd wait on it. I didn't want to add any more to your worries."

"You had no right to do that." Kate's eyes narrowed. "You listen to me, Stonewall Jackson Calhoun. I do not need some man protecting me. If there is bad news, I want to know it, and you have no right to keep it from me. Do you understand what I'm saying?"

"Yes, ma'am."

"And don't, for Christ's sake, call me ma'am."

"I'm sorry, darlin'." Calhoun was trying not to smile.

"Or that, either, God damn it."

"Mr. Elton Camby," said Calhoun, "had made a deal to sell this place out from under us. That was yesterday. Today he changes his mind and wants to give us a favorable new lease. Why don't we just call it good news?"

"Because," said Kate, "you betrayed me. You betrayed my trust." She was getting wound up. Calhoun knew there was nothing he could do but ride it out when Kate got wound up like this. "I thought," she said, "that I could count on you to share things with me like partners. Instead you're making decisions to keep things from me because you think they'll make poor weak little female me sad and upset and maybe I'll cry. So let me repeat myself. I do not want to be protected. We are equals in this. In our business and in our . . . our relationship. If you can't show me that kind of respect, that will be the end of us. Do you get it?"

"I get it," said Calhoun. "You're right. I'm sorry."

"Well, okay, then," said Kate.

"Okay," said Calhoun.

"Equals," she said.

"Sure." He nodded. "Equals."

She looked out through the glass into the store. "Customers all gone?"

"Place is empty except for you and me and Ralph, and he's snoozing out there by the fly-tying bench."

Kate got up from her chair, came over, and looked down at Calhoun. Then she sat on his lap facing him with her legs straddling his thighs. She touched his face, leaned forward, put both arms around his neck, and gave him a long wet kiss on the mouth.

Calhoun had to resist the powerful urge to put his hands on her butt and pull her tight against him. He satisfied himself by stroking her hair.

After a minute she pulled her face away. She touched his lips with her fingertip. "I'm pretty mad at you," she said softly.

"Can't blame you," he said.

"But I suppose your heart's in the right place."

"It's thumpin' pretty hard right now," said Calhoun. "I can tell you that much."

"And I am pretty happy about Walter," she said. "Also about not getting evicted from our shop."

"Me, too."

"I feel like we should celebrate, Stoney."

"Every day's a celebration, honey."

Kate smiled. "How's about tonight you pour me a short glass of bourbon and branch, toss me a green salad, broil me a T-bone, bake me a potato?"

"I think I remember how to do those things," he said. "Though it has been a while."

Kate wiggled her butt in his lap and bent to him and curtained his face with her hair and held him tight against her and kissed him again, hard and deep, and even as he felt every muscle and nerve ending and blood vessel in his body respond to her, all he could think was *I should tell her right now that I'm going to have to go away for a month or more on some kind of damned mission for the Man in the Suit and somebody who calls himself Mr. Brescia. That is the price we've got to pay for me being who I am.*

But he didn't want to spoil the moment. So he said nothing.

CHAPTER FIVE

A little before seven o'clock that evening, Calhoun was sitting in one of the Adirondack chairs out on his deck sipping from a can of Coke. Ralph, who'd already had his supper, was sprawled beside him. They were listening to the gurgle of Bitch Creek, the lovely little trout stream that ran through the woods and under the burned-out bridge behind his house, and enjoying the warmth of the late-day May sunshine. They were only a few weeks shy of the summer solstice, and even at this time in the early evening, the sun had not yet descended below the treetops.

The charcoal grill was lit. Kate's bottle of Old Grand-Dad had been dusted off and was sitting on the kitchen table. The rib eyes had been rubbed with sea salt and ground pepper. The Maine russets were brushed with olive oil and wrapped in aluminum foil. The greens and other fixings were ready to be sliced and tossed with oil and vinegar in the big wooden salad bowl.

Calhoun was never sure when she'd arrive. She usually visited Walter after they closed the shop. Sometimes she found him sleeping and didn't linger. Sometimes she stayed awhile and watched TV with him. Sometimes they talked. Sometimes they argued.

Calhoun didn't mind waiting, and he didn't mind not knowing when he'd hear her truck come growling down his driveway. In fact, he kind of enjoyed the suspense of it. Kate Balaban was worth waiting for.

When the phone inside the house rang, he mumbled, "Oh, shit," thinking it might be Kate telling him she wouldn't be coming this evening after all. That sometimes happened.

Calhoun always said, "Well, all right, then," trying not to let her hear his disappointment.

He got up, and Ralph scrambled to his feet and pressed his nose against the screen door. They went inside, and Calhoun took the phone off its wall hook. "Calhoun," he said.

"Stonewall Jackson Calhoun?" A man's deep voice he didn't recognize.

"This is Calhoun. Who's this?"

"It's Mr. Brescia. You've been expecting my call." He made it a statement, not a question.

Brescia was the guy the Man in the Suit had said would be calling. Excuse me. *Mr.* Brescia. Calhoun wondered about a man who referred to himself as Mister. He guessed Brescia wasn't his real name.

"I'm kind of busy here right now," said Calhoun. "Can't this wait?"

"Tomorrow morning," said Mr. Brescia. "Eleven o'clock at the coffee shop down the street from the Stroudwater Inn. You know where that is?"

"I do," said Calhoun.

"I'll see you then and there," said Mr. Brescia, and then he disconnected.

Calhoun hung up the phone. "Looks like it's happening," he said to Ralph.

The sun had settled behind the treeline, and the bats and swallows were chasing blackflies and mosquitoes around the opening in the woods where Calhoun's house stood when he heard the throaty second-gear grumble of Kate's Toyota pickup coming down his driveway. He stood up and went to the deck rail. Ralph scurried down the steps.

Kate's truck pulled in beside Calhoun's Ford pickup, and then she stepped out. She was wearing a pair of tight, faded blue jeans and a man's blue oxford shirt with the tails tied across her belly. Sandals with silverwork on the straps. Long dangly turquoise-and-silver earrings. Matching necklace. She'd braided her hair into two pigtails, which hung over the front of her shoulders.

He had to swallow back his heart, which had crawled up into his throat.

Kate scooched down so that Ralph could lick her face, then looked up at Calhoun and waved. "I'm about starved," she said.

"We got food, if that's what you're after."

"What else would I be after?" She came up the stairs and stepped into Calhoun's hug. She wrapped her arms around his neck and kissed him long and hard. He held her tight against his body, and after a minute she slid her mouth away from his and said, "Oh, my goodness. Will anything get cold if we don't eat right away?"

"The charcoal actually needs another hour or so to burn down to good cookin' coals," he said.

Kate grabbed his hand. "Come on, then, Mister Stonewall. We got no time to waste." She dragged him to the bedroom.

Around midnight they were sitting out on the deck. Kate was wearing a pair of Calhoun's sweatpants and one of his flannel shirts. She was sipping another glass of Old Grand-Dad on the rocks. Calhoun sat in the chair beside her holding a mug of black coffee in both hands.

They'd made love. They'd dozed. They'd cooked dinner, and they'd eaten it. They'd cleaned up the kitchen. Calhoun still didn't know whether Kate was planning to spend the night. Sometimes she did, and sometimes she kissed him good-bye and climbed into her truck and went home. He'd never figured out what impelled her to stay or to leave. It didn't matter. He liked it better when she stayed, and she knew that, but he guessed she had the right to decide for herself what she felt like doing, so he never argued with her.

The almost-full moon was high in the sky. A pair of barred owls, one off to their left and one somewhere behind the house, were hooting back and forth to each other. Ralph was inside, curled up at the foot of the bed, his belly full of steak scraps. Kate and Calhoun weren't saying much. They were pretty comfortable just sitting there listening to the owls and the gurgle of Bitch Creek.

Now's a good time, thought Calhoun. *I should tell her now, while we're both feeling good and relaxed and worry-free.* He tried it out in his head. *I'm gonna be gone for a month or so, honey. I can't tell you where or why, so please don't ask. You just gotta trust me on this. It's something I've got to do. I'll be back. Okay?*

He tried to imagine how she'd respond. Kate was a sweet, loving woman, but she stood up for herself, and she didn't take shit from anybody, including him. Especially him. She didn't think two people who loved each other should have secrets, he knew that much about her.

She might not question him or argue with him. She might not say anything more than *I guess you better just do what you gotta do, then, Stoney.*

She'd be angry and hurt, though, and she'd have every right.

Not tonight, he thought. *Let's not spoil this night. Let's hear what Mr. Brescia has to say first. Then I'll know exactly what I'm getting into. Then I'll talk to Kate.*

The Stroudwater Inn sat on a bluff overlooking the mouth of the Stroudwater River where it emptied into the Fore River in the southwest corner of Portland. The coffee shop, which appeared to have once been a brick Cape Cod house, was a hundred yards up the river past the inn, separated from it by a couple of modest private homes.

Calhoun parked in front and got out of his truck. It was about three minutes before eleven.

He headed for the front door. Alongside the building under an awning was a bricked patio area overlooking the river with about a dozen round metal tables and matching metal chairs. A single man was sitting at one of the tables reading a newspaper and sipping from a coffee mug. The other tables were vacant.

The man looked up and said, "Mr. Calhoun." Not a question. He recognized Calhoun.

Calhoun went over to the man's table. "You Mr. Brescia?"

The man pointed at the chair opposite him. "Sit down."

Calhoun sat.

"Want coffee? A sticky bun?"

As if she'd been listening, a waitress appeared. "Can I get you something, sir?" she said to Calhoun. "Coffee? Some breakfast?"

"Just coffee," he said.

"Sir?" she said to Mr. Brescia.

"I'm good," he said.

The waitress left. Brescia put his forearms on the table and leaned toward Calhoun. "I know all about you," he said.

Calhoun shrugged. "That makes one of us."

"What would you like to know, Mr. Calhoun?"

He shook his head. "Nothing. I'm all set."

Mr. Brescia smiled. He was, Calhoun guessed, somewhere in his late forties, early fifties. A bulky man, thick in the shoulders and chest, but not fat. Coarse black hair, cut very short. Swarthy coloring, big lumpy nose. "I probably know things that you'd like to know," he said. "All you've got to do is ask."

"Why don't you just tell me what you want," said Calhoun. "There's no sense trying to mess with my head. It won't do you any good."

"Fair enough." Mr. Brescia reached down and picked up a thin attaché case from the brick patio. He put it on the table between them, opened it, slid out a large manila envelope, shut the attaché case, and put it back on the patio floor beside his chair. He unclasped the envelope, reached inside, and took out an eight-by-ten black-and-white photograph. He laid it face up on the table and turned it so that Calhoun could look at it.

The photo was taken through the front windshield. It showed two people sitting in the front seat of an automobile—a man behind the wheel, his head thrown back, and a woman slumped against him in the passenger seat. They were obviously dead. The woman's face was pressing against the man's shoulder so that Calhoun couldn't see it very well. She had light-colored hair.

There was a black hole on the side of the man's head, right in front of his left ear. Calhoun put his finger on the hole in the photo and arched his eyebrows at Mr. Brescia.

Mr. Brescia nodded. "Bullet hole."

"Who're these people?"

"The man's name was McNulty. He was one of our . . . operatives. The woman was a local girl named Millie Gautier. A townie. Sixteen years old."

"She have a bullet hole, too?" said Calhoun.

Mr. Brescia put his fingertip on the middle of his forehead and nodded. "The weapon was in McNulty's left hand."

"Murder and suicide," said Calhoun.

Mr. Brescia shrugged. "Looked like that."

"But you don't think so."

"No. For one thing, McNulty wouldn't do that."

"Somebody shot both of them, then."

Mr. Brescia nodded.

"Townie," said Calhoun. "What town?"

"St. Cecelia."

The waitress appeared with a mug and a carafe of coffee on a tray. She put the mug in front of Calhoun, filled it from the carafe, and put the carafe on the table. "Anything else, gentlemen?"

Mr. Brescia waved his hand in the air. "No, thank you."

After the waitress left, Calhoun said, "St. Cecelia. That's way the hell up there in Aroostook County, ain't it?"

"Up there on the Canadian border," said Mr. Brescia. "Potato country. Potato fields and blueberry burns, mobile homes and satellite dishes and rusted-out car bodies."

"Millie had a boyfriend who didn't take kindly to her being with your McNulty?"

"We think it's more complicated than that."

"You want me to go up there and figure it out, is that it?" said Calhoun.

Mr. Brescia shrugged. "We want you to go up there and figure out what McNulty was doing that got him shot in the head."

"You don't know what he was doing?" said Calhoun. "Your own—what'd you call him?—your operative?"

"Our operatives," said Mr. Brescia, "have a good deal of latitude. Our system is unique among government agencies. We select our people for their intelligence and initiative and resourcefulness, we train them thoroughly, and then we trust them and support them. They are mostly out there on their own, and we don't necessarily expect them to keep us updated on what they're doing or even where they are." He smiled at Calhoun. "Doesn't that ring any bells with you, Stoney? I've just described your career with us."

Mr. Brescia hadn't called him by his first name before. It made Calhoun cautious. He shook his head. "Rings no bells with me."

"Our mutual friend said you'd say that."

Our mutual friend being the Man in the Suit, Calhoun assumed. "Why me?" he said.

"In spite of your, um, memory problems," said Mr. Brescia, "we are convinced that you have retained your training, that you are still a superior operative."

"I'm intelligent," said Calhoun. "I take the initiative. Resourceful. That's still me." He smiled. "What makes you think that?"

"We've kept an eye on you. As you know. We don't miss much, Stoney. You've solved two murders since you've been up here in Maine. Your sheriff calls on you to help him figure things out. You've shown intelligence, initiative, and resourcefulness—

and courage to burn—not even to mention all of the survival and self-defense and problem-solving skills that were instilled in you at great government expense."

"That make me any different from your other operatives?"

"What makes you different," said Mr. Brescia, "is that in addition to all that, you are also a registered and licensed Maine guide. Not only that, but a guide with an excellent reputation, a highly sought-after guide. One of the best, we understand."

"I'm not doing much guiding these days," said Calhoun. "I've learned I don't like it much unless I'm sharing my boat with somebody whose company I enjoy, and I'm finding there ain't all that many people who qualify. I've been happy taking care of the shop. Kate does some guiding. She's as good at it as me, and she tends to like people."

Mr. Brescia was smiling. "You even talk like I imagine a Maine guide would talk. Nobody would know you grew up in South Carolina."

"So what's my bein' a guide got to do with your McNulty getting shot in the head?"

"Last we knew of him before he turned up dead," said Mr. Brescia, "he was staying at a place called the Loon Lake Lodge, which happens to be a high-end fishing lodge on, you guessed it, Loon Lake, which is one of a series of connected lakes in the northwest corner of Aroostook County. That's genuine wilderness, Stoney, right up there on the Canadian border. Real wild country. Bears and moose and eagles and damn few people. We figure that what happened to McNulty stemmed from what he was doing at the resort. We think he ended up in St. Cecelia, which is about thirty miles south of Loon Lake, connected only by an old logging road but still the nearest township, with that poor dead girl as a way of deflecting attention from the Loon Lake Lodge."

"So you want me to hire on as a guide at Loon Lake and figure out what got McNulty killed?"

Mr. Brescia nodded. "We want to know what McNulty was investigating. We assume what got him killed was connected to that."

Calhoun smiled. "I imagine it could get me killed, too."

"Yes, it surely could," said Mr. Brescia. "McNulty was a damn good man. Knew how to take care of himself, and look what happened to him. It's a dangerous job, no doubt about it."

"So why should I do this?"

"I'd think that would be obvious by now, Stoney."

"Because you can get me and Kate kicked out of our store," said Calhoun. "Because you can get Walter kicked out of his rehab facility."

Mr. Brescia shrugged. "Because we can make anything happen."

"Say I'm willing," said Calhoun. "I can't just go knock on the door of the lodge and say, 'Here I am, ready to be hired.'"

"Don't you worry about that. They're going to come knocking on your door. We're only asking you to agree when they do."

"That's askin' a lot," said Calhoun.

Mr. Brescia shrugged. "Consider the alternatives."

Calhoun nodded. "I know I've got to do it. I don't have to like it."

"You don't have to like me, either," said Mr. Brescia, "but you do have to work with me." He fixed Calhoun with his dark, baleful eyes. "All you have to do is what I ask."

"What else do I need to know, then?"

"Two things," said Mr. Brescia. "First, we believe McNulty had latched on to a national security issue. We don't know what, or how it's related to the Loon Lake Lodge, and we realize we might be wrong. For all we know, he was there just to do some fishing and stumbled onto something. Whatever it was, now he's dead, and that doesn't seem to be a coincidence."

"National security," said Calhoun.

"Wish I could tell you more, but that's all I know, and even that is surmise. In any case, we've got to take it seriously."

Calhoun shrugged. "You said there were two things."

Mr. Brescia nodded. "The second thing," he said, "is this. Those bullets weren't what killed McNulty and Millie Gautier. They were both already dead when they got shot."

Calhoun arched his eyebrows. "Already dead, huh?"

"That's right."

"What'd they die of?"

"Since it had the appearance of a homicide," Mr. Brescia said, "the local sheriff turned both bodies over to the state's medical examiner in Augusta. The ME was the one who figured out that the gunshots were postmortem, though she hasn't yet been able to figure out what did kill them. For now she's calling it natural causes."

"Is that what you think?" Calhoun said. "Natural causes?"

Mr. Brescia shook his head. "No, I don't."

"Why shoot somebody who's already dead?" said Calhoun.

"That's something you'll find out for us," said Mr. Brescia. "It could've just been some jealous boyfriend, found the two of them parked in a car in the woods, thought they were sleeping. Hell, it could've been anybody. It might've had nothing whatsoever to do with what McNulty was investigating."

"You don't believe that."

Mr. Brescia shrugged. "No, I suppose I don't, but anything's possible."

Calhoun lifted his coffee mug to his lips. The coffee had gone cold. He put down the mug. "Okay," he said. "What else?"

"You'll be asked to hire on as a guide at Loon Lake," said Mr. Brescia. "Take the job. Go up there. Figure out what McNulty was up to. When you do, tell us. Then you can go home. That's all."

Calhoun smiled. "That's all, huh?"

Mr. Brescia nodded. "Not a word about this. To anybody. No exceptions. Understand?"

Calhoun nodded.

"No hints as to where you're going, or why. I can't emphasize this strongly enough."

"I get it." He was wondering what he could say to Kate. She wasn't going to like it, he knew that much.

"At Loon Lake," said Mr. Brescia, "you're a temporary guide. Nobody up there will know any different, even the owner. That's your cover. Don't blow it."

Calhoun nodded. "I told you. I get it."

Mr. Brescia reached into his pants pocket, took out a business card, and handed it to Calhoun.

Calhoun took it and looked at it. Two phone numbers and an e-mail address and the letter *B*. That was all. "Okay," he said.

"One more thing," said Mr. Brescia.

Calhoun looked at the man. "What?"

Mr. Brescia's eyes were dark and impenetrable. "You better not let me down."

"That a threat?" said Calhoun.

Mr. Brescia shook his head. "I don't issue threats."

"Sounded like a threat to me."

"No, Stoney. It was a statement of fact, that's all. Just get the job done. There's no room for failure. This is too important. Understand?"

"Sure," said Calhoun.

"Don't make me regret trusting you."

"I said I understand," Calhoun said.

Mr. Brescia smiled. "Okay," he said. "Good luck." He didn't stand or offer Calhoun his hand.

Calhoun got up from the table, nodded to Mr. Brescia, and headed back to his truck.

CHAPTER SIX

Toward closing time on Friday afternoon Calhoun was helping one of the local guys, a lending officer named Ben Fallows from the Portland Savings and Loan, pick out some landlocked salmon flies for his annual trip to Aziscohos and Parmachenee lakes and the Big and Little Magalloway rivers. Calhoun was pushing the old-time, traditional Maine streamer flies that presumably imitated smelt—Gray and Black Ghosts, Ballou Specials, Dark Tigers, Warden's Worries—but Mr. Fallows seemed to believe that modern flies made from flashy synthetics had to be improvements, just because they were newer. "Refinements," he called them.

Calhoun made his case, Mr. Fallows shrugged a couple of times, and Calhoun realized he didn't really give a shit what flies the banker brought with him. It didn't matter that much anyway. They'd all catch fish if they were cast to the right places and fished properly. If they weren't it didn't matter, either.

Just about then the phone rang. Kate, up at the counter, answered it, then called, "Hey, Stoney." She held the phone up in the air. "For you."

Calhoun touched Ben Fallows on the arm and said, "Grab a bunch of whatever you want and take 'em to Kate. They're all good. You can't go wrong. I gotta get the phone."

He waved to Kate and pointed to his office. She nodded.

He went into his office, shut the door, picked up the phone, and said, "Okay. I got it."

When he heard Kate disconnect, he said, "This is Calhoun."

"Stonewall Jackson Calhoun? The Maine guide?"

"I do some guiding," said Calhoun.

The voice on the other end said, "Mr. Calhoun, my name is Martin Dunlap. I own a fishing lodge up near the Canadian border, and I have a proposition for you that I think will interest you."

Here we go, thought Calhoun. *Just like Mr. Brescia said. An offer I better not refuse.* "Okay," he said. "Shoot."

"Oh, no," said Dunlap, "not on the telephone. It's too complicated for the telephone. We should be looking at each other, face-to-face. Why don't I just meet you at your shop? That will also give me the chance finally to meet the legendary Kate Balaban."

"Nope," said Calhoun. "You want to meet with me, we got to make it somewhere else."

Dunlap hesitated, then said, "Okay, I understand. I'll take you to lunch, then. Tomorrow all right with you? Can you meet me at the Sandpiper at one o'clock?"

"I can," said Calhoun, "but I'd like to have some idea what your proposition is all about."

"It's about a job, Mr. Calhoun." Dunlap paused. "I was led to believe that you would be receptive."

"Who led you to believe that?"

"Why don't we talk about it over lunch tomorrow," Dunlap said. "Would that be okay?"

"Sure," said Calhoun. "The Sandpiper. I'll be there."

"Excellent," said Martin Dunlap. "One o'clock. See you then." He hung up.

When Calhoun returned to the front of the store, Ben Fallows was at the counter, and Kate was counting the flies he'd selected.

"I got a few of everything," said Fallows. "You never know what the fish might want."

Calhoun nodded. "Some days they just lay there saying to themselves, I ain't bitin' nothin' except a yellow Matuka with three strands of Flashabou on each side tied on a 4XL Limerick hook with white thread. Other times they might wait all day for a Carrie Stevens Black Ghost, and if they don't get an authentic one, they say the hell with it, they'd rather go hungry."

Fallows frowned at Calhoun as if he thought he might be having his leg pulled but wasn't quite sure.

"Stoney's right," said Kate. "You can't have too many flies with you, because, like you said, you never know what the fish might be thinking."

Ben Fallows spent about a hundred and fifty dollars on his assortment of salmon flies. He seemed quite pleased when he left the shop.

"So," said Kate after the bell dinged behind Mr. Fallows, "who was that on the phone?"

Calhoun felt that he was sinking deeper and deeper into his deception. He hadn't exactly lied to Kate, at least not yet, but he'd withheld a ton of truth from her. Sooner or later he'd have to tell her what he was doing, and even then, he couldn't tell her much. He knew that after he had lunch with Mr. Dunlap tomorrow he'd have no more excuses. He'd have to talk to her. He didn't look forward to it.

"It was just some guy, wanted to talk about fishing," he said.

The Sandpiper was a sprightly multicolored Victorian building on Baxter Boulevard overlooking Back Cove. It had once been a run-down private residence, but then a couple of ex-schoolteachers from Boston bought it, gutted it, renovated it, hired a chef from San Francisco, named it the Sandpiper, and turned it into one of the most popular high-end restaurants in Portland. It was particularly popular with wealthy tourists and summer vacationers from out of state.

Calhoun often guided wealthy out-of-staters, and some of them had mentioned dining at the Sandpiper. They all said the food was great.

He pulled into the crushed-shell parking area beside the building a few minutes after one on Saturday afternoon. He had put on freshly washed blue jeans and a clean shirt for the occasion, and he wondered if he should've added a necktie.

A pretty college-aged girl in a short black skirt and a white shirt greeted him at a podium inside the entry. She asked if he wanted a table or would rather sit at the bar.

"I'm supposed to meet somebody," he said. "Man name of Dunlap?"

"Yes, sir," she said. "He's waiting for you. Follow me, please."

She led him through the dining room, where most of the tables were occupied, and through some French doors to a glassed-in porch that stretched across the back of the building. Beyond the wall of glass, there was a nice view of the cove, where gulls and terns wheeled in the breeze and cormorants perched on the pilings and dozens of fishing boats and pleasure craft rocked at their moorings.

The waitress led Calhoun to a table in the corner of the porch. The man sitting there had his chin in his hand and was gazing out at the water. He either didn't notice them or was pretending he didn't.

"Mr. Dunlap," said the waitress quietly. "Your guest is here."

Dunlap looked up, frowned for just an instant, and then nodded. "Mr. Calhoun?"

"Stoney," he said.

"Good," he said. "I'm Marty." Marty Dunlap stood up and held out his hand. Calhoun guessed he was in his midfifties. A compact man with thinning straw-colored hair and sloping shoulders, he was wearing a white shirt and a striped tie and round rimless glasses. A suit jacket hung on the back of his chair. "It's good to meet you finally, Stoney. Your reputation precedes you." He looked at the waitress. "Bring Mr. Calhoun a drink." To Calhoun he said, "What'll you have, Stoney?"

"Cup of coffee," said Calhoun.

Dunlap smiled at the hostess. "Okay. Coffee, then. Me, I'll have another of these." He held up a tall glass.

The hostess said, "I'll tell your server," and she left.

Dunlap and Calhoun sat down.

"You don't drink?" said Dunlap.

Calhoun shook his head. "Not anymore. I don't miss it a bit."

"I don't get down to the city much this time of year," said Dunlap. "As you can imagine, things really start hopping at the lodge once the ice goes out. When I do get away, I always come to the Sandpiper. Best food north of Boston, if you ask me. You've got to try their lobster bisque."

Calhoun nodded.

"How's business at your shop?" said Dunlap. "I'd like to meet Kate Balaban some day. She really is a legend in Maine fishing circles." He waved a hand and smiled. "But I guess you know that."

"She's a great guide," said Calhoun. "I can tell you that."

"You're no slouch yourself," said Dunlap. "Speaking of legends." He fixed Calhoun with a hard stare, as if he expected him to argue the point.

Calhoun returned Dunlap's gaze until the man smiled and looked out at the cove.

"I'm not very good at small talk," said Calhoun. "You said on the phone you had a proposition for me, and I'd just as soon hear it."

"I thought we could wait until after we'd eaten," said Dunlap.

"Why?"

Dunlap smiled. "I don't know. That's the way it's generally done."

"How I generally do things," said Calhoun, "is, when something needs to get done, I just go ahead and do it, get it out of the way so I can get on to the next thing."

A blond waitress wearing tight black pants and a pale blue jersey appeared. She put a cup of coffee in front of Calhoun and a tall glass holding what looked like a gin and tonic in front of Dunlap. "Are you ready to order, gentlemen?" she said.

Marty Dunlap waved his hand. "Give us a few minutes, hon."

She smiled and nodded. "Certainly, sir. Take your time."

When she left, Dunlap picked up his glass, took a long gulp from it, and put it down. "So, okay, Stoney," he said. "I told you I had a proposition for you, and here it is. I have been led to believe that you might be receptive. The fact that you agreed to meet me here seems to confirm that. Am I right?"

Calhoun shrugged. "Sure. I'm here."

Dunlap smiled. "Excellent. Here it is. I would like to hire you away from Kate's shop for a month, or six weeks, max, beginning as soon as possible. One of my best guides had to go home a few days ago. Some kind of family emergency involving his youngest son. Now, the thing is, Stoney, Loon Lake has a reputation to uphold. Our guides have been handpicked. We believe we have the best crew of guides in the Northeast. We pay them better than anybody, and we take care of them better than anybody. We believe that the men and women our clients spend their days with, the folks who find the fish and paddle the canoes and tell the stories and cook the shore lunches—these are the people who make or break a fishing operation." Dunlap paused to take a sip from his gin and tonic. "Our guides come back year after year," he said. "They are like family. When we have to replace one of them, we take the job as seriously as a corporation hiring a new CEO."

"And you want me," said Calhoun. "To take this poor guy's place."

"For a month or six weeks," said Dunlap. "We've given him a leave of absence—with full pay, by the way, a sabbatical, you might call it—so you don't need to feel too sorry for him."

"Generous."

"Yes. We'll make it worth your while, too, of course."

"Of all the guides in Maine," said Calhoun, "you want me."

"You're the best," said Dunlap.

"I'm pretty good," said Calhoun, "but I doubt I'm the best."

Dunlap shrugged. "Let me tell you about Loon Lake," he said. "It's the biggest and prettiest of the string of lakes that we fish. We built our lodge on Loon Lake." He began to draw with his fingertip on the tablecloth. "There are seven lakes in all. They're all connected by streams, some close to a mile long, some just a narrows at the outlet of the lake. Really, it's one big river system that goes all the way to the sea. Up there in north-western Aroostook County, the woods are all owned by the paper companies, except for what the government gave back to the Indians. We've got a ninety-nine-year lease. Virtually inaccessible except for one of those narrow roads that cut through the woods for the logging trucks. It connects us to the nearest town. We get in and out mostly with float planes, of course. Before we built our lodge—well, my grandfather built the first one back in the thirties, just a log cabin, really—these lakes were hardly ever fished."

"Your grandfather," Calhoun said. "So it's a family business, and you're—what, the third generation"

"I'm the third," said Marty Dunlap. "My son would make it four, if he . . ." He smiled quickly.

"Your son works with you?"

Dunlap nodded. "I'm trying to teach him the business so that June and I can eventually retire from it. Robert's a good man, but I'm not sure he's cut out for this. He's kind of restless, the way young people nowadays seem to be. In a big hurry to get nowhere, if you ask me." He shook his head. "If Robert doesn't want to keep Loon Lake going, I don't know what will happen. I'd hate to have to sell the place. It's part of the family, if you know what I mean, but . . ." He looked at Calhoun and shrugged.

Calhoun couldn't think of anything to say, so he said nothing.

Dunlap smiled quickly. "Well, anyway," he said, "it's still like it was a hundred years ago up there. Great fishing. Four-, five-, six-pound squaretails. Loads of big landlocked salmon. All native fish. None of the lakes've ever been stocked. We cherish our fish, and we treat 'em right. Fly-fishing only. Barbless hooks. All catch and release, except our guests are allowed to kill one trophy fish per week. A lot of folks just return all their fish unharmed, but everybody catches a trophy or two. We have an arrangement with a taxidermist in Pittsburgh. He's a true artist." Dunlap waved his hand in the air, dismissing the taxidermist from Pittsburgh. "What we've got is like the Maine of the good old days, Stoney, minus the long strings of big dead fish. Gorgeous wilderness full of moose and bear and bald eagles, the best brook trout and landlocked salmon fishing outside of Labrador, and one of the nicest, most comfortable family-owned fishing lodges in the world." Dunlap tipped up his glass and drained it. Calhoun heard the ice cubes click against his teeth. "We try to make it an attractive place for our guides. Each of them has his own private cabin. You eat the same food as the clients in the guides' own dining room. One day off a week with use of the lodge vehicles. And, of course, we pay our guides better than anybody anywhere."

"Sounds good," said Calhoun.

"As you might imagine," said Dunlap, "we charge premium rates. It's an absolutely unique experience for a fisherman or a fishing couple. Something special for a corporate group. The fish, the food, the ambience, the wilderness, all of it. We have clients who come from all over the world, and they come every year. CEOs and prime ministers, senators and movie stars and professional athletes. For our clients, money is no object."

"I can see why you need good guides," said Calhoun.

Dunlap frowned. "Huh?"

"Guides who can keep their mouths shut when they hear a lot of bullshit going on."

"Clients who don't treat our guides with respect," said Dunlap, "are not invited back. We have a long waiting list. We don't need unpleasant guests." He placed both of his forearms on the table and leaned forward. "That's my sales pitch, Stoney. My wife and my son and I, we want you to come work with us. I was told you might be interested, and I hope that's true. We're prepared to pay you enough to make it awfully difficult for you to refuse, but I'm really hoping that you'd like to do this, that you're enthusiastic about spending some time at our beautiful lodge fishing our wonderful lakes and being treated the way a professional guide should be treated."

"I don't go anywhere without my dog."

Dunlap frowned. "Nobody said anything—"

"Ralph goes with me," said Calhoun. "That ain't negotiable."

"I assume he's spent time in a boat," said Dunlap, "knows his way around people."

"Worry about me before you worry about Ralph."

Dunlap shrugged. "Well, okay, I don't see a problem, then. So are we on?"

"You never mentioned what you paid."

"I'm sorry." Dunlap ran the palm of his hand over the top of his head. "All our guides get the same. Twenty-five hundred a week. It's a salary. No tips, so as to discourage favoritism. Like I said before, one day a week off, which includes use of one of the lodge vehicles if you want to go to town." He paused. "Our guides work from May one to September thirty. For most folks around here, that adds up to a fine yearly income."

"No wonder you got the best ones workin' for you."

"Good pay, good working conditions," said Marty Dunlap. "The tried-and-true formula. Robert says I overpay the guides. I keep trying to tell him, the place lives or dies on our guides." He smiled—a bit sadly, Calhoun thought. "That's why I worry about Robert taking over the place. He doesn't quite get the human element. To him, I think it's all about the bottom line."

Calhoun nodded. "Okay," he said. "I'll do it."

Dunlap looked at him for a minute, as if he weren't quite sure what Calhoun had said. Then he reached his hand across the table. "Oh, excellent. This is wonderful, Stoney. I'm delighted."

Calhoun shook his hand.

"I'll explain all the details over lunch," said Dunlap. "Be sure to ask for the lobster bisque. I'm hoping you can come aboard next week. Thursday would be perfect."

Calhoun nodded absentmindedly. He was thinking that Martin Dunlap didn't need to give him the big sales pitch. The Man in the Suit and his buddy Mr. Brescia had given him no choice.

Now, he was thinking, came the hard part. Now he had to break it to Kate.

CHAPTER SEVEN

Calhoun got to the shop at seven thirty on Sunday morning. It was Kate's turn to open up, and he knew she'd be there well before eight, which was the time they turned the sign on the door so that the OPEN side faced out. He could talk to her then, before they opened for business. Tell her he'd be gone for a month, no more than six weeks.

He expected her to be angry at first, but he hoped that if they spent the day together in the shop, maybe she'd have a chance to think about it, get used to the idea, cool down. He didn't look forward to being away for all that time with Kate mad at him, although he knew it could happen that way.

When he pulled into the lot, he saw that Kate's truck was already there. He parked beside it, and he and Ralph went into the shop.

Kate was at the clothing display, straightening out the shirts and jackets on the hangers. When the bell over the door dinged, she looked up, and when she saw Calhoun, she gave him a big smile. "Hey, Stoney. What're you doing here at this hour? To-day's your morning to sleep in."

"I couldn't sleep, honey. You got your coffee?"

"Not yet. I just put it together a few minutes ago. It should be ready now. You want to fetch us a mug?"

He went to the back of the shop, poured two mugs full from the big stainless-steel urn, and brought them to where Kate was working on the clothing. He handed one of the mugs to her. "Honey," he said, "there's something I need to talk to you about."

She arched her eyebrows at him. "Sounds ominous. Now you gonna tell me that we're losing our lease after all?"

"Nope. Nothing like that. Let's sit, okay?"

Kate frowned at him, then went over and sat in one of the chairs at the fly-tying bench.

Calhoun took one of the other chairs. He sipped his coffee, then put the mug down. He looked Kate in the eyes. "Only way I can tell you this is to just tell you," he said. "Thing is, I'm going to be gone for a month, maybe six weeks. I—"

"What do you mean, *gone?*" she said.

"Not here," he said. "Not living at home, not coming to the shop."

"For six weeks?"

He nodded. "It might be that long."

"You said *got to.*"

He nodded again.

"Meaning it's not your choice."

"That's right." He nodded. "I don't have a choice. I've got to do this."

"You want to tell me where you've *got* to be," she said, "and what you've *got* to be doing, and who's forcing you to do it, that you won't be home and you won't be fulfilling your responsibilities at your place of business with your partner?"

He shook his head. "I can't tell you any of that, honey. I'm sorry."

"Can't or won't?"

"Can't."

"Please don't call me honey."

Calhoun nodded. "I don't blame you for being upset."

"I'm just trying to understand," she said. "You're going to be gone. Not coming to work. Not living in your house. Gone. Not your choice. And you won't—can't—even tell me where you'll be, what's going on, that's more important than your responsibilities, never mind your—your relationship with me." She glared at him. "Have I got it right?"

He shook his head. "Nothing's more important than you. Only this has got to be done, and I wish you wouldn't be mad."

"Mad?" She shook her head. "I'm not mad, Stoney. I'm disappointed. I thought we had a certain kind of relationship. Now I find out we don't. Instead, we've got secrets from each other. It's a disappointment. You're a disappointment. I feel like a fool for misunderstanding so profoundly."

"You didn't misunderstand anything," he said. "It's just, this thing I've got to do, I don't have any choice about it. I wish I could explain. Then you'd see."

"So explain. What's stopping you?"

He shook his head. "I can't."

Kate narrowed her eyes at him. Her mouth was a straight, thin line. Calhoun knew that look, and he didn't like it. It was her cold anger. Nobody did cold anger better than Kate Balaban. "When do you leave, then?" she said.

"My last day at the shop will be Tuesday," he said. "Day after tomorrow. I'm actually leaving on Thursday."

She nodded. "Thursday. Well, I hope that'll give you time to line up a replacement, at least."

"Sure," he said. "I'll do that. I'll give Adrian a call. What else? Anything else you want me to do?" He reached over to touch her arm.

She flinched and yanked her arm away.

He shrugged and took his hand back. "I wish you'd try to understand."

"Oh," she said, "I understand perfectly." She gave her head a little shake. Then she stood up, went to the front of the store, and turned the sign that hung on the door so that the OPEN side faced out.

It turned out to be a busy morning at the shop, and both Calhoun and Kate had customers to deal with most of the time. Whenever Kate needed to speak to Calhoun, she was super-polite. She'd say, "Stoney, would you mind taking Mr. Tidings out to the parking lot so he can try casting the new Winston five-weight, please?" or, "Stoney, Mr. and Mrs. Zealey wonder if you might advise them on a selection of bonefish flies for their trip to Belize."

There was a brief break around noontime when there were no customers in the shop. Kate went into the office, closed the door, and turned on her computer. Calhoun knocked on the glass to see if she wanted him to go out and get some lunch for them.

She ignored him.

The hell with it. If she wanted to go without lunch, so would he. He used the phone at the front counter to call Adrian, the kid who'd worked in the shop on a part-time basis for the past several summers. Adrian had graduated from a college in

Massachusetts with a degree in English a couple of years earlier. He was a quick learner, good with the customers, liked fishing, and didn't have a regular job.

He agreed instantly to coming on full-time for the next six weeks. He'd start on Tuesday, which would be Calhoun's last day at the shop for a while.

The rest of Sunday and all day Monday went the same way. Kate avoided Calhoun. She made sure she was in a different part of the shop from him, and when she had to speak to him, she used that cold, excessively polite tone that made it clear she'd prefer it if she didn't have to deal with him at all.

A couple of times Calhoun went up to her and said, "I wish we could talk about this," and she answered, "I don't think there's anything more to be said," and when he thought about it, he supposed she was right. There was nothing more he could tell her. All he wanted was for her to say that it was all right, that she accepted it, and that she still loved him.

It was pretty clear she had no intention of saying anything like that.

Calhoun was a volunteer sheriff's deputy, and he felt obligated to let Sheriff Dickman know he was going to be unavailable for a while. He expected this conversation to go differently from the one he'd had with Kate.

He called the sheriff after supper on Monday. "Just wanted you to know," he said, "that I'm going to be away for the next month or six weeks."

"Hope you've got some good fishing lined up," said the sheriff.

"In fact, I do," said Calhoun. "Won't be available if you need me, though."

"I expect I'll manage to muddle along."

"Oh, hey, listen," said Calhoun, as if it were an afterthought, "do you know the medical examiner in Augusta?"

"Very competent woman named Ella Grimshaw," the sheriff said. "Dr. Grimshaw. Chief medical examiner for the state of Maine. I know her, sure."

"If I ask you for a favor, will you promise not to ask me what it's about?"

"I don't see why not."

"Would you give Dr. Grimshaw a call," said Calhoun, "tell her your deputy, an honorable man name of Calhoun, would like to talk with her on Wednesday, and would she please cooperate with him?"

The sheriff chuckled. "You expect me to agree to do this and not ask you what's going on?"

"I can't tell you, so I'd rather you didn't ask."

"It's all very mysterious, Stoney. You going away for six weeks in the middle of the trout season, doing business with the ME that I don't know about." He paused. "So how's Kate taking this?"

"Not good," said Calhoun. "As expected."

"Well, I'll give Dr. Grimshaw a call," said the sheriff. "I don't know whether to tell you to be careful or to have fun."

"Both work for me," said Calhoun.

He got to the shop early on Tuesday. It was his last day for a while, and he was determined to be as useful as he possibly could be. He figured he'd take inventory and place some orders and get things organized, along with giving Adrian a refresher on how the shop ran.

Kate arrived in the middle of the morning and, as she'd been doing since Calhoun's announcement, she avoided being in the same part of the shop as he was.

Once in a while, when he glanced toward her, he caught her watching him. He couldn't read the expression on her face, but he figured it had to be a good thing that she was at least acknowledging him.

Calhoun put Adrian to work counting the flies in the bins. They'd sold a lot of flies during this early part of the fishing season, and he knew they needed to restock their supply.

Calhoun spent most of the afternoon in his office in the back of the shop, working the telephone and the computer placing orders. Kate stayed at the front counter, as far from the office as she could get and still be in the same shop.

When six o'clock—closing time—came along, she flipped the sign on the door around, went out to her truck, and drove away without glancing at Calhoun. She didn't even give Ralph a pat.

CHAPTER EIGHT

Wednesday morning Calhoun called information, got the number for the OCME in Augusta—the Office of the Chief Medical Examiner for the state of Maine—and spoke with Dr. Ella Grimshaw, the ME herself. She said that Sheriff Dickman had called her and that she was pretty busy but could meet with Deputy Calhoun at two that afternoon if he wouldn't mind telling her what was on his mind, inasmuch as the sheriff hadn't been very forthcoming.

He told her he was interested in the death of a man named McNulty along with a young girl named Millie Gautier up in St. Cecelia a couple of weeks earlier. McNulty had been shot beside his ear, and the girl was shot in the forehead. It had been made to look like a murder-suicide, but Calhoun had heard that both of them were already dead when they got plugged.

Dr. Grimshaw said she remembered the case. She'd pull the file.

———

He explained to Ralph that Augusta might be the capital city of the state of Maine, but even so, there was nothing of interest for a dog there, and if he went, he'd just have to sit in the truck, and he'd be a lot happier staying home and guarding the place. "Growl fiercely and bite all trespassers on the ass," Calhoun told him.

Ralph, who would always rather go in the truck than be left behind, sighed, curled up in a patch of sunshine on the deck, and put his back to Calhoun to show him what he thought about that plan.

Augusta was a straight shot due north up the Maine Turnpike from Portland. From his house in the woods in Dublin, it took Calhoun about two hours to get there and another five minutes to find a place to park around the corner from the OCME on Hospital Street.

Dr. Ella Grimshaw's office was on the second floor. A middle-aged receptionist who wore her reading glasses down on the tip of her nose asked him his name and told Calhoun she'd let the doctor know he was here. He could go ahead and have a seat in the otherwise empty waiting room.

Calhoun had just gotten settled in his chair with a year-old copy of *Field & Stream* when the door behind the receptionist's desk opened and a tall, lanky woman stepped out. She started toward Calhoun.

He stood up. "Dr. Grimshaw?"

She smiled and held out her hand. She had short gray hair and sharp blue eyes. Calhoun guessed she was around fifty. "Deputy Calhoun," she said. "Nice to meet you."

They shook hands. She had a man-sized hand and a firm grip.

"Let's go into my office," said Dr. Grimshaw. "Would you like some coffee or something?"

"I'm good," said Calhoun. "Thanks."

He followed her into a big sun-filled office. The wall that looked down on Hospital Street had four floor-to-ceiling windows. On one of the side walls were built-in bookshelves stuffed with serious-looking volumes. The other wall displayed framed diplomas and family photographs. Backed up to the windows was a big oak desk littered with papers and manila folders. In one corner of the office, four comfortable-looking upholstered chairs were angled around a glass-topped coffee table.

Dr. Grimshaw gestured at the chairs. "Let's sit." She picked up a manila folder from her desk, then sat in one of the upholstered chairs.

Calhoun sat across from her.

She tapped the edge of the folder against her chin and fixed Calhoun with those icy eyes. "So tell me, Deputy. Why does a nonmurder in Aroostook County interest the sheriff's department in Cumberland County?"

Calhoun had expected this question. "Didn't Sheriff Dickman talk to you about that?"

Dr. Grimshaw smiled. "Actually, my old friend the sheriff was rather evasive."

Calhoun smiled and flapped his hands. "Well . . ."

She nodded. "So I guess I should expect his deputy to be equally evasive."

"To tell you the truth, ma'am, there's really not much I can say at this point."

Dr. Grimshaw shrugged. "Then I don't see why I should share my information with you."

Calhoun looked at her. "I wish you'd told me that before I drove all the way up here."

She waved a hand in the air. "I didn't say I wouldn't share. I will. Just so you know I'm doing you a favor, since you're of no mind to reciprocate."

Calhoun nodded. "Thank you. I appreciate it."

"It's all right," she said. "I really don't mind. We're all on the same side here, aren't we?"

Calhoun figured that was a rhetorical question, but he nodded anyway.

Dr. Grimshaw put the folder on the coffee table, opened it, and took out a sheet of paper. She squinted at it, then looked at Calhoun. "When the man's body came to me from St. Cecelia, he was a John Doe with a bullet hole inflicted by a .32 caliber weapon in his head. Subsequently we learned that his name was McNulty. Along with his body came that of a sixteen-year-old girl, a resident of St. Cecelia named Millie Gautier, who also had a .32 bullet wound from the same weapon in her head. A .32 caliber revolver was found in McNulty's hand, but we quickly determined that both bullet wounds were postmortem. Hence, it was neither a double murder nor a murder-suicide." She looked up at Calhoun with her eyebrows arched.

"Shooting bullets into dead people must be some kind of crime," he said.

Dr. Grimshaw smiled and nodded. "I suppose it is," she said, "but it's not murder."

"I suppose you couldn't trace the ownership of that .32."

"No," she said. "The handgun was not registered."

"So since it's not a murder," he said, "this case is not top priority for you. Right?"

"A different priority," she said. "Both deaths were unattended, so we needed to come up with a cause. That is easier said than done sometimes."

"You must have some idea what they died of," said Calhoun.

"Well," said Dr. Grimshaw, "without more evidence, I'd rather not even speculate." She put the paper down on the table.

"Bottom line, Deputy Calhoun, is that we don't know what killed them, and it's frankly quite worrisome. We did all of the standard tests for poisons and diseases and came up with blanks. Something unusual killed these two, and it's very important that we figure out what. I have sent tissue and blood samples from both victims to the CDC in Georgia. The Centers for Disease Control. Frankly, while I'm always interested in solving mysteries—and the circumstances that lead somebody to shoot two dead bodies and try to make it look like a murder-suicide surely make an interesting mystery—professionally speaking, I am far more concerned that there might be some unknown bird flu mutation or a virulent new strain of the West Nile virus going around in the wilds of northern Maine."

"Is that what you think?" said Calhoun. "The two of them got some rare disease?"

"Like I said," she said, "I'm trying not to speculate. I don't have a hypothesis at this point. I'm just telling you what worries me. I'm hoping the CDC will identify it for us and tell us it's not something we need to be worried about."

"When do you expect to hear from them?"

"Hard to say," said Dr. Grimshaw. "I've asked them to consider it urgent. Could be this afternoon. Of course, knowing how the bureaucracy works, it might not be for another few weeks."

"Will you let me know?" said Calhoun.

She cocked her head and peered at him. "I would like to understand your interest in the case."

He shrugged. "Some cases slop over county lines."

"Aroostook is pretty far from Cumberland," she said.

"You can drive from one to the other in half a day."

She smiled. "I'll let you know what I hear from the CDC. I don't have a problem with that, reciprocity or not. It is pretty intriguing. And if you can figure out why somebody shoots two dead people and wants it to look like a suicide and a murder rather than whatever it is, I'll be all ears."

Calhoun recited his cell phone number to her, and she wrote it down on the inside of the manila folder. She glanced at her wristwatch, then looked up at him. "Was there anything else, Deputy Calhoun?"

He shrugged. "I was wondering whether you heard anything from the folks up in Aroostook County about who they think did the shooting—and why."

"You probably will want to talk with them," said Dr. Grimshaw. "Last I heard, they hadn't progressed very far with their investigation. The two bodies were found in a car parked beside an old logging road in the woods. The police up there interviewed some people—the girl's father, a boyfriend, a few people who might've seen Mr. McNulty and the girl together. No suspects, no arrests." She tapped the manila folder. "Their entire report takes up less than three pages."

"As if they're not pursuing it very hard," said Calhoun.

"There are aspects of the case that might be embarrassing to people," said Dr. Grimshaw. "There might be some, um, pressure not to pursue it too hard." She shrugged. "I don't know that for a fact. Reading between the lines. They don't have a murder. The only apparent crime is shooting bullets into already-dead bodies. If they did find somebody to arrest, it's unclear what they'd charge him with."

Calhoun nodded. "They've got a point." He stood up. "I won't take any more of your time. Thanks for seeing me."

Dr. Grimshaw stood up, also. She was nearly as tall as Calhoun. She went to her office door and opened it. "I'll let you know when I hear something from the CDC."

Calhoun nodded. "Thank you."

She held out her hand, and he shook it.

"Good luck, Deputy."

"Thanks for your help."

"One of these days," she said, "maybe you'll tell me what your real interest is in this case."

"Oh," he said, "I'm just doing my job."

"Of course." She smiled, then handed him a business card. "Call me."

After supper that night Calhoun opened a duffel bag on his bed and filled it with clothes for a month at the Loon Lake Lodge. Plenty of warm socks, flannel shirts, a few pairs of blue jeans, a couple of windbreakers. Boots and moccasins. Sweaters. Underwear. Toilet articles. Books. The charger for his cell phone, though he doubted that there would be service at Loon Lake.

It didn't take very long to pack. He wasn't that interested in clothing.

Then he loaded a big bag with fishing gear. This took more thought. From the dozens of fly boxes that were piled on a shelf in his living room, he selected those that contained land-locked salmon flies. Then he threw in a few that held trout flies, and on third thought, he added a couple with smallmouth bass and pickerel flies. He wasn't sure what he'd run into up at Loon Lake.

He dumped in a dozen fly reels, plenty of spools of tippet material, and a few containers of bug dope. He added his Colt Woodsman .22 pistol, which he liked to carry in the woods, a box of long-rifle bullets, a filleting knife, and a hunting knife in its leather scabbard. Finally he selected eight fly rods that he or his clients might use for trolling and casting.

When he was done packing, he poured himself a mug of

coffee, took it out onto the deck, and sat on one of his Adirondack chairs. Ralph came along and lay down beside him.

Calhoun reached down and gave the top of Ralph's head a scratch. "I'd rather we didn't have to do this," he said.

Ralph did not reply.

"Well, it's got to be done," Calhoun continued. "I'm glad you'll be with me, anyway."

They watched the color fade from the evening sky and listened to the owls and other night creatures hoot and peep and squawk in the surrounding woods. In front of the house, some bats were flapping around chasing insects. Calhoun tried to think of something he'd failed to pack that he'd need. Six weeks was a long time to be gone. He figured he'd overpacked. He probably wouldn't need half of the stuff he'd jammed into his bags.

He was supposed to meet the float plane at the Balsam Street dock on Moosehead Lake in Greenville at two the next day—Thursday afternoon. Marty Dunlap hadn't said anything about limiting the weight of his gear. He'd told Calhoun that the pilot's name was Swenson, readily recognized by his red bush of a beard and his Hawaiian shirt, not to mention the fact that the plane would have the Loon Lake Lodge name and its triple-*L* logo painted on its fuselage.

His mug of coffee was almost empty when he heard the whine of a truck engine turning off the road onto his driveway a quarter of a mile away. When it downshifted he recognized it by its sound. "It's Kate," he said to Ralph. "I'll be damned."

A couple of minutes later headlights cut through the woods, and then Kate's truck pulled up beside Calhoun's in the opening in front of the house.

She shut off the lights and the engine, stepped out of the cab, and used her hand as a visor to look up at the house. She was wearing a pair of tight-fitting jeans and a red-and-black checked flannel shirt.

She looked spectacular.

Calhoun waved at her. "Come on up. I got bourbon. Or coffee, if you'd rather."

"I can't stay but a minute," she said, getting that issue out of the way right off. "I just wanted to talk a little bit."

"I still got bourbon and coffee," he said.

"Bourbon, I guess," she said, and then she came over and started up the stairs.

Ralph waited at the top of the steps with his stubby tail wagging. Calhoun went inside and poured an inch from Kate's bottle of Old Grand-Dad into a tumbler, added two ice cubes, and took it back out onto the deck.

Kate was sitting in one of the wooden chairs. Ralph had his chin on her knee, and she was scratching his muzzle.

Calhoun handed the glass to her.

She took it. "I didn't want to leave things that way with you gone for a month."

He sat down and said nothing.

"The way—I mean, how I was acting—I thought about it. Thing is, Stoney, you've never given me any reason not to trust you. I should trust you, that if you say you can't tell me what you're doing, it means you can't, and who am I to tell you you're wrong. This doesn't mean I'm not mad about it, because I am. I mean, it makes no damn sense. If you can't tell me what you're gonna be doing for six weeks, and where you're gonna be doing it, the least you could do is tell me why you can't tell me."

She looked at him with her eyebrows arched.

All Calhoun could do was shrug.

She took a big gulp of bourbon. It was pretty obvious she was working herself up. "Dammit all to hell, Stoney," she continued. "You know, it ain't just about do I trust you. It's about sharing our lives. People who share their lives together aren't supposed to have secrets. Not to mention, I don't like being left by myself this way. I don't know how I'm going to manage for six weeks without you. I've come to depend on you, damn you. At the shop . . . well, I can handle the shop, I guess. Adrian's good. We'll be all right. It's the rest of it, Stoney. Who'm I going to talk to about Walter when he gets all nasty and abusive, or when he's doing so bad it looks like he's about to die? Who's going to hug me when I need it? Where am I going to go when I need a night of lovin'?"

Calhoun held out his hand. Kate narrowed her eyes at him for a minute, then got up from her chair, came over, and sat on his lap.

"You don't need to say anything," he said into her hair. "I don't blame you for being upset."

"I *am* upset," she said. "I'm not spending the night with you, either. I just wanted you to know that I love you anyway, and I'll be all right. I'll get by. And whatever you're doing, you damn well better be careful and come back in one piece. You hear me?"

He enveloped her in his arms. "Yes, ma'am. I hear you."

"I have the feeling it's dangerous," she said.

Calhoun said nothing.

"If something happens to you, Stonewall Jackson Calhoun, you'll have to answer to me."

"I'll be careful," he said.

She snuggled against him for a minute.

Then she sat up straight. "Don't think I'm not mad," she said.

"I understand," Calhoun said.

"Tell me this," she said. "How long did you know before you told me?"

He shrugged. "A few days."

"A few days?" Kate shook her head. "So what the hell were you waiting for?"

"Working up the courage, I guess," he said.

"Courage? You? Men have shot at you with the intention of killing you, and you, you just hunched your shoulders and plowed straight ahead. No, Stoney. I'm not buying that. It ain't courage that you're lacking. Consideration, I'd call it."

"Courage or consideration or whatever," he said. "You've just got to accept it."

"Accept it?" She shook her head. "You telling me I've got a choice?" She glowered at him for a moment, then abruptly she got off his lap, turned, went down the stairs, and got into her truck. He followed along behind her and stood there beside her vehicle while she started it up.

She shifted into first gear, then leaned her head out the window. "I'm mad as hell at you, Stonewall Calhoun. Don't forget that. I got a feeling I'm just going to get madder, too. I don't know why I came here tonight. I guess I expected something out of you that you can't give me. It ain't fair, what you're doing. I know you know that. That's why it took you so damn long to tell me." She glared at him. "Anyway, whatever it is, good luck with it, and you better be careful. If you don't come back safely to me, I'll never speak to you again." She narrowed her eyes at him. "Might not even if you do."

Then, with a little spray of gravel, she pulled out of the parking area and headed up the driveway.

Calhoun watched her drive away.

"I guess we better be careful and come back safe," he said to Ralph. "I can't hardly stand it when she won't talk to me."

CHAPTER NINE

Calhoun was supposed to meet the bush pilot, Swenson, at the dock in Greenville at the foot of Moosehead Lake at two o'clock on Thursday afternoon. Greenville was a little more than two hundred miles north of Portland, and narrow, meandering secondary roads covered the last third of that distance. He figured it would take close to five hours of driving. He left at eight that morning to give himself an hour's cushion.

The first leg of the trip was a straight shot north on the Maine Turnpike. Ralph rode shotgun. Calhoun found a classical music station on the truck's radio, and when it faded away, he trolled the dial until he found another one. He was trying to keep his mind from wandering to Kate and not having good luck with it. The music didn't help. They often played the Portland classical music station on the shop radio, and the symphonies and sonatas and concertos all reminded him of her. It made his stomach feel empty and twisted.

They were still south of Augusta when he noticed that the clouds ahead of him to the north were thickening. A few minutes later a light mist began to appear on the windshield.

He wondered if the float plane would fly in the rain. He thought about being grounded in Greenville for a few days. The idea did not appeal to him.

He exited the turnpike north of Waterville and stopped at a gas station to fill the truck's tank. Now the mist had turned to a soft steady rain.

When he went inside to pay, he bought three plain doughnuts and a big cardboard cup of black coffee. Back in the truck, he gave one of the doughnuts to Ralph and ate the other two himself between sips of coffee. When he finished eating, he took his cell phone from his pocket. He was hoping for a message from Kate, though he honestly didn't expect one. He wasn't surprised to see the NO SERVICE message on the phone's window.

They pulled into Greenville a few minutes after one o'clock. The rain had stopped, but the low clouds hung dark and foreboding overhead.

Greenville's main road followed the contours of the foot of Moosehead Lake, and pretty soon Calhoun came to Balsam Street. He turned onto it, and as expected, it ended up behind a row of stores in a big open area on the shore of the lake. Some vehicles, mostly pickup trucks, were parked behind the stores, and a wide wooden dock stretched into the water.

Moosehead was the biggest lake in Maine, and today a northerly wind was chopping its surface into little whitecaps. The lake lay gray and hostile-looking under the black overcast. Good weather for trolling flies for landlocked salmon, actually, and Moosehead was one of the best salmon lakes in the world. Calhoun rolled down the truck window to get a better look. A low bank of mist hung over the water so that the far shore was a blur. It smelled like a rainy afternoon on the ocean, damp and organic and salty.

Parked in the water and tied off on the pilings down toward the end of the dock sat a big float plane, a de Havilland Twin Otter, if Calhoun wasn't mistaken. The Twin Otter was the workhorse of float planes. It had two turboprops and could carry ten or a dozen men and hundreds of pounds of gear. This was the plane that they used to transport lumber and generators and woodstoves when they built cabins and fishing lodges on remote Maine lakes.

Calhoun parked his truck among the other vehicles behind the row of stores and fished his cell phone from his pants pocket. When he flipped it open, he saw that there was service here in Greenville.

He had a voice mail message waiting. It came from a number he didn't recognize. He called up his messages and a woman's voice said, "Hello, Deputy Calhoun. This is Ella Grimshaw calling you on Thursday morning from the medical examiner's office here in Augusta. When I saw you yesterday, I promised I'd let you know when I heard from the CDC. Their report just came in a short time ago, and I'm relieved to tell you that those two victims from St. Cecelia, who we determined were not killed by gunshot wounds, appear not to have died from some rare mutated virus or some insidious new strain of influenza, either. I don't know if you're interested in the details, but they are public record, and I'd be happy to share them with you if you want. You may call me here at the office or on my cell phone." She recited two numbers, and Calhoun knew he'd remember them without writing them down.

He tried Dr. Grimshaw's office number and reached a receptionist, who asked his name and put him through.

A moment later Dr. Grimshaw said, "Deputy Calhoun. Hello."

"Hi," he said. "I'm returning your call."

"Right," she said. "I told you I'd call when I had something new about the McNulty and Gautier deaths, right?"

"Yes, ma'am."

"Well, I got the report from the CDC just this morning," she said. "They both died of botulism poisoning."

"Botulism," said Calhoun.

"That's right."

"I don't know anything about botulism," he said. "It's pretty deadly, isn't it?"

"Very deadly," she said. "Fortunately, it's quite rare. We have only about a hundred and fifty cases a year in the United States. The botulinum neurotoxins kill you by paralyzing your respiratory system. Not a pleasant way to die. It's actually the most poisonous substance known to man." She hesitated, then said, "It's no wonder that we worry about terrorists."

"You saying that stuff's a biological weapon?" He remembered how Mr. Brescia had told him that he thought McNulty was working on something involving national security when he died. A biological weapon in the hands of terrorists would certainly qualify.

"Not a weapon," she said. "Not as far as we know. Not yet, anyway. We worry that it could be, though. Just a matter of figuring out how to package it and deliver it efficiently."

"So how did McNulty and Millie Gautier get botulism? Not from terrorists, I assume."

"No," said Dr. Grimshaw. "There have been no terrorist incidents lately in Aroostook County." Dr. Grimshaw chuckled softly. "No, so far this is good news. Most likely they both just ate the same tainted food. They apparently died at about the same time."

"That's good news, huh?"

"If no one else ate that food, if it's not an outbreak, it's good news, yes."

"How long between when you eat the bad food and when you die?"

"It can be as little as six hours or as much as several days," she said. "Why do you ask?"

"Just wondering," he said, though since he intended to investigate McNulty's and Millie Gautier's deaths, he was thinking that the information could prove helpful. "How do you figure it?" he said. "They were driving in their car, and both of them started to feel sick, so they pulled off the road there where they happened to be, which was in the woods on the outskirts of St. Cecelia, and they sat there in their car until they were dead? Then somebody came along and shot them both and tried to make it look like a murder and a suicide?"

"I guess so, Mr. Calhoun," said the doctor. "It's a hard one to figure, isn't it? Frankly, right now I'm more concerned with the health of the people living in and around the town of St. Cecelia than I am with the details of these two deaths. With botulism, one fatal case is an isolated incident, but two deaths at the same time and place could portend a full-blown outbreak. That is a cause for worry."

"Have they had any other cases of botulism poisoning in St. Cecelia?"

"So far, we've heard of none, thank God. That, as I said, is the good news."

"If it was a terrorist incident . . . ?"

"There would surely have been more deaths, but——" She paused. "What? Oh. Excuse me for a minute, Deputy Calhoun."

Calhoun heard her muffled voice. It sounded like she had put her hand over the receiver on her phone to talk to somebody.

"I'm sorry," she said a minute later. "I've got to go now. Anyway, that's all the information I have for you. If I learn anything more, I'll call you."

"Thank you," Calhoun said. "I appreciate it."

"If you hear anything," she said, "I hope you'll share."

"Sure," he said.

After he disconnected with Dr. Grimshaw, Calhoun sat there for a minute, thinking about what she'd told him. The two of them, McNulty and the girl, dying from botulism poisoning was strange enough, but somebody shooting their corpses, trying to make it look like a murder-suicide, was downright weird. It made no sense.

Well, that's why he was here. To make sense out of it.

He got out of his truck, held the door for Ralph and told him to heel, and headed out onto the dock.

A panel truck was parked there next to the plane. When Calhoun got closer, he saw that the truck had the Stop & Shop logo on its side and that two men were transferring stuff from the truck to the plane, which sported its own logo, a fancy scrolled triple *L* with a leaping salmon and crossed fly rods.

One of the men was wearing a short-sleeved shirt covered with orange and yellow tropical flowers. He had a reddish beard with a lot of gray in it, and he was wearing a Detroit Tigers cap backward. Lanky strands of gray hair poked out from under the cap. He wore his aloha shirt untucked, which did little to camouflage his big stomach.

Calhoun went up to him. "I'm looking for Mr. Swenson."

The man nodded. "I'm Swenson. Who're you?"

"Calhoun. I hope you're expecting me."

"Yeah, okay," said Swenson. "Good. Glad you're here. Hoped I wouldn't have to wait for you. Soon's we get these supplies loaded, I want to take off. I don't like the looks of this sky."

"Can I help?" said Calhoun.

Swenson shook his head. "Me 'n' Eddie here know what we're doing. Got it down to a science. Whyn't you bring your gear down." He looked at Ralph, who was sitting on the wooden dock beside Calhoun. "The mutt yours?"

"His name's Ralph," said Calhoun, "and he's not a mutt. He's a Brittany."

Swenson dismissed the issue of Ralph's parentage with a wave of his hand. "You planning on bringing him on the plane with you?"

"Yes."

"He gonna be all right with the noise? What about air sickness? Will he sit still? I can't have some dog puking all over the seats or moving around while—"

"Ralph won't be a problem," said Calhoun.

Swenson cocked his head, then shrugged. His face was deeply creased and sunburned, and his eyes were a washed-out blue. He looked like he'd lived hard. Calhoun guessed he was somewhere in his late fifties.

Swenson turned his back on Calhoun and resumed taking the stuff Eddie handed to him and stowing it in the cargo hold of the plane.

Calhoun gave Ralph a whistle and headed back to his truck. He hefted his duffel and his gear bag and lugged them back to the plane. He dumped them on the dock, then went back to the truck and got the rest of his stuff.

By the time he piled all his gear on the dock next to the plane, Eddie was behind the wheel of the Stop & Shop truck, and Swenson was talking to him through the window.

After a minute, the truck started up and rolled down the dock to the parking area, and Swenson climbed into the cargo hold of the plane. "Hand your stuff to me," he said to Calhoun.

So Calhoun passed his bags and aluminum fly-rod tubes to Swenson, who stowed them away. Then he closed the cargo door, went up to the front of the plane, and said, "Well, let's get going. You sit up front with me. Your dog can sit behind us if he'll stay quiet."

Calhoun climbed into the front seat on the right. Ralph scampered onto the seat behind him. Swenson cast off the lines, then took the pilot's seat beside Calhoun. He turned and held out his hand. "I'm Curtis Swenson," he said.

Calhoun shook his hand. "Stoney Calhoun," he said.

"Your seat belt," Swenson said. He buckled his own.

Calhoun buckled up.

"You're taking Bud Smith's place while he's off tending to his family, I understand," said Swenson.

Calhoun nodded. "I'm just filling in."

"Nice opportunity for you."

Calhoun shrugged. "It should be interesting."

"Bud's a pretty good guide."

"So'm I," said Calhoun.

Curtis Swenson handed a headset to Calhoun. "Put this on. Then we can talk. It gets pretty damned noisy up here." He clamped his own earphones on over his Tigers cap, then turned and looked at Ralph. "You gonna be all right, pooch?"

"He'll be fine," said Calhoun.

Swenson leaned forward and squinted up at the sky. "I figure we got an hour before this settles into something serious. Let's do it."

He started the left engine, then the right one. The plane's cab filled with the roar, only partially muffled in Calhoun's ears by the headset. Swenson fiddled with some switches, then put the plane in gear and began taxiing out onto the lake. Calhoun watched what Swenson did, and he realized that there was a memory in his body and his brain of how the stick felt vibrating in his hands, and how his feet could feel the air pressuring the fuselage when they worked the rudder pedals, and he knew he'd flown a plane such as this one low and fast over woods and lakes. This memory, like all of his memories from the time before he was zapped by lightning, was imprecise and refused to be pinned down, but Calhoun could feel it in his fingers and toes.

Swenson taxied about half a mile down the lake, then pivoted the plane around so that it was headed into the north wind. "Ready?" he said. His voice crackled through the earphones.

"I'm ready, Captain," Calhoun said.

The plane began moving forward. As it accelerated, the roar of the engines became louder. Pretty soon they were skimming across the top of the wind-rippled water, and then they were aloft.

"We got about an hour's flight," said Swenson. "You gonna be all right?"

"I'm fine," said Calhoun. He turned in his seat to check Ralph, who was sitting there looking out the window as if they were riding in Calhoun's pickup truck.

"You ever been to Loon Lake?" said Swenson.

"Nope."

"Fancy place," he said. "Awfully good fishing. You like fancy places?"

"Not particularly. I like good fishing, though."

"They got a Russian couple staying there now. Rumor has it he used to torture political prisoners for the KGB. She's about forty years younger than him. There's a country singer and her boyfriend. She's a big star, they say, and he's a heroin addict. Some actor's there with his two teenage boys. An outdoor writer and his wife, some rich couple from Texas, pair of CEOs from Chicago. That's how it is. A lot of big shots. You or I, we couldn't afford the place."

"They're having good fishing?" said Calhoun.

"The salmon are bitin' like snakes, they say. I couldn't tell you from personal experience."

"You don't fish?"

Swenson turned and looked at Calhoun. "I'm an employee. I'm not invited to fish."

"You like to fish, though, huh?"

"Sure. Who doesn't?"

"You can come out with me sometime," said Calhoun.

"Get yourself in trouble with management," said Swenson, "hobnobbing with the help."

Calhoun smiled. "I can live with that. Hell, I'm the help, too."

They fell silent for a few minutes. Below them it appeared to be all pine woods, with the occasional stream or pond. Now and then Calhoun glimpsed one of the sandy roads that had been cut out of the woods by the lumber companies for their big trucks to haul the logs. The roads looked like pale scars on the green landscape.

"How long've you been flying?" said Calhoun, mostly by way of making conversation.

"Choppers in Vietnam got me started," said Swenson. "When I got out, I flew the bush in Alaska for twenty-five years, and I'm not prepared to say which was more dangerous. Crashed and burned in both places. This here is sort of my retirement. Compared to Alaska, Maine's easy."

"The weather?"

"Exactly," said Swenson. "Well, in Nam, of course, we had people shooting rockets at us. In Alaska you have a different weather system in every river valley. You never know which one's going to show up where you're flying. Nobody can predict them. The pilots understand the weather better than anybody, because their lives depend on it, but nobody's perfect. Sooner or later, everybody goes down. Then it's a matter of if you survive it."

"You went down?"

"More than once," said Swenson.

"Ever go down up here?"

"In Maine?" Swenson shook his head. "Nope. Not yet."

"That's comforting," said Calhoun.

"In Maine the weather's more predictable. You can understand it if you pay attention. Like today. I'm pretty sure we got a good hour before these clouds drop down too low for safe flying."

"*Pretty* sure?"

"Sure enough to be flying," said Swenson.

"My life is in your hands," said Calhoun.

"You watch what I do," said Swenson. "If I have a stroke or a heart attack or something, it'll be up to you to bring us down."

"I'm watching," said Calhoun. "I'd just as soon you stayed healthy, though."

Calhoun understood that he didn't need to watch. He'd flown planes before, and if he had to, he knew, the muscle memory of it would click in and he could do it again.

They were quiet for a little while as the wooded landscape passed under them. Then Calhoun said, "Did you know McNulty?"

"McNulty," said Swenson.

"He was a guest at the lodge."

"I know who he was," said Swenson. "What's your interest in McNulty?"

"Nothing, really. I just heard about him is all."

"What'd you hear?"

"That he got killed."

"You want some advice," said Swenson, "my advice is, don't say anything about McNulty and that girl getting shot."

"When I'm at the lodge, you mean."

"Yes, sir. That's what I mean."

"They're sensitive about it, are they?"

"Management is," said Swenson.

"Meaning Marty Dunlap."

"And his wife. And his son."

"Tell me about them."

Swenson gave his head a little shake. "Not much to tell. The wife's in charge of the kitchen help and the chambermaids. June's her name. She's pretty interested in religion. The son—Robert—he does the booking and tends to the guests. You don't want to cross Robert. Marty oversees everything and deals with the guides and the other help. He's a pretty straight shooter."

"Robert's not a straight shooter?"

"Robert's ambitious. He'll run you over if he has to."

"So what's their problem with McNulty?"

"Obvious," said Swenson. "McNulty was a guest at the lodge, and he got killed. Embarrassing. The guests aren't supposed to die at Loon Lake. We had the sheriff up there interrogating everybody, including the guests. Not exactly the image they're looking for. So now it's over and done with and hopefully forgotten, and I'm giving you good advice when I tell you not to bring up the subject of Mr. McNulty."

"I'll keep it in mind," said Calhoun.

CHAPTER TEN

From the air, Loon Lake reminded Calhoun of a lumpy half-deflated football. It was the biggest of seven lakes, which were all connected by thin silvery ribbons of water like a string of odd-sized, misshapen pearls. Some of the streams that ran between the lakes appeared to be several hundred yards or more of boulder-strewn whitewater. Others were just the narrows linking the foot of one lake with the head of the next. This system of interconnected streams and lakes was, Calhoun understood, one long riverway meandering its way to the Atlantic Ocean.

Curtis Swenson dropped the plane so that they were flying just a few hundred feet above the treetops. "Big Hairy," he said as they swooped over one of the lakes. Then, pointing to another, smaller lake, "Little Hairy. Don't ask me who named them. They all have old Indian names, too, but at the lodge, they use these American names. This one here is Drake Pond. Loon's the biggest, almost three miles long. Down there you can see Muddy Pond and Crescent Lake and June's Pond. Marty named that one after his wife, I know that. Fishing's good in all of them. The rivers, too. And don't overlook the currents in the narrows at the head and foot of every lake." A minute later, he said, "There's the lodge."

Swenson made a turn over the lodge. It was perched on a knoll overlooking a cove on Loon Lake where an E-shaped dock stretched into the water next to a big boathouse. Another float plane, this one smaller than the Twin Otter, was tied up at the dock.

The lodge was sided with raw cedar. It featured a lot of glass. It was a big rambling many-angled structure with ells on both sides. It seemed to crouch on the knoll like a native animal. There were a couple of other smaller buildings, and snuggled into a grove of pine trees on the lakeshore was a cluster of cabins.

Swenson flew to the south end of Loon Lake and turned the plane so that it was heading north into the wind. "Here comes the tricky part," he said. "Landing and taking off. You've got to watch out for logs and boulders just under the surface. A chop like we've got here, they're hard to see."

"Where do the logs come from?"

"They still cut a lot of lumber around here," Swenson said. "They load the logs in trucks to take 'em to the mills. They used to run logs down the lakes, but that's illegal now. Still, sometimes a big rogue log finds its way into a river or lake, and it gets semiwaterlogged and drifts along just under the surface, and if you hit it with your pontoon, it will blow up your airplane. *Boom.* Quick as that."

Comforting, Calhoun thought.

Swenson brought the plane down. Calhoun held his breath. The water seemed to zoom up to meet the pontoons, but they landed so lightly on the corrugated surface of the lake that Calhoun couldn't tell exactly when the pontoons touched the water.

They taxied up to the dock. Two men were there to help

bring the plane alongside and tie it off. One of the men was Marty Dunlap. The other was younger, somewhere in his late twenties, Calhoun guessed. Both were wearing khaki pants and green flannel shirts. The younger man had his face jutted forward at Marty, and his hand gripped Marty's shoulder. Calhoun read anger on the man's face and in the tension in his neck and shoulders.

Marty shrugged the younger guy's hand away and turned to help ease the plane alongside the dock. The other guy stood there for a moment glaring at Marty's back before helping with the plane.

Calhoun stepped onto the dock, turned, and gave a whistle, and Ralph came bounding out of the plane. The dog headed for dry land. Calhoun knew what he had in mind.

Marty Dunlap came up to him, clapped him on the shoulder, and gave his hand a shake. "Stoney," he said. "Great to see you. Glad you could make it." Calhoun saw that his green shirt had the triple-*L* logo, the same one that was on the fuselage of the float plane, stitched onto the left breast pocket.

"I had a good pilot," he said.

"That must be your dog," said Dunlap, jerking his head in Ralph's direction.

"His name's Ralph," said Calhoun.

"This is my son, Robert," said Dunlap. "Robert, come here and meet Mr. Calhoun."

Robert Dunlap had black hair and pale blue eyes and neatly trimmed black stubble on his cheeks and chin. He was a few inches shorter than Calhoun but stocky and strong looking. His green shirt was identical to Marty's.

Robert held out his hand. The anger and tension Calhoun had seen in him a few minutes earlier was gone. Now he was smiling. "Welcome to Loon Lake, Mr. Calhoun," he said.

Calhoun nodded. "You can call me Stoney."

Robert nodded. "Sure."

There was a golf cart parked on the dock. Marty Dunlap went over and spoke to the young man who was sitting behind the wheel, a lanky redheaded guy who looked like a college kid, also wearing a dark green shirt with the triple-*L* logo over the pocket. The young guy nodded and steered the cart over to where the Twin Otter was parked, and he and Curtis Swenson began unloading supplies from the plane and piling them into the little wagon that the golf cart was towing.

Marty Dunlap came back to Calhoun and said, "Let's show you your cabin. You can settle in, get your gear stowed away. Dinner's not for a couple hours. Robert, let's help Stoney with his stuff."

Robert gave a little shrug, then hefted Calhoun's duffel onto his shoulder. Marty took a couple of gear bags. Calhoun carried the bundle of fly rods and the last gear bag, and they all trooped off the dock and along a path that followed the rocky lakeshore past a big boathouse to the cluster of cabins.

All of the cabins had screened porches across the front. Marty pushed open the screened porch door of one of the cabins. The porch was furnished with a small square table and chairs plus two comfortable-looking rocking chairs, and there was a wood box full of cut and split firewood.

Robert opened the cabin door and they went inside. It was a single big room with a kitchen area at one end and a bed at the other end and plenty of windows. On the back wall was a woodstove with a sofa and some chairs clustered around it. Under a double window on the front wall was an eating table with four wooden chairs. There was a big closet in the back corner by the head of the bed, and a chest of drawers sat at the foot. A bookcase in the corner was packed with paperback books.

Marty opened a door on the back wall. "Bathroom," he said. "You got a toilet and a shower and plenty of hot water."

"All the comforts of home," said Calhoun.

"No TV," said Robert.

"I don't have a TV at home, either."

"No telephone," said Marty, "and no cell phone reception, I'm afraid. We've got a satellite phone at the lodge that our guests can use for emergencies."

"That's the way it should be," said Calhoun. "Place like this, up here in the howling wilderness."

"Wilderness, all right," Robert said. "Though it doesn't exactly howl. Electricity from our generators and hot running water and flush toilets. Not to mention gourmet food."

"It's wilderness enough," said Marty.

"Sure," said Robert. "Luxury wilderness for the rich dudes." He jerked his head at the door. "Come on. Let's let Stoney get himself settled in."

"Right." Marty nodded. "Dinner's at six in the main lodge. Use the back door. Guides' dining room'll be right there on your left."

After the Dunlap men left in their matching khaki pants and green shirts and their quiet father-son tension, Calhoun found a bowl, filled it with water, and put it on the floor next to the sink. Ralph drank half of it, then lay down on the braided rug in front of the woodstove and went to sleep. Calhoun opened his duffel on the bed, hung his shirts and pants in the closet, and dumped his socks and underwear in the chest of drawers. Then he took his fly boxes and reels and other fishing stuff out of the gear bags and laid it all out on the table. He stuck his Colt Woodsman .22 in the drawer of the table beside his bed, and he propped up the aluminum tubes holding his fly rods in the corner.

He turned on his cell phone, saw that there was no service, turned it off, and stuck it in the bureau drawer where he'd dumped his socks. He put his deputy's badge in that drawer, too.

After he finished unpacking, he lay down on the bed, laced his hands behind his neck, and closed his eyes. He thought about Kate. No phone service meant he wouldn't be able to talk to her while he was up here. Marty Dunlap had been pretty clear that his satellite phone was for guests with emergencies, by which he meant that it was not for guides, whether or not they had emergencies. Not that most people would think talking to Kate would constitute an emergency, but it felt fairly urgent to Calhoun.

It had been sweet of her to come to his house last night to try to patch things up between them, even if it didn't work out. She'd wanted something from him that he couldn't give her, which was nothing new. So she went home madder than when she'd arrived, and now he faced a month without any chance to patch things up with her.

If he'd played it differently, if he'd defied Mr. Brescia and made Kate promise not to say anything to anybody and then hinted to her, at least, about why he had to come to Loon Lake, she might've kissed him before she left, might've even stayed for a sleepover . . .

He drifted off, thinking about Kate, the smell of her hair in his face, the feel of her skin against his, and then he was easing along a jungle path holding a machete in both hands. There were shouts coming from behind him, and he tried to run, but the path was muddy, and his bare feet kept getting sucked down. When he came to a bend in the path, he saw a woman's face peering out from a box with bars made from thick twisted vines. She was naked, and through the leafy vines Calhoun caught a glimpse of a breast and a bare leg. He stood there ankle deep in the muddy pathway holding his machete like a baseball bat. The woman was whispering to him in some foreign language he didn't understand. She seemed to be laughing and crying at the same time. He tried to move closer to her, but his feet were stuck in the mud, and then she began shouting at him, and he tried to tell her that he was going to save her, but the words stuck in his throat. He swung his machete at the bars that imprisoned her, but he couldn't reach them, and the shouting from behind him became louder. They were shooting at him, and cannons were going *boom, boom,* and then the woman's face disappeared . . .

Even as he dreamed it, he knew this was one of his old nightmares. As he forced himself to wake up, the cannons shooting in the dream became a fist pounding on his cabin door.

He sat up, rubbed his face, and tried to shake away the disorienting remnants of his dream.

There were several variants to this dream, but they always featured the same woman, and she always needed to be rescued, and Calhoun always failed. He wondered who she was. Somebody from his unremembered life, he was sure of that. Someone he'd once loved. He knew that from how he felt about her in his dreams.

He blew out a breath and called, "Come on in. It ain't locked."

The door opened and a tall, lanky man stepped into the cabin. He had a long, deeply tanned, creased face, dark eyes, and black hair pulled straight back into a ponytail. It was hard to guess his age. He could've been forty or sixty.

Ralph uncoiled himself from the braided rug and went over to sniff the man's cuffs.

"That's Ralph," said Calhoun. "I'm Stoney. Stoney Calhoun."

"I'm Franklin," said the man. He reached down and scratched the back of Ralph's neck. "Franklin Delano Redbird. Your fellow guide. Sorry if I woke you up."

Calhoun shrugged. "That's okay."

"I came to take you to dinner," said Franklin Delano Redbird. "Your dog, too. He's welcome in the guides' dining room. I can show you how things work around here, if you want."

Calhoun went over to where Franklin Redbird was standing inside the door and held out his hand. "That's very generous of you," he said. "I accept. I appreciate it."

"I got the day off tomorrow," said Franklin Redbird. "We can take out a canoe, do some fishing, give you a feel for the lakes, if you'd like."

"You must have something better to do on your day off," said Calhoun.

Franklin shrugged. "I got no interest in driving down to St. Cecelia, picking up a woman, getting drunk, gambling away my paycheck. That's the other option. I'd rather go fishing."

"Well," Calhoun said, "thank you. I'd love to go fishing with you."

"It's a date, then."

"Excuse my manners," said Calhoun. "Come on in. Have a seat." He gestured at the chairs by the woodstove. "I don't know what I've got here to offer you."

Franklin went over and sat down. "There should be a six-pack of beer and some Cokes stocked in your refrigerator," he said. "I'll have a Coke."

Calhoun went to the refrigerator and took out two Cokes. He went over, handed one of them to Franklin Redbird, then sat beside him.

Franklin talked about the fishing, which had been good, and the food, which was always excellent, and the sports, who were mostly rich and powerful and demanding. Once in a while you'd get a client who really loved fishing, but most of them already had so much excitement in their important lives that catching a few fish, even wild native brook trout and landlocked salmon, didn't seem to matter very much, although if you couldn't put them on some fish, they wouldn't hesitate to let you know that they didn't like it. "Well," he said, narrowing his dark eyes at Calhoun, "you're a guide. You know how it is."

Calhoun nodded. "Lately I've been trying to guide only people whose company I think I'll enjoy."

"You won't have that luxury at Loon Lake."

He shrugged. "I'm only here for a month. Six weeks at the most. I'll do what I have to do."

Franklin nodded. "It was odd, about Bud."

"Bud," said Calhoun. "The guide whose place I'm taking?"

"Yes. One day he's out guiding, the next morning he's in the Cessna and Curtis is flying him home. No warning, nothing. He didn't even say good-bye to anybody."

"I heard he had a sick child at home," said Calhoun, although he knew the whole thing had been orchestrated by Mr. Brescia to create the opportunity for Calhoun to come up here and figure out what McNulty had been up to.

Franklin nodded. "That's what they told us. A sick child. It just seemed kind of fishy to me."

"What else could it be?"

"I don't know. It was almost as if they wanted to get rid of him." Franklin shrugged. "Bud was lazier than most guides. Maybe that was it. Though if that was the case, I don't know why they didn't just fire him."

"He'll be back," said Calhoun, "and when he comes back, I'll be gone. Doesn't sound like somebody they're trying to get rid of."

"Peculiar," said Franklin. "That's how it seemed to me. Something's not right."

"This all happened right after McNulty got killed, didn't it?"

Franklin snapped his head around and looked hard at Calhoun. "What's your interest in McNulty?"

Calhoun shrugged. "Nothing. I just heard about this guy named McNulty who was a guest here and ended up getting killed."

"No connection to Bud Smith at all," said Franklin, "and if you want my advice, you won't mention anything about McNulty and that girl getting shot. It's a sore subject."

"Embarrassing, huh?" said Calhoun. "Bad for business."

"I'm serious," said Franklin. "Forget about McNulty."

I don't see how I can, Calhoun thought. *Finding out about McNulty is why I'm here.*

"Okay," he said. "I get it. Thanks for the advice."

Franklin stood up. "Dinner's in an hour. I'm headed back to my cabin, get cleaned up. See you there."

Calhoun nodded. He stood up and held out his hand. "Thanks for everything. I'm looking forward to tomorrow."

"Me, too," said Franklin Redbird. Then he walked out of the cabin.

CHAPTER ELEVEN

Dinner was thick slices of pork tenderloin with homemade applesauce, boiled red potatoes drenched in butter and sprinkled with chives and parsley, fresh peas, tossed green salad, and hot biscuits, all served family style on platters and in bowls, with big slabs of warm apple pie for dessert. Calhoun couldn't remember the last time he'd eaten such a delicious meal.

The food was delivered by a young woman who Calhoun guessed was a college student. Her name was Robin. She wore a green T-shirt with the Loon Lake Lodge logo over her left breast and snug-fitting blue jeans and sneakers. She had short blond hair and long legs and a pretty smile. When she saw Ralph lying beside Calhoun's chair, she went down onto her knees and bent her head close to his and patted him and talked to him for a minute. Then she went back to the kitchen. When she returned, she had a bowl of dog food for Ralph.

She put it on the floor near him. He scrambled to his feet and attacked the food bowl.

"Thanks," said Calhoun. "On behalf of my dog, whose manners could stand some improvement."

"Does he like breakfast, too?"

Calhoun nodded. "He'll eat anytime, all the time. He's a dog. I generally feed him in the morning and evening."

Robin smiled. "We'll take care of feeding him when you're here, if you want. Just bring him with you. He's a sweetie."

The guides' dining room was right off the kitchen. It was a pleasant wood-paneled space with a wall-sized window on one end overlooking the lake. A mounted brook trout that might've weighed eight pounds and a salmon that must've gone close to six, plus several antlered deer heads and a bearskin, hung on the walls.

The other guides all introduced themselves. Calhoun hoped he'd be able to remember their names.

Two were women. One was a soft-spoken redhead named Elaine. She had pale skin and chocolate brown eyes, and she looked delicate until you noticed her big knuckly hands and the ropy muscles of her wrists and forearms. Calhoun caught Elaine looking at him a couple of times during dinner. She seemed to have a little smile for him, as if they shared some intimate secret. When Calhoun caught her eye, he returned her smile, and she quickly looked away.

The other female guide was a big sloppy gal with a loud bawdy laugh named Kim. There were two young guys—late twenties, Calhoun guessed—named Peter and Ben who didn't say much of anything beyond "Please pass the potatoes" during dinner. Ben was the tall, skinny one—he must've stood at least six-six. Peter was built like a fullback, with a thick chest and bulky shoulders. There was a heavyset guy with a salt-and-pepper beard who they called Mush and a sinewy bald guy named Leon who seemed to be the elder statesman of the group. Calhoun guessed Leon was close to seventy.

Franklin Redbird and Stoney Calhoun completed the roster

of Loon Lake guides. Eight of them in all. Curtis Swenson ate at the guides' table, too. He was wearing a different Hawaiian shirt from the one he'd had on that afternoon. This one featured parrots. A paperback book was propped up against his water glass, and he ignored the conversation that floated around him.

Calhoun didn't mention McNulty during dinner, and neither did anybody else. Both Swenson and Franklin Redbird had warned him not to raise the subject of McNulty lest he offend people. Well, he didn't see how he was going to do his job up here if he didn't ruffle some feathers, and Mr. Brescia had made it clear that he had better get the job done. Calhoun had no desire to see how that merciless man would respond to failure.

The sooner he got a handle on the situation, the better. He was pretty eager to get back to Portland.

He figured he'd have to keep asking about McNulty, see how the others reacted. He assumed nobody knew that Mc-Nulty and Millie Gautier had died of botulism poisoning. When he'd brought the subject up to Curtis Swenson and Franklin Redbird, both of them had mentioned that McNulty had been shot.

He guessed that somebody up here had something to hide, and he aimed to make it uncomfortable for anybody with a secret. Sooner or later they'd do something that would give themselves away.

The trick would be to avoid blowing his cover in the process.

They were finishing up their pie and coffee when Robert Dunlap came into the guide's dining room. He had changed out of his khaki pants and green flannel shirt into a sports jacket and necktie. "How was dinner?" he said, and all the guides murmured their approval.

"Stoney," he said, "if you wouldn't mind, I'd like to introduce you to our guests. You and Ralph."

So Calhoun, with Ralph at heel, followed Marty Dunlap's son to the big living room on the other side of the building. This room featured a cathedral ceiling and a solid wall of glass overlooking the lake. The sun was just setting behind the hills, bathing the lake in pink and orange. There were a dozen or so people there—four or five attractive women wearing dresses or tailored pants and blouses, the rest middle-aged and older men in sports jackets or blazers and neckties. They were all holding brandy snifters or highball glasses, and several of them were puffing cigars or cigarettes. Some classical music was playing from hidden speakers up in the rafters of the spacious room. It was all quite grand, Calhoun thought.

Robert cleared his throat and said, "Can I have your attention for a minute?"

The guests all turned and looked at him.

"I want to introduce our newest guide to you," he said. He put his arm around Calhoun's shoulders. "This is Stoney Calhoun. Stoney's one of the best guides in the state of Maine. He works out of a fly shop in Portland and specializes in landlocked salmon and striped bass. He's a great fly tier, too. And this"—Robert reached down and gave Ralph a pat—"this is Ralph, Stoney's bird dog."

The Loon Lake guests held up their glasses and snifters in a toast to Calhoun and Ralph.

"Ralph and I are looking forward to fishing with you," said Calhoun.

"Can you teach my wife how to cast a fly rod?" said one guy.

The others laughed.

"I can teach any of you how to cast," Calhoun said. "Women pick it up faster, in my experience."

"You haven't tried to teach my wife," the guy said.

"We'll go out for a lesson," said one of the women, "just Stoney and me. Then we'll see how fast I pick things up. I've got a feeling Stoney's an excellent teacher. He certainly is cute."

More laughter.

Calhoun didn't want to be in the middle of this. He raised his hand in a wave and said, "Thank you. Nice to meet you all. I'll see you on the water." Then he patted Robert Dunlap's shoulder, turned, and left the room.

When he was outside, he took a deep breath and blew it out. More than once he'd found himself trapped in a boat with a married couple who were more interested in playing out their issues and conflicts for the benefit of a stranger than in catching fish. Wives flirted with him. Husbands told him sexist jokes. Both husbands and wives directed snide comments about each other to him, as if they expected his agreement and support.

He had yet to devise a comfortable way of extricating himself from these situations. All he could do was ignore them, play dumb, and pretend he didn't understand what was going on.

He and Ralph walked down the slope in front of the lodge to the dock. The skies had cleared, the sun had set, and the moon glowed from behind the trees on the horizon. Its light rippled on the lake's surface. They went out to the end of the dock. Calhoun sat down, took off his shoes and socks, and dangled his legs over the side, letting his feet hang in the cold lake water. Ralph sprawled on the planks beside him.

Tomorrow he'd go fishing with Franklin Redbird. It would be a quick, down-and-dirty introduction to the Loon Lake watershed. It takes a long time to get to know one lake, never mind seven of them, intimately enough to fish them effectively, but Calhoun figured it would be enough to enable him to find some fish for his sports.

"Is there room there for me?"

Calhoun jerked his head around. Elaine, the guide with the strong hands and soft smile, was standing behind him. He hadn't heard her.

He patted the dock beside him. "Plenty of room. Have a seat."

She sat beside him. He noticed that she had bare feet. She dangled them in the water. "So what do you think so far?"

"About what?" said Calhoun.

"Our place here. The people. Marty and Robert and June." She laughed softly. "Hell, I'm just trying to make conversation."

"It seems like a good place," he said. "The food's excellent. I haven't met June yet."

"You still got that pleasure to look forward to, huh?"

"Do I detect some sarcasm in your tone?"

She chuckled. "June's a piece of work. You'll see."

"How long've you been guiding here?" said Calhoun.

"Six years." Elaine smiled. "I can't honestly imagine a better place to work. You'll like it. I understand you're taking Bud Smith's place. You're leaving when he comes back?"

He nodded. "I got my own life down in Portland. I just agreed to help out Marty."

"Too bad. I got a feeling that you're gonna fit right in."

"I've got to learn the water pretty fast."

"Franklin's going to take you out tomorrow, right?"

"That's right. Damned nice of him."

Elaine chuckled. "He pulled the short straw."

Calhoun smiled and nodded. "I figured it was something like that. Man's giving up his day off."

She gave his biceps a gentle punch. "I was kidding. Franklin's just a nice man. This water's not hard to learn. Fish are pretty much where you'd expect them to be. This time of year, along the drop-offs, around the rock piles, in the moving water, anywhere a brook comes into the lake. That's where you'll find the smelt spawning. Salmon and trout both love those smelt." She smiled. "I bet you already know all that."

Calhoun nodded. "I suppose I do. Nice to have it confirmed, though."

They sat there on the end of the dock in comfortable silence while the moon rose from behind the forest across the lake.

"Franklin told me you've been asking about that McNulty man," Elaine said.

"I'm surprised Franklin mentioned it."

"He wondered if I knew anything about what happened to him," Elaine said. "What he might've been up to. Why he got shot."

"Franklin asked you that?"

She nodded. "He said you were interested."

"I didn't think he'd say anything," said Calhoun. "Really, it's just idle curiosity. Franklin was kind of horrified when I mentioned McNulty."

"Well," she said, "he pulled me aside before dinner."

"What'd you tell him?"

She cocked her head and looked at Calhoun. "Nothing. I don't know anything about McNulty. Franklin didn't seem to believe me. He got a little upset."

"Upset?"

"He raised his voice at me, called me a liar. I just walked away. That quiet Indian is a nice person, but he's got a temper."

"I'm sorry," said Calhoun. "I guess that was my fault."

"No," said Elaine. "That was Franklin Redbird's fault."

"I was the one who raised the subject with Franklin. He was asking on my behalf."

"Don't worry about it," she said. "I can handle Franklin Redbird."

They sat there in silence for a few minutes, watching the moon come up over the trees across the lake. Then Calhoun said, "Everybody tells me I shouldn't mention McNulty. Apparently he's a big embarrassment to this place."

"He was a guest here," Elaine said, "and he got shot, ended up dead in a car with a teenage girl. It raised a lot of questions. That sort of thing isn't great for a place's reputation."

"I was just wondering about it," Calhoun said. "It's no big deal."

Elaine turned and looked at him. "No? Really? No big deal?"

He nodded. "Really."

She smiled. "So why do you keep asking about it?"

"When it happened," he said, "people were talking about it all the way down to Portland. It was in the news. How this guy who's staying at the fanciest fishing lodge east of the Rocky Mountains ends up dead in a car in the woods with an under-age girl, both of them shot in the head. Maybe a murder-suicide, maybe not. If not, no known motive, no perpetrator apprehended. It's interesting, that's all. Now, here I am, and I bet you knew McNulty. So what am I missing?"

"I didn't really know him," Elaine said. "I never guided him. Not sure I ever exchanged more than three words with him. He was a quiet guy. He was here by himself, had his own room, and when he went fishing, it was just him and his guide in the boat. Like I tried to tell Franklin, I don't know anything about McNulty." She shrugged. "I don't think you should keep asking about him."

"Who did guide him?"

She laughed softly. "You are persistent, aren't you?"

"Just curious," he said. "When people don't want to talk about something, it makes me more curious."

"I don't remember who guided him," she said with a shrug.

"Could you find out for me?"

She hesitated, then said, "I guess I could, if it's that important to you."

"I'd appreciate it," said Calhoun.

Elaine was frowning at him.

"What?" said Calhoun.

"Huh?"

"You were looking at me funny."

She smiled quickly. "I guess I don't understand your interest in McNulty, that's all."

Calhoun flapped his hand. "You've got to admit, it's an interesting case."

She shrugged. "I guess so."

They were silent for a few minutes. Then Elaine said, "Talking with you about McNulty makes me curious, too. It is kind of strange how the people up here don't want his name even mentioned. As if we had something to hide. Which I don't really get. I mean, it didn't even happen here." She put her hand on Calhoun's shoulder to brace herself as she pushed herself to her feet. "Well, bedtime for me," she said. "Long day on the water tomorrow."

Calhoun stood up, too. He picked up his shoes and socks and snapped his fingers at Ralph. "Me, too," he said.

They walked barefoot off the dock and onto the pine-needle-carpeted path that followed the lakeshore past the boathouse to the guides' cabins. They stopped outside Calhoun's door.

"If you need anything," said Elaine, "I'm just two cabins down from you." She pointed. "Don't hesitate. Anytime."

"Thanks," he said. "It looks like I got everything I'll need, but I appreciate it."

She patted his arm. "Well, good night, then, Stoney Calhoun. I'm glad you're here." She gave him a nice smile, then turned and headed down the path.

"Good night, Elaine," said Calhoun. He watched her go into her cabin.

CHAPTER TWELVE

Breakfast for the guides at Loon Lake Lodge started at six and went until eight thirty in the morning. Calhoun and Ralph got there a little before seven. On the table were pitchers of chilled orange juice and carafes of hot coffee, covered platters of bacon and sausages and ham steaks, bowls holding bananas and oranges, boxes of Cheerios and Wheaties and Raisin Bran, and cloth-covered trays piled with toast and biscuits and bagels and English muffins.

Calhoun sat beside Franklin Redbird, who was holding a coffee mug in both hands and sipping from it. "You eat already?" said Calhoun.

"Flapjacks, Maine maple syrup, sausages," said Franklin. "What I always have. Flapjacks and sausages stick to a man's ribs all day long."

Calhoun poured himself a mug of coffee. Curtis Swenson, the bush pilot, wearing his usual gaudy Hawaiian shirt, this one featuring multicolored toucans, was sitting down at the other end of the table sipping coffee and reading a newspaper and ignoring everybody. The two young guides, Peter and Ben, were shoveling in the food, and the heavyset guide they called Mush was sipping his coffee. The others apparently had either already eaten or hadn't showed up yet.

Robin, the waitress, came in and asked Calhoun if he wanted some eggs or pancakes or French toast or some combination thereof. Or maybe some oatmeal?

He asked for three eggs over easy.

"You ready to go fishin' today?" said Franklin.

"Rarin' to go," said Calhoun.

"I got rods and flies and lunch and everything," Franklin said. "It'll be a treat, having a real fisherman and a good bird dog in my canoe. You and Ralph just meet me on the dock after you're done with breakfast." He wiped his mouth on a napkin and stood up. "See you there." He patted Calhoun's shoulder and left the dining room.

"The Indian's taking you out today, huh?" said Mush around a mouthful of Wheaties.

"Franklin's going to show me around, yes," said Calhoun. He didn't like the way the burly guy used the word "Indian," with just the hint of a sneer.

"That old Penobscot grew up around here," said Mush, "knows the water better'n anybody, and knowin' him, he'll probably show you all his best spots." He grinned. "Me, I'd rather hang on to my secrets. So it's a good thing you got him, not me."

Calhoun smiled. "I agree with you on that."

Mush frowned, then shrugged, and returned his attention to his cereal.

A couple of minutes later, Robin returned with a plate of eggs for Calhoun and a bowl of dog food for Ralph.

"Thank you," said Calhoun.

"You want anything else," said Robin, "just holler."

After they finished eating, Calhoun and Ralph went back to the cabin. Even though Franklin said he had all the gear they'd need, Calhoun put a couple of his own fly boxes into his shirt pockets. He preferred to fish with flies he'd tied himself, and he had some patterns he'd invented that he thought Franklin might like to try.

He strapped his sheathed hunting knife onto his belt, put on his sunglasses and a long-billed cap, and grabbed his rain jacket, and he and Ralph went down to the dock.

Franklin Redbird was sitting in the stern of a classic Grand Lake canoe tinkering with the outboard motor. Calhoun was happy to see that the lodge used Grand Lakers. They were sleek twenty-foot-long square-ended canoes, wood skeletons covered with green fiberglass, with elegant upswept bows. Franklin's had what looked like an eight- or nine-horsepower outboard motor clamped on the transom. The broad-beamed Grand Lake canoes were stable and dry in a heavy chop, they could navigate shallow water, and they carried three adults and piles of gear with room to spare.

Calhoun saw that Franklin had two fly rods already strung up and stowed on pegs under the gunwales. "Shall I cast us off?" he said.

Franklin nodded. "Let's go fishin'."

Calhoun pointed to the middle of the canoe and said to Ralph, "Get in and lie down."

Ralph jumped softly into the canoe and curled up near the middle thwart.

Calhoun untied the lines, then climbed in and took the bow seat. He pushed the canoe away from the dock. Franklin took a few strokes with a paddle, then started up the motor, and they were cruising across the lake.

It was a cloudy, warm, soft day. The air smelled moist.

Sometime in the night the wind had turned from the north to the southwest—an excellent quarter for salmon fishing—and there was just enough chop on the water. Calhoun put on his rain jacket against the spray that the bow occasionally threw up.

When they got to the other side of the lake, Franklin said, "Let's put out some lines, see what happens." He handed one of the fly rods up to Calhoun.

Calhoun took it and decided not to replace the flies Franklin had chosen. There was a Ballou Special tied to the point and a Black Ghost on the dropper. Classic old Maine salmon streamers. He approved of Franklin's choices, and besides, he was afraid he'd insult the man if he replaced them with his own flies.

He turned around and sat facing the back so he could watch his line as it trailed out behind them. Franklin cut the motor down to a slow trolling speed. "This here is a good shoreline this time of year," he said, raising his voice a little to be heard over the low grumble of the motor. "This wind coming out of the southwest blows onto it, and that seems to push the baitfish into the rocks. Plus there are several brooks that come into the lake along here where the smelt like to spawn."

A few minutes later Calhoun's rod bounced, and then it bent steeply, and line began peeling off his reel. "Hey," he said. He lifted his rod and felt the weight of a good fish. "I got one."

Franklin cut the motor and reeled in his own line. Far behind the boat a large landlocked salmon jumped. Then it ran toward the deep water. Calhoun lowered his rod so that it was parallel to the water and held it to the side and tried to turn the fish. He liked to bully them, to land them fast so they wouldn't be dangerously exhausted when he netted them. If you babied it, a fish like a salmon could kill itself pulling against the resistance of the rod by overdosing its muscles with lactic acid. Once in a while he broke off a fish this way, but Calhoun figured that was a reasonable price to pay for returning a healthy fish to the water.

With unrelenting down-and-dirty pressure from the long, limber fly rod, he got the fish close to the boat quickly, and Franklin netted it with the long-handled boat net. He held the net down to Calhoun so he could reach in and twist the fly from the salmon's mouth. He didn't even touch the fish. "A lovely salmon," he said.

"A beauty," said Franklin. "Close to four pounds, I'd say. Nice job of fighting him, too." Then he put the net back into the water and flipped it over, and after a moment, the salmon realized it was free and swam slowly away.

They caught three more salmon and one nice brook trout in the morning, trolling along the shoreline of Loon Lake. A little after noontime, Franklin Redbird beached the canoe on a sandy point of land. Ralph hopped out and went to explore the bushes. Franklin and Calhoun hefted the big cooler out of the canoe, then gathered dead wood and got a fire going.

"Now you relax," said Franklin. "Take a nap or something while these coals burn down and I get lunch going."

"I'd rather help," said Calhoun.

"One-man job," said Franklin. "I'm all over it. Take a nap."

"A nap," said Calhoun.

"Why not?"

It went against Calhoun's grain to let somebody else do all the work, but that was how Franklin wanted it. So he found a mossy place in the sun and lay down and closed his eyes, and Ralph came over, turned around three times, and lay down tight against Calhoun's hip, and to his surprise, the next thing he knew Franklin was poking his arm and telling him lunch was all ready.

It was a typical Maine guide's shore lunch—a bubbling pot of chili, grilled rib-eye steaks, slices of tomatoes, a loaf of sourdough bread, a bag of Toll House cookies, and a pot of coffee.

"This is great," said Calhoun. He tossed a hunk of steak to Ralph, who swallowed it whole. "You do this every day?"

Franklin nodded. "Some of the guides have the cook make sandwiches, but I like to give my sports the traditional Maine shore lunch experience. The cook'll pack whatever you want. Steaks, sliced potatoes and onions, beans, soup, chili, pies and cookies, soft drinks, coffee and tea. All you gotta do is build a fire."

"No beer?"

Franklin shook his head. "Not in my canoe. You can bring some if you want. In my experience, it tends to make your sports crabby and argumentative. Or else they just end up falling asleep in the boat."

"I don't bring beer when I go guiding, either," said Calhoun. "There are plenty of times and places for drinking beer besides on a fishing boat."

While they were eating, Franklin said, "I asked around about McNulty last night."

"You didn't have to do that," Calhoun said. "I don't want you to get in trouble."

"No trouble," he said. "Didn't learn anything, though. Sorry. I tried."

"That's okay."

"Either nobody knows anything," said Franklin, "or they just ain't talking about it."

"It's not important," Calhoun said.

A few minutes later there came the sound of an airplane passing over the lake. Both Calhoun and Franklin Redbird used their hands as visors and peered up at the cloudy sky, but the plane did not come into their view.

"That'd be Curtis," said Franklin. "Picking up some clients in Canada probably."

"Canada," said Calhoun.

"A lot of the international sports come in through Canada. We're real close to the border here. It's a much shorter flight than the one from Greenville you took yesterday. Just a quick hop from their wilderness lake to ours."

"And no passport needed," said Calhoun.

Franklin shrugged. "You're right about that."

Calhoun listened to the diminishing roar of the plane's engine. He didn't recognize it. He remembered the distinctive sound of engines, and this was not the Twin Otter that had brought him to Loon Lake, the float plane that Curtis Swenson piloted. He didn't bother correcting Franklin, though. He didn't feel like trying to explain his gift for identifying engine sounds.

After they finished eating, they cleaned up their campsite, loaded the canoe, and went exploring. At the head of the lake, Franklin showed Calhoun how to paddle upstream through the narrows to get to Big Hairy Lake. Then he beached the canoe at a place where a small brook entered Loon Lake, and the three of them, with Ralph leading the way, walked about a mile on a path the followed the meandering brook until they came to another, smaller lake. This was Little Hairy, where a rowboat with a pair of oars lay overturned on a sand beach. Franklin pointed out good fishing spots along the shoreline of Little Hairy.

Then they walked back to the canoe and motored down to the foot of Loon Lake, where Franklin showed Calhoun how to get to the other lakes—Muddy, Crescent, Drake, and June's.

This time of year, he said, they all fished well. Look for rocky shorelines and drop-offs and the places where brooks came into the lake.

By now it was getting on toward late afternoon, and they decided to troll their way back to the lodge.

They caught a couple more salmon on the way. When they rounded a rocky point and came into the cove where the lodge was located, Calhoun saw that there were three seaplanes tied off at the E-shaped dock—the lodge's Twin Otter, the smaller Cessna, and another Twin Otter that hadn't been there in the morning, which he assumed was the one they'd heard when then were eating lunch.

"That's the sheriff's plane," Franklin shouted over the roar of the outboard. "From Houlton. Something's going on."

As they approached the dock, Calhoun saw that there were four men standing there. Two of them were Marty and Robert Dunlap in their green shirts. The other two wore khaki-colored shirts with matching pants and Smokey the Bear hats. They'd be the Aroostook County sheriff and a deputy, one of whom doubled as a float-plane pilot, he guessed.

Franklin shut off the outboard motor as they approached the dock, and they glided up to it. Robert Dunlap knelt down and eased the bow against a piling. Calhoun climbed out and tied them off. Then he whistled at Ralph, who jumped up onto the dock and trotted to the bushes that grew along the shore.

Calhoun reached down and gave Franklin Redbird a hand up.

Franklin mumbled, "Thanks, Stoney." He was looking hard at the two men in khaki.

They both approached Franklin. One of them looked to be about fifty. He had a florid face and straw-colored hair and a big, hard-looking belly. The other was younger and thinner, with black hair and pale skin and a slim mustache that curved down at the ends.

"Franklin Redbird?" the older one said.

"That's me, Sheriff," said Franklin. "You know me. We've met a number of times."

The sheriff nodded. "I'm arresting you for the murder of Elaine Hoffman. You have the right to an attorney. You have the right to remain silent. Anything you say can and will be used against you in a court of law. Do you understand what I just told you?"

"You saying Elaine got murdered?"

"That's right," said the sheriff.

"What the hell?" said Franklin. "I didn't murder anybody. Least of all Elaine."

"Please," said the sheriff. "Do you understand your rights?"

"Of course I do," said Franklin. "Will you tell me what's going on?"

"We'll be the ones asking the questions," the sheriff said. He turned to his deputy. "Henry, cuff this man, put him in the plane, and stay there with him, will you?"

Henry came over, pulled Franklin's arms behind him, and handcuffed him. Then, holding his arm, he steered him over to their float plane, which had AROOSTOOK COUNTY SHERIFF'S DEPARTMENT, HOULTON, MAINE printed on its fuselage. Both of them climbed in.

The sheriff turned to Calhoun. "You're Calhoun, right?"

"That's right."

"Stonewall Jackson Calhoun?"

Calhoun nodded.

"Well, Mr. Calhoun," said the sheriff, "me and Henry have had a chance to talk to everybody else here except you. I hope you don't mind if I ask you some questions."

Calhoun shrugged. "I don't mind. I can tell you, you got the wrong man."

The sheriff jerked his head at the lodge. "Why don't we go inside, get comfortable, have some coffee. That all right, Marty?"

Marty Dunlap, who'd been standing there with Robert watching, said, "That's fine. Nobody'll be in the guides' dining room this time of the day. You can use that. We'll make sure there's some fresh coffee." He turned to Robert. "Why don't you go on up there, fill a carafe with coffee, put out some cream and sugar and mugs for them."

Robert hesitated, then shrugged and headed up to the lodge. Calhoun guessed that Robert didn't appreciate being asked to do menial chores that the help should be doing, even—or maybe especially—if it was his own father who did the asking.

Calhoun and the sheriff strolled up to the lodge, went into the guides' dining room, and sat across the table from each other. Robert came in with the coffee. The sheriff poured his mug full, then handed the carafe to Calhoun, who filled a mug for himself.

The sheriff waited for Robert to leave the room. Then he leaned forward on his forearms and said, "You're a deputy sheriff. What're you doing up here?"

"I'm guiding," Calhoun said. "That's what I mainly do. A fishing guide down in Portland. I help out Sheriff Dickman now and then when he needs a hand with something. I'm just a part-time unpaid deputy. It ain't my job or anything."

"That's not how I heard it," said the sheriff.

"Well," said Calhoun, "I can't help what you might've heard. Give Sheriff Dickman a call, ask him. He'll tell you what I just told you."

The sheriff shrugged. "I wasn't accusing you of anything. Just curious."

"I'm here because one of their regular guides got called home. I'm filling in for a month because this is their busy season. That's all."

The sheriff held up both hands. "Okay, okay. I believe you. That's what Marty told me. Except he didn't say anything about you being a deputy sheriff." He reached into his shirt pocket and pulled out a small leather-covered notebook. He opened it and squinted at it, then looked up at Calhoun. "Some people have told me that you were with Elaine Hoffman last night."

"She and I sat on the dock for maybe half an hour after dinner, just talking, getting to know each other a little," Calhoun said. He remembered the sound of Elaine's soft voice, her gentle smile. He was having a hard time with the idea that she was dead. "Why don't you tell me what happened to her and why you're arresting Franklin Redbird."

"What did you talk about?"

Calhoun shrugged. "I don't remember. Not much. Fishing. Elaine told me how much she liked it here. Said it was the best job she ever had."

"Did she mention having any problems with anybody?"

"Like Franklin Redbird, you mean?"

"Anybody," said the sheriff.

"Actually, she said she'd had an argument of some kind with Franklin."

"What'd she say they argued about?"

About McNulty, Calhoun thought. *Franklin asked her about McNulty, and she said she didn't know anything about the man, and Franklin didn't believe her.*

Calhoun wasn't ready to mention McNulty to this sheriff. "She didn't tell me what the issue was," he said, "and I didn't ask. None of my business. I had the feeling it wasn't very important and that neither of them was overly upset about it."

"Well," said the sheriff, "Mr. Redbird was upset enough that he went to Ms. Hoffman's cabin sometime in the night while she was sleeping in her bed and plugged her three times in the chest with his .22."

"You're sure it was him?"

The sheriff nodded. "We found his pistol in a drawer in his cabin. It had been recently fired, and three cartridges were missing from the clip."

"What kind of pistol?"

"Colt Woodsman," said the sheriff. "Look. I know you were out fishing with Redbird today. I assume you're friends and that you like him and can't believe he'd do something like this. Yet several people told me that they overheard him and Elaine Hoffman having a bad argument, and then the murder weapon turns up in his cabin. What do you think?"

"I think anybody could've put that gun in Franklin's cabin," said Calhoun. "None of the guides lock their cabins. They don't even give us a key. You think Franklin is so stupid that he'd go shoot somebody and then stick the gun back in his own drawer?" He shook his head. "I also think folks could easily misunderstand when they overhear a conversation, think it's an argument when it isn't. You're right. I got to know Franklin pretty well, fishing with him today. You can learn a lot about a man, spending a day on the water with him. He's a peaceful man with a clear conscience."

"Well, then, Mr. Calhoun, why don't you help me out. You're a deputy. You know how this works. If it wasn't Franklin Redbird, who could've done this?"

"Look," said Calhoun, "I've barely been here twenty-four hours. Except for Franklin, and that half hour or so last night talking with Elaine, and a float plane flight with Curtis Swenson, I don't know anything about anybody up here. Oh, and

Marty interviewed me before he hired me. The others, I've barely said hello to. I have no idea about grudges or conflicts worth committing murder for."

The sheriff picked up his coffee mug, took a sip, put it down, and looked at Calhoun. "People who heard Redbird and Ms. Hoffman arguing," he said, "a couple of them told me that your name was mentioned."

Calhoun shrugged. "I wouldn't know about that."

"No? No idea why they might've been arguing about you?"

"No. Not a clue. When was this so-called argument?"

"Just before dinner last night."

"Elaine and I didn't even meet each other until dinnertime. I'd met Franklin briefly before that. He came to my cabin to welcome me and to tell me he wanted to take me fishing."

"That was it?"

"That was it," said Calhoun. "We talked about fishing, that's all."

The sheriff peered into his notebook again. Then he closed it and tucked it in his shirt pocket. "Okay, Mr. Calhoun. I got no more questions for you right now. I guess if I come up with some later, I'll be able to find you."

"I'll be here for a month or so."

"Marty's going to have to scramble for guides," said the sheriff, "with Elaine Hoffman dead and Franklin Redbird under arrest." He pushed himself back from the table and stood up.

"What happened to Elaine?" said Calhoun. "Her body, I mean."

"The coroner from St. Cecelia drove up, examined her, declared her dead, speculated that the three bullet holes in her chest were the cause of death, zipped her into a body bag, got Robert Dunlap to help him lug her out to his van, and took her back to St. Cecelia with him."

"Did he speculate about the time of death?"

"Around midnight last night," said the sheriff. "Give or take an hour or two." He picked up his hat from where he'd put it on the table, fitted it onto his head, and turned for the door.

"Wait a minute, Sheriff," said Calhoun. "About that Colt Woodsman. Your murder weapon."

"What about it?"

"I own a Colt Woodsman. I kept it in the drawer of my bedside table. I'm wondering . . ."

"You think someone took your .22 and used it to murder Elaine Hoffman?"

"Could be," said Calhoun. "They could've gone into my cabin during dinner or after that, when I was talking to Elaine out on the dock."

"Why would anyone do that?"

Calhoun shrugged. "Because the Woodsman's a good murder weapon, I guess."

The sheriff cocked his head and narrowed his eyes at Calhoun. "You said Franklin Redbird welcomed you and invited you to go fishing with him yesterday afternoon. Did he come into your cabin?"

Calhoun nodded. "We had a Coke."

"What about your Colt? Might he have noticed it when he was there?"

"It was in the drawer of my bedside table. I don't see how he could've seen it. He didn't go prowling through my drawers when he was there."

"Maybe you left the room while he was there?"

"There's only one room," Calhoun said, "and I didn't leave it."

The sheriff shrugged. "So maybe you mentioned something about the weapon to him."

Calhoun shook his head. "No, I don't believe I did. He would've had no way to know about that gun. You got the wrong man."

"If he went into your cabin and poked around, he'd have found it easily enough."

Calhoun shrugged. "I suppose so. Anybody could've done that. The Colt was just sitting there in the drawer. Not exactly well hidden."

"Well," said the sheriff, "Colt stopped making the Woodsman .22 about thirty years ago, but it's still a pretty common sidearm around here. Why don't you take me to your cabin. Let's see if yours is still there."

CHAPTER THIRTEEN

The sheriff and Calhoun walked along the path from the lodge to his cabin, with Ralph trotting on ahead of them. When they got there, the sheriff said, "Why don't you wait out here. I'll go in and check out that drawer where you put that Woodsman of yours."

Calhoun shrugged. "Okay by me." He snapped his fingers at Ralph. "You wait here with me."

Ralph sat down.

The sheriff went inside. He came back out a few minutes later shaking his head.

"It's not there, huh?" said Calhoun.

"No gun in that drawer."

"It's probably your murder weapon, then," said Calhoun.

The sheriff looked hard at him. "Did you shoot Elaine Hoffman and plant the murder weapon in Franklin Redbird's cabin?"

"Me?" Calhoun shook his head. "No. Why would I do that?"

"That's for me to figure out, I guess," said the sheriff.

"Neither of us did it," Calhoun said. "Whoever planted the gun had to've done it while Franklin and I were out fishing."

The sheriff gave a little shrug.

"You think I did it?" said Calhoun.

"I don't know. You could have. It looks like the murder weapon belongs to you."

"I've got less motive than Franklin," Calhoun said. "I only just met Elaine Hoffman. Why would I want to kill her?"

The sheriff shrugged again. "We'll figure that out."

"So who you going to arrest here," Calhoun said, "me or Franklin?"

"Him," said the sheriff, "but I got a feeling you're not telling me everything, Mr. Calhoun, and when I figure out what it is you're not saying and why you're not saying it, maybe I'll come back and arrest you. Maybe I'll arrest you both, you and Redbird. Maybe you two have got some kind of conspiracy thing going on here, hm?"

"And *maybe* what you're going to figure out," Calhoun said, "is that neither of us did this."

The sheriff shrugged. "Maybe so. We'll see."

"You check the serial number on that gun. If it's mine, you'll see that it's properly registered. Also, you might want to remember, I'm the one who told you that the murder weapon could've belonged to me. I didn't need to do that."

"I guess we would've figured it out pretty quick without your helpfulness," said the sheriff, "looking up the gun's serial number in our computer files, seeing who it was registered to. It would've appeared more suspicious if you hadn't said anything."

Calhoun nodded. "I guess you're right about that. I had no quarrel with Elaine Hoffman, though."

"Franklin Redbird did." The sheriff shook his head. "I'm

enjoying this chitchat, Mr. Calhoun, but it's growing repetitive, and I've got a prisoner to fly to Houlton for processing. I expect I'll be back here at Loon Lake before we're done with this case. So I'll be seeing you again."

The sheriff touched the brim of his hat with his forefinger, turned, and headed back toward the dock.

Calhoun sat on the front steps of his cabin. Ralph came over and plopped his chin on Calhoun's knee. He scratched the dog's muzzle. "So how do you think all this is connected to McNulty?" he said.

Ralph didn't say anything.

"It's my fault, you know," Calhoun said. "What happened to Elaine. Me asking about McNulty, and her having that argument with Franklin. It's got to have something to do with McNulty. I'm feeling awfully bad about Elaine. I liked her. I can't imagine somebody shooting her. A terrible thing. I feel bad about Franklin getting arrested, too, though I don't see how they can hold him very long if all they've got is some hearsay about an argument and that gun of mine that was obviously planted."

Without lifting his chin, Ralph rolled up his eyes to give Calhoun a look of sympathy and understanding.

"But look at all we've learned," said Calhoun, giving the dog's ears a rub. "We've learned that just mentioning McNulty's name around here is enough to get somebody riled up to the point of committing murder. We know we got a killer among us, and I'll be awfully surprised if it turns out to be Franklin Redbird. We can guess that Elaine knew something about McNulty, even though she said she didn't, and if she did, others probably do, too. All that's pretty good work for just being here twenty-four hours, wouldn't you say?"

Ralph didn't have much to say on the subject.

Calhoun looked at his watch. "Well, it's time for dinner." He stood up. "Ready?"

Ralph knew the word "dinner." The dog had an extensive vocabulary of words related to food. He scrambled quickly to his feet and started trotting down the path to the dining room.

Calhoun heard the guides talking as he and Ralph went down the short hallway to the dining room. Muffled, conspiratorial voices. He guessed there was plenty to gossip about, with Elaine getting shot and Franklin Redbird getting arrested and the sheriff questioning everybody.

The voices stopped suddenly when he and Ralph entered the room. "Evening," he said, nodding to everybody as he took an empty seat.

A couple of the guides nodded to him. The others kept their eyes averted. Curtis Swenson, as usual, was reading at the table. This time he had a magazine open in front of him. He didn't even look up when Calhoun walked in.

"You don't have to stop your conversations on my account," Calhoun said.

After a few minutes, some of them began talking about the fishing they'd had that day.

Mush, the heavyset guide, who was sitting beside Calhoun, said, "The sheriff give away any secrets to you?"

"Secrets on what subject?" said Calhoun innocently.

Mush rolled his eyes. "The murder. The Indian. You spent the day in a canoe with him. So did he do it, you think? Did he say anything?"

"You mean Franklin?"

Mush nodded. "The Penobscot. Yes."

"He didn't do it," Calhoun said.

"You know this?"

Calhoun nodded. "I do."

"The sheriff thinks he did."

"The sheriff's wrong," Calhoun said.

"Did you tell him that?"

"I did."

"I guess he don't believe you," Mush said, "or else they wouldn't've taken Redbird away on the plane."

"I suppose they think he did it, but he didn't." He turned to Mush and, imitating the soft voices he'd heard as he came in, he whispered, "I bet you got a thought. You think it was Franklin Redbird?"

"Nah, I don't reckon it was him," said Mush. "Maybe he's an Indian, but I happen to know he's a peaceful feller. Wouldn't hurt anything or anybody. He don't even hunt."

"So who do you think did it, then? Who killed Elaine?"

Mush's eyes darted around the room. He leaned his head toward Calhoun and whispered, "I don't want to say nothing."

"If you think you know," Calhoun said, "you gotta tell the sheriff."

"Oh, I talked to the sheriff. Yes, sir. I talked to him, all right."

At that moment Robin came into the room carrying a big tray of food. She put the platters and bowls on the table. Baked halibut steaks, mashed potatoes, string beans, loaves of hot bread, green salad.

Robin knelt down beside Ralph where he lay beside Calhoun's seat and rubbed the dog's belly. "I bet you're hungry," she said softly.

Ralph lifted his head and looked at her with liquid eyes, which was as good as saying, "I'm starved." "Hungry" was another one of his food words. With dogs, it's all about food.

Robin straightened up, looked at Calhoun, and said, "I'll bring Ralph's supper right out." She looked around the table. "Can I get anybody anything else?"

They all shook their heads, and Robin left the room.

Calhoun wanted to ask the guides questions about Elaine—who her enemies were, what secrets she kept, what there was about this pretty, quiet woman that didn't meet the eye—but if anybody knew anything, they were either keeping it to themselves or they'd already told the sheriff. They'd be unlikely to reveal anything along those lines at the dinner table.

So they all focused on their food.

After Robin came in to clear the table and bring the blueberry pies and vanilla ice cream, Kim, the other female guide, said, "So, Stoney. How'd you enjoy the fishing today?"

"We had excellent fishing," he said. "We actually spent much of the day just looking around. Franklin gave me a quick lesson on your lakes and where the fish like to lie. We did catch several nice salmon and one squaretail that must've gone at least four pounds. That Franklin, he's a helluva guide. Made us a terrific shore lunch."

"He's a good guide, all right," Kim said. She looked around the table with narrowed eyes. "A good guy, too. He's just the sweetest man. Anybody who thinks he could've murdered somebody is plain crazy."

As Calhoun was leaving the lodge after dinner, Marty Dunlap hurried over to him and said, "Stoney. Got a minute?"

"Sure. What's up?"

"Well, as you know, we're suddenly finding ourselves short of guides, with Franklin getting arrested and Elaine . . . um, Elaine getting killed. We've still got a business to run here. I'm going to have to press you into service a little sooner than I expected."

Calhoun nodded. "Okay by me. Franklin showed me around. I think I can find the folks some fish. Just tell me when."

"Monday," said Marty. "Tomorrow's Saturday, a getaway day for most of our guests, and we'll have some new sports coming in on Sunday. The regulars can handle those who'll be fishing over the weekend. Monday we'll definitely need you."

"Okay. That's what I'm here for."

Marty gripped Calhoun's arm. "Good. Thanks." He paused. "Listen. I don't know what Franklin might've told you . . ."

"About what?"

Marty shrugged. "Just . . . anything."

About McNulty, Calhoun thought. *You want to know if Franklin talked to me about McNulty.*

"We just talked about fishing," Calhoun said. "Franklin knows his stuff. Made a helluva shore lunch."

"He's a good guide, all right." He patted Calhoun's shoulder. "Everything satisfactory in your cabin? Anything we can do for you?"

"The cabin's good," he said. "Very comfortable." He thought about mentioning the fact that somebody had entered his cabin, which had no locks for the doors, and stolen the Colt Woodsman that was used to murder Elaine Hoffman, but he decided not to. Until he knew whom he could trust, he figured the less he said to anybody the better. "Oh," he said. "There is one thing."

"What's that?"

"When we had lunch at the Sandpiper, you told me the guides would have access to an automobile on their days off, and sometimes they'd drive down to St. Cecelia."

"That's right," Marty said. "You want to take a car?"

"Tomorrow," said Calhoun. "Would that be all right?"

"I guess so." Marty smiled. "Hell, Stoney. You've only been here a couple days. You feel like you've gotta get away already?"

"That ain't it," said Calhoun. "I got some business I didn't have a chance to finish up before I came here, that's all. I'd like to get it out of the way. Of course, if you don't think . . ."

"No, that's fine," Marty said. "I was just kidding. I'll meet you over by the car barn after breakfast tomorrow morning, get you fixed up. It's not a problem. As long as you're ready to do some guiding on Monday."

"I'll be good to go," said Calhoun. He hesitated, then said, "Has Franklin got a lawyer, do you know?"

Marty nodded. "I hooked him up with an attorney I know in Houlton."

"Is he any good?"

"Sure he's good. We take care of our people."

"If he's any good," Calhoun said, "Franklin should be back in a day or two. They don't have any evidence against him."

Marty shrugged. "I don't know. We'll see, I guess."

"You think Franklin did it?"

"I don't know, Stoney. I can't imagine anybody doing it, but it was done. I guess Franklin Redbird could've done it as well as anybody else."

After Marty went back into the lodge, Calhoun and Ralph headed down to the dock. He took off his shoes and socks and sat on the end dangling his feet in the water as he had the previous night with Elaine. Ralph sprawled beside him. Calhoun reached over and scratched the back of the dog's neck.

The sun had gone down, and the moon was obscured by the clouds. Only faint ambient light seeping through the cloud cover prevented the darkness from being total. Some night birds were swooping over the surface of the lake catching insects.

From the woods behind the lodge came the hoots and whoops of a pair of barred owls. Then, echoing from somewhere out on the lake, came the crazy, haunting laugh of a loon, and a moment later, another loon answered. The call of a loon was the wildest sound in nature, Calhoun thought, and it never failed to send a shiver up his spine.

A minute later, Ralph lifted up his head, and a low growl rumbled in the dog's chest.

Calhoun said, "Shh." He put his hand on Ralph's back and turned to look around.

Somebody was coming down the dock. In the darkness, it was just a shadowy shape, and Calhoun couldn't tell who it was, although by the way he walked, it appeared to be a man. He was sticking to the darkest shadows along the dock, moving silently. Surreptitiously, Calhoun thought. Sneaky.

The man stopped beside the Twin Otter float plane. He hesitated, and it appeared that he was looking around to see if anybody had followed him. Then he climbed out onto one of the pontoons and disappeared in the darkness.

A moment later Calhoun saw the narrow beam of a small flashlight flickering through the windshield of the plane.

He kept his hand on Ralph's back. He wasn't sure what to do. If he got up and walked down the dock to the landing, he'd go right past the plane, and whoever was in it would be likely to see Calhoun and figure Calhoun had seen him. It was pretty apparent by the way he'd been slinking around in the darkness that this person on the plane didn't want to be seen, and Calhoun didn't want to be identified as a person who'd seen somebody who didn't want to be seen.

On the other hand, if he just kept sitting there on the end of the dock, the man inside the plane might spot him, and he'd know that Calhoun had been there the whole time.

Well, that seemed the better of two bad options. So he and Ralph slid down to the corner where their shapes would be hidden in the shadow of the pilings, and they remained sitting there on the end of the dock listening to the loons while somebody prowled around inside the Twin Otter.

Calhoun kept glancing back at the plane. The light from inside was moving around. It flickered dimly through the windshield. Calhoun guessed the prowler was searching for something down in the cargo area of the big plane.

He figured the person had actually been on the plane for no more than two or three minutes, although it seemed much longer than that, when the light went out and the shadowy figure climbed out of the plane and began walking back along the dock. Something dangled from his hand, something he hadn't had with him when he walked out onto the dock. He'd picked it up from somewhere inside the plane. It looked like a small suitcase.

Calhoun looked hard at the departing figure, trying to figure out if he recognized him. He didn't. It was just a man's shape seen from behind in the darkness.

It could've been Curtis Swenson, Calhoun thought. The pilot was the only one he could think of who might have a reason to poke around the plane. If it *was* Swenson, it raised the question of why he would feel he had to sneak around in the darkness to go into his own plane.

The figure reached the end of the dock and turned right onto the path that skirted the edge of the lake, heading away from the lodge and in the direction of the boathouse. A moment later the darkness swallowed him up.

Calhoun gave him about ten minutes. Then he put his socks and shoes on, stood up, snapped his fingers at Ralph, and headed back to his cabin.

When they got there, Ralph hopped up the steps, put his nose against the door, and growled.

"Again?" said Calhoun. "That's two growls in less than an hour. What is it this time?" He knew enough to trust Ralph. If the dog growled, something was going on. "Somebody's in our cabin," he whispered to the dog. "Is that what you're telling me?"

Ralph kept his nose against the door and continued to growl softly. No lights showed in the cabin windows. If somebody was waiting inside, they wanted it to be a surprise.

Calhoun was mindful of the fact that somebody had shot Elaine Hoffman in her cabin the previous night. Now, if Ralph was to be believed, somebody had snuck into his cabin and was waiting there in the darkness.

Well, it was his damn cabin, and he had no intention of not going in.

He guessed whoever was inside, if somebody was indeed in there, had heard them by now. He wasn't going to surprise anybody. He just had to hope they wouldn't open fire on him when he walked through the doorway.

"Well, old dog," he said loudly, for the benefit of whoever might be inside, "here we are. You tired? I'm pooped. We had ourselves a hard day of fishing, didn't we? Let's go to bed."

He turned the knob, pushed the door open, slipped inside, and moved quickly away from the open doorway where his silhouette would make an easy target. "Who are you?" he said. "Who's here?"

A sound in the darkness came from the direction of his bed. It was a soft human sound. If Calhoun wasn't mistaken, it was the sound of a woman crying.

CHAPTER FOURTEEN

"It's me," came a soft voice in the darkness. "It's Robin. I'm sorry."

Calhoun reached over and hit the switch on the wall. When the ceiling light came on, he saw that Robin, the young waitress, was sitting on the edge of his bed. She was hunched over and hugging herself. A wrinkled handkerchief was clutched in one of her hands. Her face was red, and her eyes were swollen.

He went over to where she was sitting and squatted down on the floor in front of her. "So what's up?" he said to her. "What's going on?"

"I'm sorry," she said. "I hope it's all right. I didn't know who to talk to. I'm not sure who I can trust anymore. I figured, you just got here, you couldn't . . ." She looked up at him with her wet eyes.

"I couldn't what?" he said.

She shook her head. "Just, things that've been going on here, they started before you came. So I figure you didn't have anything to do with them."

"Well, you're right," Calhoun said. "You can talk to me. I won't say anything to anybody."

Robin dabbed her eyes with her handkerchief. Then she blew her nose into it. "I'm the one who found her. Her body."

"Elaine, you mean?"

She nodded. "She didn't show up for breakfast. Then her clients were waiting for her down on the dock, all set to go fishing, and she wasn't there. That's not like Elaine at all. So Mr. Dunlap asked me if I'd run down to her cabin and tell her that her sports were ready to go. So I—"

"Robert or Marty?" said Calhoun.

"Marty." Robin frowned at him. "Does it matter?"

Calhoun smiled. "No, I guess not."

She blew out a quick breath. "So anyway," she said, "I knocked on her cabin door and called in to her, but there was no answer. It was totally quiet in there. I knocked again, a little louder. Still no answer. So I pushed open the door and poked my head in. I saw that Elaine was still in bed. It looked like she was sleeping. I spoke to her, asked her if she was feeling okay, but she didn't answer me. Then I got worried that she'd taken drugs or something and was unconscious, so I—"

"Did Elaine do drugs?"

"Huh?" Robin frowned. "Oh. Well, no, I don't think so. I mean, I'm sure she didn't. That was just the thought I had. That maybe she'd OD'd or passed out or something." She shrugged. "So anyway, I went over to her bed. I was going to shake her and speak to her and see if anything was wrong. Then I saw the blood. A big patch of dried blood on the sheet where it covered her chest. Elaine was lying there with her eyes staring up at the ceiling, and she was all gray and . . . and dead. So then I—"

"The blood was dry?" said Calhoun.

Robin nodded. "It was dark and dried. Not shiny like— like fresh blood."

"So she'd been dead for a while."

Robin shrugged. "I guess so. I don't know much about that stuff."

"Okay," said Calhoun. "Then what happened?"

"Then," she said, "I completely lost it. I guess I just sat down on the floor and started screaming, because after a while some people came, and they took me back to my room, and I remember that June stayed with me for a while. I cried a lot. I guess I might've been in shock or something. After a while I went to sleep, and when I woke up, I was okay." Robin looked at Calhoun and gave him a little smile. "Well, obviously not really okay, but I'm a lot better now. Anyway, that's what happened. It was pretty traumatic. I never saw a dead person before, never mind a friend."

"You and Elaine were friends, huh?"

"She was like ten years older than me," she said, "but we were best friends."

"You shared secrets?"

Robin nodded.

"Intimate, personal things?"

"Sure. That's what best friends do."

"What secrets did Elaine share with you?"

Robin shook her head. "I don't think I should say. I mean, they're secrets, you know?"

"Elaine's dead," said Calhoun. "Maybe whoever shot her did it because of one of those secrets."

"I thought of that."

"Did you say anything to the sheriff about Elaine's secrets?"

"Not really. I guess I should have, and he did ask me pretty directly if I knew anything about her, about why somebody might want to—to kill her, but . . . well, I didn't quite trust him.

He didn't seem like the kind of man I should tell Elaine's secrets to. Even if he was trying to catch the murderer. I mean, I was thinking, Elaine told me some things in private. She trusted me with her personal stuff because she knew I'd never tell anybody. So I wasn't going to tell this stranger, even if he was the sheriff and even if Elaine was . . . even if she was dead. I just couldn't do that."

"So you *do* think whoever killed her might've done it because of one of her secrets?"

Robin shrugged. "I guess so."

"Robin," said Calhoun, "you've got to tell me."

She frowned. "Why? I mean, why you? I like you and trust you and everything, but, well, no offense, but you're just a fishing guide."

Calhoun looked at her. "Why did you come here tonight?"

She frowned. "Huh?"

"Tell me why you came into my cabin."

"I did. I told you. I needed somebody to talk to. I didn't know who else I could trust."

"You thought you could trust me, though, huh?"

She shrugged. "You're new here. Like I said. You couldn't be involved in . . . in the things that have been happening here."

Calhoun nodded. "Okay."

"Don't you believe me?"

He smiled. "Sure. I believe you." He hesitated. "Can I tell you a secret?"

Robin smiled. "Oh, just what I need. Somebody else telling me their secrets."

"I'll try not to get shot," said Calhoun. "Listen. I'd rather you didn't tell anybody, but in my regular life back in Portland I'm a part-time deputy sheriff. I know how all this business works. I know how to deal with evidence, and I know the procedures. So talking to me wouldn't be like giving away a friend's secrets to another friend. It would be like telling the authorities what they should know."

"You're a policeman?"

He smiled. "Not really a policeman. I'm a volunteer deputy sheriff. I can't arrest people or anything like that. I'm just a helper. I am pretty good at it, though."

"You got a badge?"

He nodded.

"Can I see it?"

"Sure." When he unpacked, he'd dropped the badge in its leather folder, along with his cell phone, in with his socks in the top drawer of the bureau. He opened the drawer, found the badge, and showed it to Robin.

"Cool," she said.

"Believe me now?"

"I believed you before. I just wanted to see it."

"I'd just as soon the others didn't know about me being a deputy," Calhoun said. "Can I trust you with the secret?"

Robin nodded. "I'm good with secrets."

He put the badge back in the drawer. He wondered if whoever had come into his cabin to steal his .22 pistol had prowled through his other drawers and seen the badge.

He turned to Robin. "So I've got the feeling you have a theory about who killed Elaine and why."

"Not who," she said. "I have no idea who might have done it. But why? Yeah, maybe."

"How about a glass of water, or a Coke or something?"

She nodded. "Water would be good."

Calhoun got up, went to the sink, and filled a glass with water from the tap. He took it to the table. "Let's sit here and talk," he said to Robin.

She got up from the bed and sat at the table.

Calhoun sat across from her. "Tell me about Elaine," he said.

She nodded. "Her secret, you mean."

"Yes."

She picked up her glass and took a sip of water. "There was this man staying here. A client. A fisherman. He was by himself, had a single room, went out fishing alone. With just a guide, I mean. A really good-looking man. He was, I don't know, about forty, I guess. Anyway, he and Elaine, they, um, they had a thing going on."

She meant McNulty, Calhoun assumed. "A thing?" he said.

Robin nodded. "She slept with him."

"Probably against the rules, huh?" Calhoun remembered that Elaine had told him she barely knew McNulty. He wondered what she'd lied to her friend Robin about.

"Oh, definitely," said Robin. "Sleeping with one of the clients? If the Dunlaps ever found out, Elaine would've been fired. They were very discreet. He used to sneak down to her cabin after dark. The guides all knew what was going on, I think, but none of them would ever say anything. Elaine told me. I think she was in love with him, though she just said she liked him and they were having some fun."

"This man," said Calhoun. "What was his name?"

"McNulty," she said. "I never heard his first name. Elaine always referred to him by his last name. McNulty. He got killed. He went down to St. Cecelia one day, and they found him dead. In a car. With a woman. A girl, actually. A teenager. They'd both been shot. Needless to say, Elaine was pretty upset."

"About him being with a girl."

Robin nodded. "Well, about him being killed, too, of course."

"Tell me what you can about this McNulty."

"I thought he was kind of spooky, to tell you the truth," Robin said. "He was the strong silent type, if you know what I mean. Elaine liked that, but it kind of freaked me out. He always seemed to have a lot going on in his head, but he never had much to say. From what Elaine told me, he didn't like to talk about himself. He didn't tell her where he was from or what he did for a living or anything like that. She used to say she figured he was married, that he came here to get away from his wife. That was all right with her. Elaine was pretty liberal about things like that." She paused, took a sip of water. "I told Elaine I thought he was dangerous. That he'd get her in trouble." She looked up at Calhoun and smiled quickly. "I guess I was right about that."

"Dangerous," said Calhoun. "Dangerous how?"

Robin shook her head. "I'm not sure I could explain it. It was just the impression I got. It's how he seemed to me. Like he lived out on the edge, took a lot of risks. It's like he was always calculating the odds. When you were in a room with McNulty, you had the feeling he was studying you, like he was looking right into your head. Looking for your weaknesses." She hesitated. "One of my jobs here, besides serving meals, is to make the guests' beds, put out clean towels, straighten out their rooms. One time I was working in McNulty's room and I saw a gun on his bureau. It was one of those square pistols like policemen on TV use."

"Confirming your suspicion that he was dangerous."

"Well," she said, "that he wasn't just some fisherman on vacation, anyway."

"You say he got shot," Calhoun said, as if this were the first he'd heard of it. "Who did it?"

She shrugged. "The rumor was it might've been some jealous boyfriend of the girl he was with, but I don't think they've arrested anybody."

"I bet you've got a theory."

She shook her head. "I really don't. If it was somebody from here—from the lodge—I can't imagine who. I know all these people, you know what I mean?"

Calhoun looked up at the ceiling for a minute. Then he said, "So now Elaine has been shot. You don't think that's just a coincidence, do you?"

"No," she said. "I think it's connected. To what happened to McNulty. It's got to be. I don't think I could stand it if things like that just happened randomly. I can't believe our world is like that."

Oh, it is, Calhoun thought. *When you get older, you'll see. It's a world crammed full of randomness.*

"So how do you think Elaine's death is connected to McNulty's?" he said.

"Well," she said, "he was definitely into something up here, and I figure he said something about it to Elaine. Or maybe he even got her involved in it. Whatever it was got him shot. And now Elaine."

"Into something," Calhoun repeated. "Into what?"

Elaine shook her head. "I don't know. He just didn't seem like the kind of man who'd come to a place like this to go fishing."

"So you're not buying the jealous boyfriend theory, huh?"

"I don't know. I guess not. They would've arrested him by now, if there even is a jealous boyfriend, wouldn't they?" She looked at him. "I certainly don't think it was Franklin Redbird. He's just the sweetest, gentlest man."

"So did Elaine tell you about what McNulty might've been involved in?"

Robin shook her head. "No. One day, instead of going fishing, he borrowed one of the lodge's cars and went down to

St. Cece. He told Elaine he had some business to transact down there. Two days later he was dead."

"Business."

Robin shrugged. "That's what she told me."

Calhoun was thinking that McNulty, who was really an elite government operative, a superspy, one of Mr. Brescia's highly trained agents—like Calhoun himself—had found whatever it was he was looking for at the Loon Lake Lodge. So he went to St. Cecelia, and probably intended to keep going. The girl, Millie Gautier, joined him, for some reason. Along the way they contracted botulism poisoning, and they died in their car. Then someone came along and shot them.

It still didn't make much sense.

Calhoun leaned back in his chair. "Can you think of anything else?"

Robin yawned. "I can't hardly think at all anymore." She looked at him. "You won't tell anybody I was here, will you?"

"No. Of course not."

"Or that I told you these things."

He shook his head. "If you happen to think of anything else . . ."

"Sure," she said. "I'll tell you." She covered another yawn with her hand. "So what're you gonna do?"

"A little snooping, I guess," Calhoun said.

"That's your job as a deputy sheriff, huh?"

He smiled. "That's right."

"Be careful, okay?"

"Oh, don't worry about me."

Robin stood up. "I better get back to my room. I have to get up early for breakfast."

"Ralph and I will walk back with you."

She shook her head. "You know what? I'm not sure it would

be a good idea to be seen together this time of night. If you have a flashlight I can borrow . . ."

"No," said Calhoun. "We're going with you. We'll be careful not to be seen together. Okay? I'll feel a lot better knowing you're safe."

She shrugged. "Well, okay."

Robin held on to Calhoun's hand, and they walked along the shadowy pathway from Calhoun's cabin, past the boathouse and past the dock, to the big lodge. The moon had risen over the treeline across the lake. It bathed the landscape in its yellow light. From out on the lake came the eerie laughter of the loons.

Ralph scampered ahead of them, leading the way, protecting them against monsters.

When they got to the back entrance to the lodge, Robin turned to Calhoun. "Thank you."

"I didn't do anything," he said.

"You listened. You got me talking. I needed that. Now I feel better." She put her hands on his shoulders, leaned toward him, and kissed him softly on his jaw. Then she wrapped her arms around his neck and hugged him hard against her.

He put his hands on her hips and gently pushed her away.

She looked into his eyes. "I'm sorry."

"No, don't be," he said. "That was nice."

"You're probably married or something."

He nodded. "Virtually," he said.

She laughed softly. "That's—" She stopped and pulled quickly away from him.

"What's the matter?" he said.

Robin put her finger on his lips, then pointed her chin back down to the shadowed pathway where they'd just walked.

Calhoun saw the shape of a person coming in their direction.

Robin squeezed Calhoun's arm, opened the door, and slipped into the lodge.

Calhoun snapped his fingers at Ralph. He moved away from the door and stood in the shadow of a big pine tree. Ralph came over and sat on the ground beside him.

The shadowy person came walking up the path, but instead of heading for the rear entrance where Robin had just entered, he disappeared around the corner, heading for the front of the lodge.

In the darkness, Calhoun couldn't see who it was—but the shape and the way he moved reminded Calhoun of the shape of the person who'd been sneaking around on the float plane.

CHAPTER FIFTEEN

After breakfast the next morning, Calhoun and Ralph walked out to the garage behind the lodge. It was made of peeled spruce logs and was the size of a small airplane hangar. A dark green Range Rover with the Loon Lake Lodge triple-*L* logo painted on the door panel was parked in front, and the two Dunlap men, Marty and Robert, were leaning against the hood. They seemed to be deep in some serious discussion, and as Calhoun approached them, they looked up, shifted their positions, and ended their conversation.

Calhoun went up to them and shook each of their hands. "I appreciate this," he said.

"One of the perks of the job," said Marty. "This is your vehicle. You got a full tank of gas. You'll be back today, I hope."

"I'm aiming to be back for dinner," Calhoun said.

"Looking for a little recreation in St. Cece?" said Robert.

"Huh? Recreation?"

"You never been to St. Cecelia, Stoney?"

"Nope."

Robert shrugged. "You'll see."

"I got some business to take care of," Calhoun said. "That's all. Not interested in recreation."

Robert clapped him on the shoulder. "Well, I hope it all goes well." He held out his hand. A key on a chain dangled from it. "Here you go. Drive safely."

Calhoun took the key. "Thanks."

"Just head out this driveway," said Marty, pointing to the rutted dirt road that started beside the garage and twisted into the forest. "About half a mile, you'll come to the lumber company road. Go left. From there it's about thirty miles to St. Cece. It'll take you well over an hour. It's a pretty bad road. High crown, rocks and potholes. Drive slow and careful, and watch out for the lumber trucks. They go fast and won't slow down or pull over for you. You don't pull to the side, they'll run you over. Oh, and be alert going around the corners. You don't want to run into a moose."

"I'll watch out for trucks and moose," Calhoun said. "Thanks." He opened the car door for Ralph, who hopped in and took his usual place on the passenger seat. Then he got in behind the wheel. He shut the door, started the engine, and rolled down the window. "Thanks again," he said.

Marty held up a finger and came over to the open car window. He braced his forearms on the roof and leaned in. "I been meaning to ask you, Stoney," he said. "You doing okay?"

"Sure."

"Getting along with your fellow guides? Enjoying the food? Finding your way around?"

"It's all good," said Calhoun.

"Sorry about what happened yesterday," he said. "Elaine getting killed, Franklin being arrested, you getting interrogated by the sheriff."

"It was a terrible thing."

"I wouldn't want you to think we had murders happening here every day."

Calhoun nodded.

"You probably got pretty friendly with Franklin Redbird," said Marty.

"Sure. I fished with him for a day. You can get pretty friendly with a man that way."

"I don't think he killed anybody," Marty said. "Robert, here, he's a little more cynical than I am."

Robert, who'd been standing there listening, said, "It's not cynicism. It's just the facts. Anyway, what you and I think doesn't count. The sheriff thinks Franklin did it, and that's what counts."

"He didn't do it," said Calhoun.

"Really?" said Robert.

Calhoun nodded.

"You're pretty sure of that, are you?"

"Yep. Pretty sure."

"So who did it, then?" said Marty.

Calhoun shrugged. "I got no idea." He shifted into first gear. "If I don't get going, I'll miss dinner, and I don't want to miss dinner."

Marty slapped the roof of the car and stepped away from the window. "Have a good day."

Calhoun waved and started down the driveway. In the rearview mirror he saw Marty and Robert Dunlap, father and son, standing there outside the garage with their arms folded across their chests, watching him go.

The paper company road was originally cut through the forest so that their big flatbed trucks with the high wooden sides could transport pulp logs to the paper mills near the coast. It was apparent to Calhoun that the road hadn't been used by the big trucks very much recently. Now the alders and poplars and hemlocks were crowding both sides, making it barely wide enough for the Range Rover to pass. Even sticking to the center of the road, here and there tree branches scraped against the sides of the vehicle. Weeds and saplings sprouted from the ruts, and rocks had pushed through the earth's crust. In the low places, spring seeps trickled across the road.

They'd been driving for about half an hour when they rounded a bend and came upon a mother ruffed grouse and her brood of seven chicks pecking gravel beside the road. Calhoun hit the brakes, and when Ralph spotted the grouse, his bird-dog genes kicked in, and he pushed his nose against the windshield and began to whine.

The mother grouse lifted her head and looked directly at the Range Rover, and through the open car window, Calhoun could see the glitter of her beady little eyes and hear her panicky little cries. Instantly the fuzzy little brown chicks scurried into the underbrush beside the road. There, Calhoun knew, they'd crouch motionless in the grass and dead leaves and be impossible to see, and they wouldn't budge no matter how close to them you stepped.

The mother bird staggered across the road in the opposite direction, dragging her wing, feigning vulnerability. It was a great act. Once she'd succeeded in enticing her enemy to follow her a safe distance away from her precious brood, she'd burst into sudden, noisy flight and disappear into the woods.

These were survival behaviors that had evolved over hundreds of generations of ruffed grouse. All creatures had repertoires of survival behaviors, and Calhoun never tired of observing them.

All creatures except humans, he thought.

Humans just killed each other.

They'd been driving for about an hour and a half, rarely going much over twenty miles per hour, when they came upon a square wooden building beside the road with a sign reading CASINO over the door. Half a dozen vehicles—one old yellow Volkswagen van and five or six pickup trucks—were parked in the dusty side lot.

A few hundred yards later they passed a used car lot. Then a garage with gas pumps out front and a side lot full of rusty broken-down vehicles. A cluster of trailers with satellite dishes in front. Then a potato field. Then a diner. Here and there a small ranch-style house. A lumberyard, rich with the sweet scent of pine sawdust. Another casino, a roadhouse with a sign reading GIRLS, a café. The road gradually flattened and widened, and then it became paved, and pretty soon Calhoun found himself in what he guessed was downtown St. Cecelia. The street was lined on both sides with commercial establishments—restaurants, bars, clothing stores, a hardware store, a florist, a real estate office, a bank, a food market, a stationery store, a pharmacy. There were two intersections, both regulated by blinking yellow traffic lights. A few people were strolling along the sidewalk. Parked cars lined both sides of the street. St. Cecelia appeared to be a thriving little community in the middle of the geographically biggest, and one of the least populated, counties in the United States.

Calhoun kept driving along the main drag, and pretty soon he came to a police station and a post office, then an elementary school, and then a Catholic church with a cemetery beside it. Past the cemetery, the road became dirt and again entered the woods.

Now that he had a feel for the town, he turned around,

headed back the way he'd come, and stopped in front of the police station, which was a simple square wooden building painted
green. Two black-and-whites were parked in the side lot.

He fished his cell phone out of his pocket and was happy to
see that there was service here in St. Cecelia. He poked out the
number for the shop in Portland.

After a couple of rings, a male voice said, "Kate's Bait, Tackle,
and Woolly Buggers. This is Adrian. Can I help you?"

"You can help me by putting Kate on the line," Calhoun said.

"Oh, hey, Stoney. How you doin'?"

"Good. You?"

"Tell the truth," said Adrian, "I wouldn't mind if you decided not to come back. This is a good job. I like this job a lot."

"Afraid you're gonna be shit out of luck, sonnyboy, because
I'll be back. But I'm glad you like it. Now gimme Kate."

"She's not here, Stoney."

"Of course she is. It's Saturday morning. She's always there
on Saturdays. Put her on."

Adrian hesitated, then said, "I can't."

Calhoun blew out a breath. "She tell you she didn't want to
talk to me? Is that what's going on here?"

"I'm sorry, man."

"Just tell her I got something I need to tell her. Tell her I got
some news for her."

"I do that," Adrian said, "she'll fire me. She's pretty mad at
you, I can tell you that much."

"She say why?"

"No. She didn't say anything to me. Just 'If that Stoney Calhoun man calls, I ain't here.'"

"Well, listen to me," said Calhoun. "You take that phone
you're holding and you go find Kate and hand it to her right
now. Don't tell her it's me. Just say it's a call for her."

"Sorry, Stoney. I'm not going to do that."

"Why the hell not?"

"Because she'll ask me who it is, which I'm always supposed to ask when I answer the phone, and when I tell her it's you, she'll just get mad at me, and she'll still refuse to talk to you."

"Okay," Calhoun said. "I guess you're right." He was quiet for a minute. Then he said, "You have any idea at all why she's mad at me?"

"Me?" said Adrian. "Not me. Kate doesn't talk about things like that with me."

Calhoun sighed. "Okay, then," he said. "This is what I want you to do. Write this number down, not that she doesn't know it. Got a pencil?"

"I do."

Calhoun recited his cell phone number. "You got that?"

"I got it."

"Good. Now, you tell Kate that Stoney called, and you tell her that you were a good boy and told him she wasn't there. Then you give her that phone number, and you tell her that I'll only be in a place that has cell phone service for another few hours, and I'd deeply appreciate it if she'd give me a buzz. You got that?"

"I bet she already knows your cell phone number, Stoney."

"Maybe she does," Calhoun said. "Just do what I'm asking anyway, will you?"

"Sure. I'll do it."

"And if she says she ain't gonna do it, you tell her that Stoney sounded like he had something important to tell her."

"All right. Sure."

"Remember who hired you."

"I do," said Adrian. "It was you."

"I can fire you, too, you know."

"I'll do exactly what you said, Stoney. You don't need to threaten me."

"I wasn't serious, you know. About firing you."

"I can't always tell with you," said Adrian.

"Good," said Calhoun.

After he disconnected from Adrian, he sat there trying to figure out why Kate was still mad at him. She'd been mad when he first told her he was going to be gone for a month and wouldn't tell her why, and he understood that, but then she came to his house, and she didn't seem so mad at all, and then for some reason she got mad all over again, and now she was refusing to talk to him, and he couldn't keep up with how her moods kept changing.

The easiest way to understand it, he guessed, was to not bother trying, to recognize the obvious fact that women were different from men, and to keep in mind that he, Stonewall Jackson Calhoun, did not understand them, and he just had to accept it. Women didn't think like men, they didn't have the same emotions as men, they didn't behave like men. They didn't love the way men did, either.

Calhoun loved women—or at least, he loved Kate Balaban—but he had no idea what made her tick. In fact, he was in awe of her. She was utterly unpredictable, and as far as he was concerned, that made her endlessly fascinating.

Now she'd decided not to talk to him, and there was no sense in trying to figure out why, because the reason was buried somewhere in that inscrutable woman-ness that he loved about her but that sometimes frustrated him beyond tolerance.

While he was sitting there in front of the St. Cecelia police station pondering the mystery of Kate Balaban, a cruiser pulled into the side lot, and a uniformed officer got out. He glanced over at Calhoun, hesitated, then came strolling over. He bent down to the open side window and said, "You're from Loon Lake, huh?"

"How'd you know that?"

The cop jerked his chin at the side of the car. "It's written all over your vehicle."

"Right." Calhoun nodded. "My name's Stoney Calhoun. I'm a guide up there. Just started." The cop's nameplate, which was pinned to his uniform shirt over the pocket on the left side, read SGT. A. CURRIER.

Sergeant Currier bent down, looked into the car as if he expected to find something illegal there, and saw Ralph. "Hi, dog," he said.

"His name's Ralph," said Calhoun.

The cop shrugged. "Last time I seen one of these Range Rovers," he said, "there were two dead bodies in it. You don't see Range Rovers in St. Cecelia very much."

"It's not mine," said Calhoun. "It belongs to the lodge. I borrowed it."

"I figured," said Currier. "I hope to hell you don't end up dead in it, Mr. Calhoun."

"Well, me, too. So were you the one who found the vehicle with McNulty and the Gautier gal in it?"

He frowned. "What do you know about that?"

Calhoun shrugged. "Just what I heard."

"Yeah, big story around here," Currier said. "I wasn't the one who came upon them—that was a civilian—but I did catch the call, and I was the first officer at the scene. They'd been shot. The two of 'em in the front seat. I figured we had a murder on our hands. Murder and suicide is what it looked like, though somebody could've shot 'em both and set it up to look that way. Around here we have husbands and wives arguing and stabbing each other on a regular basis. Once in a while a bar fight gets out of hand. This looked like it was gonna be a real murder case, though. Then the ME reports that the two of them had already died before they got shot, and the only mystery left is, who'd bother shooting bullets into a couple of dead bodies?"

"What'd they die of?" said Calhoun. He wondered if the St. Cecelia police had been told about the botulism.

The cop shrugged. "All I know is, it wasn't gunshot wounds."

"Where were they found?"

Sergeant Currier pointed down the street in the direction of the church and the cemetery. "An old logging road in the woods south of town. Their Range Rover was pulled up under the branches of a big hemlock tree, and the two of them were deader'n doornails in the front. Bullet holes in their heads, weapon in the man's hand."

"So who in the world would shoot them if they were already dead?" said Calhoun.

"Everybody figured it was Harry Saulnier. He had a thing with the girl. Folks figured he was mad that she was cheating on him."

"This was the boyfriend?"

"If you want to call him that, a thirty-six-year-old good-for-nothin' drunk and a crazy sixteen-year-old girl." The cop waved the back of his hand in the air. "Anyway, it wasn't Harry. He was out of town when it happened. Not that it matters, since shooting people who are already dead isn't much of a crime."

"How did McNulty and the girl know each other?" said Calhoun.

Currier frowned. "I don't know why I'm telling you all this."

"I'm interested," said Calhoun.

"What do you know about it?"

"Me?" Calhoun shrugged. "Nothing. But you probably heard,

they found one of the guides up to Loon Lake murdered yesterday. Maybe there's some connection."

Sergeant Currier nodded. "I did hear about that, and that
occurred to me, too. I guess the sheriff's got himself a suspect."

"They arrested one of the other guides, but he didn't do it."

"No?"

"No," said Calhoun. "So how come this McNulty and the
Gautier girl were together? You must've looked into that."

"Oh, sure. We don't know much about them. We do know
they were at Tiny's the day before they died."

"What's Tiny's?"

"It's a roadhouse. Strippers and booze. Food's not so bad,
actually. If you drove down from Loon Lake, you had to've
passed it. It would've been on your left, the other side of the road
from the big potato field."

"I remember the field," Calhoun said.

"A couple witnesses said they saw McNulty and the girl in
there in the afternoon. I questioned Tiny myself. He said the
man was there first, nursed a beer at the bar, and she come in a
little later and joined him."

"She picked him up?"

Currier shook his head. "That's not how Tiny saw it."

"Like they already knew each other, you mean?" said Calhoun.

"That's right," said Currier. "Like they had planned to meet
there at Tiny's."

"Did they eat there?" Calhoun said. He was thinking they
might've gotten botulism poisoning from something they ate
at Tiny's.

Currier nodded. "The two of them sat at the bar, had lunch,
watched the TV. After they ate they left together."

"This was the day before they were found dead?"

Currier nodded.

"Any idea where they were before they went into Tiny's?"

He shook his head. "He probably came from out of town. From your place on Loon Lake, I'd guess. As for her, who knows?"

"Or how they met in the first place?"

"Nobody seems to know."

"Did anybody see them after they left Tiny's?"

"No witnesses in St. Cece turned up who'd seen them. The truth is, once the coroner said those bullets were shot into them after they were already dead, which might not even amount to a crime, we didn't work very hard at finding witnesses."

"Weren't you interested in what they did die of?"

He shrugged. "I guess so, but that's up to the medical examiner."

"And you haven't had any more mysterious deaths like those two in your town here?"

Sergeant Currier shook his head. "Nope. No deaths at all in the past couple weeks." He straightened up and slapped the roof of the Range Rover. "I gotta get going."

Calhoun nodded. "Take it easy."

Currier nodded. "You, too." He bent down and peered into the car. "See you, pooch," he said to Ralph. He straightened up. "I hope you're not planning to go snooping around in our town here, Mr. Calhoun."

"Snooping? Why would I do that?"

Sergeant Currier shrugged. "You seem like a snoopy guy."

"Not me."

"Well, that's good," Currier said. "Wouldn't want you to get yourself in trouble."

CHAPTER SIXTEEN

After Sergeant Currier went into the police station, Calhoun started up the Range Rover and drove south again, heading out of town, until he'd gone past the cemetery and left St. Cecelia behind. The paved road wound past a potato farm and some blueberry burns, and then it entered a pine forest. Here and there a little dirt road angled into the woods. He wondered if one of these old cartpaths was the one where McNulty stopped his car on the day he and Millie Gautier died.

When he came to a pretty little brook trickling under an old stone bridge, he pulled into an open area beside the road. He got out and held the door for Ralph.

While Ralph was watering the bushes and drinking from the brook, Calhoun took out his cell phone. He checked his voice mail to see if perhaps Kate had called while he'd been talking with Sergeant Currier. He figured she probably hadn't, but Kate was just unpredictable enough that she might've.

She hadn't.

He thought about calling the shop again, but he decided that he'd just be humiliating himself. Not that he particularly minded humiliating himself, if it meant he might speak to Kate, but he figured she was no more likely to agree to talk to him now than she had been an hour ago.

He whistled to Ralph, and then they both got back into the Range Rover. Calhoun followed the road south through the woods, heading out of town. He wanted to get a feeling for the area, to see it the way McNulty had seen it. Maybe he'd have an insight. Sheriff Dickman liked to describe investigating as turning over rocks and kicking bushes and seeing what might crawl out or fly away. Calhoun guessed that's what he was doing.

They'd gone eight or ten miles, and nothing had crawled out from any rocks or flown out from under any bushes, and the road didn't get any better, so he turned around and headed back to St. Cecelia.

They drove through town and picked up the road heading north to the lodge. After about a mile, they came to the potato field, and sure enough, just as Sergeant Currier had said, there on the other side of the road was a rectangular wooden building with a painted sign hanging from a post out front that read TINY'S CAFÉ—EXOTIC DANCERS. Red and green neon beer logos— Budweiser, Coors Light, Molson's—glowed in the big front window. Three motorcycles were parked out front, and a few pickup trucks and dinged-up old sedans sat in the side lot.

Calhoun pulled into the lot and turned off the ignition. "You're gonna have to stay and guard the vehicle," he said to Ralph.

Ralph looked at him, then turned his head away. He understood the word "stay," and he didn't like being left behind.

Calhoun made sure all the windows were cracked open, and then he got out of the Range Rover and went into Tiny's Café.

He stopped for a moment inside the doorway and blinked

against the gloom. Some kind of canned music was playing softly from hidden speakers. Calhoun recognized the tune. It was the Beatles' song "Norwegian Wood," but it was performed by an orchestra heavy on the violins, with an exaggerated up-beat tempo that the Beatles never intended. Elevator music. Or more likely, he guessed, stripper music.

All of the windows were covered with heavy curtains, so that you couldn't tell what time of day or night it was. The odor of stale beer and tobacco smoke burned in his nostrils. The half of the big interior to the left of the entry was washed with dreary fluorescent overhead lights. Here there was a bar, with a few booths along the wall and a scattering of tables. The right side of the room was dark except for a single pale blue flood-light focused on a small stage.

Eight or ten people—two were women—were sitting at the long bar. Several of them wore black leather jackets and ban-dannas on their heads. One of the booths was occupied by a middle-aged couple. Nobody was sitting at the tables.

A burly, barrel-chested man with a full black beard and black hair pulled back in a ponytail and a hoop in his left ear worked behind the bar. A television mounted on brackets over the bar was showing a tennis match with no sound.

Calhoun went over and sat on a stool at the end of the bar. Two stools over, a young guy wearing overalls and work boots glanced at Calhoun and lifted his chin by way of greeting.

Calhoun lifted his own chin and looked up at the tennis match. Two women were playing. They had strong bodies, thick, muscular legs. He marveled at their athleticism.

After a minute or two the bartender came over. "What'll you have, friend?"

"Can I get something to eat?"

"Ayuh. This here is a café. We got food." He reached under

the bar and handed Calhoun a typed piece of paper sandwiched in transparent plastic. "This is what we got. How about a beer?"

"Coffee," said Calhoun.

"You got it." He went to the other end of the bar and returned a minute later with a heavy white mug full of coffee. "Milk and sugar?"

Calhoun shook his head. "Black is good. So are you Tiny?"

The bartender grinned. His white teeth flashed from the depths of his black beard. "How'd you guess?"

"Well, you're anything but tiny."

"Tiny Cormier. My parents named me Roland."

"I'm Stoney Calhoun." He held out his hand.

Tiny shook it. "You're a stranger hereabouts. Least, I never seen you before. I'd've remembered you."

Calhoun nodded. "I'm guiding up at Loon Lake. Just started a few days ago. This is my first visit to St. Cecilia."

"Well, Mr. Calhoun, you come to the right place if you're looking for some fun. The girls don't start performing till evening, but if you want . . ." He arched his eyebrows.

"No," said Calhoun. "All I want is some lunch." He frowned at the menu. "Cheeseburger, I guess. Medium. Slice of onion on top. And some fries."

"You got it." Tiny turned and went down to the other end of the bar.

The guy sitting beside him said, "You said you was guidin' at the fishing lodge up there at Loon Lake? That right?"

"Yes, that's right," said Calhoun.

"Had a murder up there, huh?"

"Yup."

"I heard they nailed an Indian for it."

"They arrested a man, but he's not the one who did it."

"No, huh?"

"No," said Calhoun.

"So who did?"

Calhoun shrugged. "I don't know."

"You probably heard about the shooting we had down here few weeks ago. That involved a fella who was staying at your lodge."

"I heard about it," Calhoun said. "That was before I started at Loon Lake. A girl from St. Cecelia was involved, too, I understand."

"Yep. That was Millie Gautier. Edwin, her old man, he's pretty shook up by it."

"Hard to blame him," Calhoun said. "Man loses his daughter? That's a rough one."

"Actually," said the guy, "it's hard to tell how Edwin's feeling about it. Some folks are saying he's the one who shot those two."

"What do you think?" said Calhoun.

"Shit, I don't know. It ain't any of my business. I hardly know Edwin. Run into him at the lumberyard a few times is all. That's where he works. That little girl was a wild one, though. Everybody knows that. What's a daddy to do, huh?"

"You saying her father abused her?"

"Abused?" The guy shrugged. "I don't know about abused. He probably took his belt to her a few times. Ask me, she had it coming."

"Well," said Calhoun, "it's an interesting case, all right." This man hadn't indicated that he knew that McNulty and Millie had not died of gunshot wounds. Calhoun guessed it wasn't up to him to set him straight.

Tiny had returned with a knife and a fork rolled in a napkin. He put them on the bartop in front of Calhoun. "Ayup," Tiny said. "Interesting. Them two were in here for lunch the day they got killed. Cops come in, asked me some questions."

"Like what?"

"Oh, like what time they got here, what time they left, what'd they have to say when they were here, did they talk to anybody else. I answered 'em as best as I could."

"Did they ask what the two of them had to eat?"

Tiny frowned at Calhoun. "Huh? Eat? What makes the difference, what they had to eat?"

Calhoun shrugged. "I was just wondering."

"The cops didn't ask that question, no." Tiny shrugged. "The guy, he had a cheeseburger, like what you ordered except no onion. Fries and a beer. The little gal with him . . ." Tiny looked up at the ceiling for a minute. "Hm. I seem to remember she asked for a BLT. On white toast. Bag of chips and, um, an iced tea. She being too young to drink alcohol."

"That's a good memory," said Calhoun. He was thinking that it was unlikely that McNulty and Millie Gautier had contracted botulism here at Tiny's, because they had eaten entirely different things.

"Tiny's famous for his memory," said the guy on the bar stool. "You notice he didn't need to write down your order? He remembers everything. Anyone who ever come in here, he'll remember the face and the name, too."

"You're Stoney Calhoun," said Tiny. "You come back in a couple years, I'll remember, all right. And I'll bring you coffee and ask if you want a medium cheeseburger with onion and fries."

"That's impressive," Calhoun said. "So you're the one who served those two that day, then."

Tiny rolled his eyes. "I'm the one who serves everybody all the time in this place."

"Do you remember overhearing anything they said to each other while they were sitting here having lunch?"

"The cops asked me that."

"What did you tell them?"

Tiny cocked his head and peered at Calhoun. "Why you asking all these questions about them two?"

"Like I said," Calhoun said, "I think it's an unusual case." He shrugged. "I find things like that interesting, that's all. Plus, well, the man who was arrested for the murder at Loon Lake is a friend of mine. I can't help thinking the two cases are connected."

"Yes, sir," said Tiny. "It is interesting, and I see what you mean about them being connected. Your lodge, there, being the connection." He hesitated. "Those two were having themselves a quiet little argument when they were here. Didn't raise their voices or curse or start throwing things. Nothing like that. A polite disagreement, I guess you'd call it. That's what I told the cops."

"Did you catch what they were arguing about?" Calhoun said.

"Not much," Tiny said. "The man, it seemed he was going somewhere, and the gal—she was just a kid, a teenager—she wanted to go with him, and he kept saying no, she couldn't. She kept at him, and he just kept shaking his head. When they walked out of here, they were still going at it." He shrugged. "That's all. The man, he hardly said anything. Just, 'No, that won't work, honey. Now leave it be, okay?' Like that. But she did keep at him." He grinned. "Women, huh?"

Calhoun thought of Kate. He smiled and nodded. "Ayuh. Women."

Tiny said, "Lemme get your burger for you." He turned and walked away and was back a minute later with Calhoun's lunch. "More coffee?"

"Sure. Thanks."

Calhoun watched the tennis match while he ate. Tiny's burger was thin and greasy and overcooked, and the fries were limp, but he was hungry, and ketchup made it more than acceptable, and the coffee was pretty good. He saved a hunk of burger for Ralph.

When he was done, he put a twenty-dollar bill on the bartop. Tiny came over and took the bill, and a minute later he slapped down some change.

Calhoun left a five for a tip. "Thanks," he said to Tiny. "That burger hit the spot."

"You come back in the evening, Stoney," said Tiny. "We got some pretty gals dancin' here. We bring 'em all the way down from Montreal."

"Sounds good," said Calhoun. He slipped off his stool and walked out of the café.

When he got outside, he had to blink a few times against the brightness of the early afternoon sunshine. Then he headed over to the Range Rover. When he got in, Ralph, who was curled up on the backseat, ignored him. He slipped the dog the hunk of Tiny's burger. Ralph gobbled it down as if it had been cooked perfectly, then licked the side of Calhoun's face. With dogs, it was, indeed, all about food.

CHAPTER SEVENTEEN

Less than a mile down the road heading back toward St. Cecelia, Calhoun came to the sawmill where the guy sitting at the bar in Tiny's had told him that Edwin Gautier, Millie Gautier's father, worked.

He parked in the sandy lot beside a small shingled building with the word OFFICE over the door. He told Ralph he'd have to stay in the car and got the expected scowl from the dog. When he slid out of the Range Rover, he saw that there was a steel building the size and shape of an airplane hangar at the foot of the slope out back. Huge piles of pine logs with their limbs lopped off but their bark still on were stacked in a big open area. The smell of fresh-cut sawdust that hung over the place was strong and pleasant.

He went into the office. A bulky middle-aged woman was sitting behind a messy steel desk peering at a computer monitor. She wore big round glasses and a man's oxford shirt with the sleeves rolled halfway up her forearms. The walls were all covered with cheap pine paneling. Sitting against the walls were a couple of straight-backed wooden chairs and several file cabinets. A doorway behind the woman's desk led into another part of the building.

She glanced up at Calhoun. "Hang on a sec," she said and returned her attention to her computer. She hit a couple of keys, shook her head, typed in something else, then nodded and sat back. She looked up at Calhoun. "Okay. What can I do for you?"

Calhoun took the leather folder that held his deputy badge out of his pocket, opened it, and showed it to her. "I need to speak with Edwin Gautier."

She glanced at the badge, then frowned at Calhoun. "You're new around here, ain't you?"

"I'm not from around here," he said. "I have an interest in Mr. Gautier's daughter's death."

"Well, you ain't the only one. Poor ol' Edwin's been questioned a bunch of times already."

"I need to do it one more time," said Calhoun. "Can you tell me how to find him? I understand he works here."

"I'll have to git him for you," she said. "You can't go out in the yard. Insurance, you know."

"That's fine," said Calhoun. "Thank you."

The woman picked up a phone, hit a couple of buttons, gazed up at the ceiling for a moment, then said, "Chester? Listen, send Edwin up here to the office, would you? Somebody here needs to talk to him." She chuckled, glanced at Calhoun, then said, "Yeah, yeah. I know. Okay, thanks." She hung up the phone. "He'll be right along," she said to Calhoun, "soon as he dumps his load. Edwin drives the forklift. You might as well meet him out front, talk to him there."

"Thank you, ma'am," said Calhoun.

He went outside and sat on the steps, and about ten minutes later a man came around the corner of the building. He was wearing a green shirt and matching pants, with work boots and a yellow hard hat. A cigarette dangled from the corner of his mouth. When he saw Calhoun sitting on the steps of the office building, he stopped, dropped the butt on the ground, and stomped on it. Then he took off his hard hat and wiped his forehead with the back of his wrist. "You lookin' for me?" he said.

"Are you Edwin Gautier?"

Gautier nodded cautiously. He was a small man, wiry and compact, late thirties, early forties, Calhoun guessed. His pale, stringy hair was thin on top and hung to his collar on the sides.

Calhoun fished out his deputy badge and showed it to the man.

Gautier shrugged. "Why don't you guys just figure out what happened to Millie and leave me alone? I told you everything I know."

"I apologize for putting you through this all over again," Calhoun said, "but it's a peculiar case, and we're not making much headway with it. So I got to ask you some questions you might've already answered."

"What if I don't feel like talking about it anymore?"

Calhoun shrugged. "I guess we can drag you down to the police station and hold on to you till you do feel like talking about it."

"You threatening me?"

"Nope. Just answering your question. Clarifying your options."

Gautier sighed. "So what do you want to know?"

Calhoun patted the step beside him. "Why don't you sit down."

Gautier shrugged and sat.

"So tell me about Millie," said Calhoun.

"What about her?"

"Well, for starters, what was she doing hanging out with a man old enough to be her father?"

"How'm I supposed to know?" said Gautier.

"She was your daughter."

"Look," he said. "I done my best with Millie, and I know that wasn't good enough. Her mother run away when Millie was seven. She was a willful child, just like her old lady, and she grew into a willful girl. I tried to discipline her, but it didn't do no good. She just did what she wanted, and lately that included hanging around grown-up men. Her big dream was to find some guy who'd take her out of St. Cecelia. She knowed it wouldn't be me."

"That must have been difficult for you."

Gautier shrugged. "From the time she was about thirteen, she was a wild one. She had a reputation, Millie did."

Calhoun said nothing.

"When some of the guys you work with, have a beer with, they've, um, been with your daughter?" Gautier shook his head. "Downright embarrassing."

"I guess I would've given her a good whipping if she was mine," said Calhoun.

"Oh, I done that. Yes I did. It wasn't that I didn't care. I did. That's why I whupped her. I never gave up on Millie. I tried to show her the error of her ways. Smacked her bare little butt with my belt more than once. Little devil, she'd just laugh at me. 'Hit me harder, Eddie,' she'd say. Bitchly child always refused to call me Daddy."

Again, for the ten-thousandth time, Calhoun wondered if, in his previous, unremembered life, his life before a lightning bolt obliterated his memory, he'd had children, and if he did, whether he'd beaten them.

He doubted it. It took a certain kind of man to beat a child, and Calhoun didn't see how he could ever have been such a man.

Edwin Gautier was such a man, and Calhoun had to stifle an urge to punch the ignorant man in the face.

It was no wonder that Millie wanted to get away from St. Cecelia.

"What can you tell me about McNulty?" Calhoun said. "The man Millie was found with."

"I never met the man, myself," said Gautier.

Calhoun said nothing.

After a minute, Gautier shrugged. "I heard some things."

Calhoun nodded encouragingly.

"Millie thought this McNulty was gonna take her away from here. He was her ticket. He was a rich guy, staying at that fancy fishing lodge up to Loon Lake. Millie would've done any-thing for him. The night before she . . . she died—she didn't come home. She was with him."

"With McNulty."

Gautier nodded. "Yes, sir.

"How do you know?"

"She come home in the morning to change her clothes, and we had a conversation. I asked her where she'd been at, and she said it was none of my business, as usual. Then she told me she was leaving for good and I better not try to stop her, she'd found herself a nice rich man who was gonna take care of her."

"Did she say where they were going?"

"She said this man—it was McNulty, I guess, though she didn't mention any name that I recall—he had business in

Augusta, and then maybe they'd go to Florida. Millie was always talking about Florida. I suppose she might've made that part up. About going to Florida. To make me jealous or something, as if everybody dreamed about going to Florida the way she did."

"Did she say what the man's business was in Augusta?"

Gautier shook his head. "She was just trying to make him sound important, I suppose."

"So she said they were leaving that day?"

"Yes. The day she died."

"You saw her that morning?"

Gautier nodded.

"And she was okay?"

"Okay? What do you mean?"

"Healthy. Not sick."

"Oh, she was healthy, all right. Rarin' to go, she was."

"Did she seem afraid?"

Gautier frowned. "How so?"

"Worried? Nervous that something bad might happen?"

"Not that I noticed. Anyway, Millie wasn't like that. Nothing fazed her."

"It was later that day that they found her?"

"That night," Gautier said. "In the woods south of town. In his vehicle."

"So," said Calhoun, "I know I'm not the first person to ask you, but I got to do it again. Did you follow them and find them parked there in the woods, looked like they were sleeping, maybe, and shoot the both of them and leave it to look like a murder and suicide? Was that you who did that?"

"You're right," said Gautier. "You ain't the first person to accuse me of that."

"I wasn't accusing. I was just asking."

"Same difference, ain't it?"

"You saying you didn't do it?" said Calhoun.

"That's right. I did not do that."

"I bet you have an idea who did."

He shook his head. "No, I don't. I figure it was about the man, McNulty, not about Millie. She was just in the wrong place at the wrong time."

"Why is that?"

He shrugged. "Because Millie didn't have any enemies. She was just a kid. No reason to kill her. Everybody liked Millie."

"Except you," said Calhoun.

Edwin Gautier turned his head to look straight at Calhoun. "You're wrong about that," he said. "I liked Millie a lot." He swallowed and blinked, and Calhoun saw the man's eyes brimming. "I loved her, sir. She might've been a bitch sometimes, and she surely was a wild one, but she was always my little girl."

After Edwin Gautier twisted his yellow hard hat back onto his head and shambled down the slope to the steel hangar where his forklift was waiting for him, Calhoun went back to the Loon Lake Range Rover and let Ralph out. While the dog snuffled around the sandy area, lifting his leg on certain bushes, selected for reasons known only to him, and ignoring others, Calhoun fished out his cell phone and checked it again for messages.

There were none.

He'd hoped Kate would change her mind and leave him a voice mail. "Hey, how you doing?" would have been fine. "I still love you" would have been excellent.

It was a little after four on this Saturday afternoon. She'd still be at the shop. He thought about calling again, and this time not letting Adrian off the hook. He'd demand to talk to Kate, and when she came on the line, however reluctantly, he'd just tell her he missed her and loved her no matter what she might be thinking and feeling about him.

Still, he didn't do it. He figured if she hadn't called and left him a message, it meant she was still mad and would just refuse to talk to him. So he snapped the phone shut and stuck it in his pocket. Once he headed back to Loon Lake, he'd be out of cell phone service, and then there would be no chance of talking with Kate. It was frustrating.

He whistled to Ralph, and the two of them climbed into the Range Rover. He started it up, turned onto the dusty lumber company road, and headed north, back to the lodge.

As he drove slowly over the humpy dirt road, he tried to figure out what, if anything, he'd learned.

He'd learned that Edwin Gautier loved his daughter and was an unlikely suspect for shooting her and McNulty's already-dead bodies. Anyway, even if he had done that, it had nothing to do with McNulty's mission at Loon Lake.

McNulty and Millie had died of botulism poisoning, most likely contracted from eating the same food, but it didn't appear that they'd had that food at Tiny's Café. They'd eaten entirely different lunches that day, and besides, nobody else who'd eaten there had died from botulism. In fact, no one in St. Cecelia except for McNulty and Millie had died from botulism. That meant it had come from someplace else.

Millie Gautier had told her father that McNulty was headed for Augusta, the state capital. Assuming that was true, and that McNulty did not plan to return to Loon Lake, it meant that he'd found what he was looking for up there and was going to Augusta to submit a report. Whatever McNulty had uncovered at Loon Lake—Mr. Brescia suggested it might have something to do with national security—he did not have the chance to report it. He died of botulism poisoning first. Then somebody, who apparently didn't realize they were already dead, shot him and Millie. The shooter, Calhoun guessed, aimed to prevent McNulty from submitting his report. The shooter was the man whose name McNulty would have turned in.

It was most likely somebody from the lodge. That narrowed it down considerably.

Calhoun remembered seeing the shadowy figure prowling around the float plane and then leaving with something in his hand. It looked like a small suitcase, and he hadn't had it with him when he arrived. Calhoun guessed the snooper was Curtis Swenson, the pilot, sneaking around in the darkness so he wouldn't be seen, collecting something illicit that he'd hidden on his plane.

Somebody—Calhoun guessed that shadowy figure was the same man, probably Swenson—had followed him and Robin when he'd walked her back to her room the night after Elaine Hoffman was killed.

The more he thought about it, the more Calhoun kept circling back to Swenson. The pilot, unlike the guides at the lodge, had the freedom and flexibility to go to St. Cecelia almost anytime. He could fly back and forth across the border to Canada, and he could go anywhere in Maine where there was a lake to deliver whatever he kept hidden on the plane.

Swenson could've followed McNulty to St. Cecelia and shot him and Millie in their car. He could've killed Elaine Hoffman with Calhoun's Colt Woodsman .22 pistol, too.

Now if he was following Calhoun and Robin around, it meant they weren't safe, either.

Calhoun needed to figure out what Swenson was up to. If he could discover what was in the suitcase he kept hidden on his float plane, he guessed he'd know what McNulty had known, and if he could then avoid getting himself killed, he'd be able to submit a report to Mr. Brescia.

Then he could go home.

CHAPTER EIGHTEEN

Calhoun got back to the lodge in time to take a shower and relax for a few minutes before supper. He'd just finished toweling
his hair and getting dressed when somebody knocked on the
cabin door.

He said, "Come on in," and the door opened, and Robin
stepped into the cabin.

"Hey," said Calhoun.

She smiled. "Hey, yourself."

"Aren't you supposed to be serving dinner tonight?"

"It's Saturday," she said. "My night off."

"And you're still here?"

"Where would I go?"

"Home?"

She rolled her eyes. "I don't think so. And there's no place
around here except St. Cece. Nothing for me there."

He nodded. "I was down to St. Cecelia today. It's not much
of a place. Want a Coke?"

"I wouldn't mind," the girl said. She was wearing shorts
and a T-shirt. Her feet were bare, and her shaggy blond hair

was damp, as if she'd just gotten out of the shower, too. Calhoun thought she looked about twelve years old, except for her strong legs and her grown-up chest.

He fetched two cans of Coke. "Why don't we sit out on the porch," he said. "There's a nice breeze comes off the lake this time of day."

They went out to the screen porch and sat in the rockers. Ralph followed along and plopped down in front of the door.

"So what's up?" Calhoun said.

She turned and smiled at him. "Does something need to be up?"

"Huh? Oh. No, I guess not." He shrugged. "So tell me something."

"What?"

"Do they pay you really well here?"

Robin smiled. "You mean, what's a nice girl like me doing in a place like this?"

Calhoun shrugged. "Something like that, I guess."

She nodded. "Yes, they pay very well. Way better than I could do back in Madrid." She pronounced it MAD-rid, with the emphasis on the first syllable.

"Madrid," Calhoun said, repeating her pronunciation, "being your hometown?"

"Ayuh," she said, "and I can't wait to get away from there. I want to go to college, Stoney. I want to go far, far away. Arizona or Colorado sounds good to me. Someplace as different from Madrid, Maine, as I can find. My dad is dead, and my mother has no money, but I'm willing to work hard and make sacrifices to earn enough money to get where I want to go. Like serve food and make beds and vacuum floors and anything else June Dunlap tells me to do."

Calhoun remembered Edwin Gautier telling him about

Millie's dream of going to Florida. He guessed it had to be hard, being a small-town Maine girl with big dreams.

"Half of my high school friends got pregnant before they graduated," Robin said. "The other half are working at the supermarket and planning on getting married to their boyfriends who work at the mill." She shook her head. "Not me, mister."

Calhoun smiled. "Can't blame you."

"I'm a good worker," she said, "and I'm pretty smart. I deserve better." She frowned. "Oh, the reason I came to see you, actually, was to tell you something. Mr. Redbird has been released. He's coming back. I know you're his friend. I thought you'd like to know."

"Well, yes," he said. "Thank you. I'm glad about that. Franklin was wrongly accused."

"I guess they didn't have enough to hold him on," Robin said. "So they had to let him go. I heard that Curtis Swenson is flying to Houlton tomorrow to pick him up."

Calhoun nodded. An idea had occurred to him.

That Saturday evening, Robin's night off, it was June, Marty Dunlap's wife, who brought the food from the kitchen into the guides' dining room: a big bowl of baked kidney beans with salt pork, a platter of hot dogs, another of brown bread, baskets of fresh-baked corn muffins, a plate of sliced cucumbers and tomatoes, and a bowl of potato salad—beans and franks, the traditional New England Saturday night supper. After she'd put everything on the table, June touched Calhoun's shoulder.

He turned and looked up at her. She had wide-spaced green eyes with squint lines in the corners and a small, turned-up nose. Her brown hair was liberally sprinkled with gray. Calhoun thought June Dunlap was a very attractive woman.

"You've been here three days already, Mr. Calhoun, and we haven't been introduced," she said. "I'm June."

Calhoun smiled. "I'm Stoney." He held up his hand to her. "Nice to meet you."

She gave his hand a quick shake. "I hear you drove down to St. Cecelia today."

"I did," he said. "It's quite a town."

June rolled her eyes. "It's a depraved and malignant town. Good for nothing except gambling and boozing and whoring."

He nodded. "That's what I meant. Nothing of interest to me, but I'm glad I got to see it for myself."

June patted his shoulder and went back to the kitchen, and the guides began passing around the bowls and platters of food.

"So'd you do some whoring and gambling and boozing today, Stoney?" said Ben, the lanky young college-aged guide.

"You bet," Calhoun said. "Guess I had myself enough debauchery today to last me at least till my next day off."

Ben grinned, and Peter, the other young guide, said, "Unless I'm mistaken, you've got tomorrow off. Heading right back to St. Cece, are you?"

"Oh, I doubt that," Calhoun said. "I'm too old for two straight days of St. Cecelia." He glanced at Curtis Swenson, who, as usual, was reading a magazine and ignoring everybody. "Hey, Curtis," he said.

Swenson looked up. "What?" He was wearing his signature Hawaiian shirt. This one featured orange and red parrots in a green and purple jungle.

"I heard you're flying to Houlton tomorrow to fetch Franklin Redbird."

Swenson nodded. "I heard the same damn thing. That must mean it's true."

"Want some company?"

"Huh? What do you mean?"

"Suppose I went along with you?"

"Why'd you want to do something like that?"

Calhoun shrugged. "Franklin's my friend. I just thought it would be a nice thing to do, to be there to greet him. Give you some company, too."

"I don't care about company," Swenson said.

"I'd like to go," said Calhoun.

Swenson shrugged. "If you want to go, I guess I can't stop you. Meet me at the dock at eight thirty, and don't be late, because I ain't going to wait for you. Oh, and leave the dog home. I'll be taking the Cessna, and there ain't that much room in it."

"There's got to be room for a dog."

"Just leave him this time, okay?"

"Sure," said Calhoun. "Ralph doesn't need to come. I'll explain it to him."

"Good," said Swenson. "You do that." He took a bite out of a muffin, then turned a page in his magazine and resumed his reading.

When Calhoun walked out of the dining room, June Dunlap came up behind him and said, "Stoney? Got a minute?"

"Sure," he said.

They walked outside and stood there on the deck. "It's about Robin," June said. "My kitchen girl."

"I know Robin," he said.

"I know you do. That's what I wanted to mention to you." She looked away for a minute, then swung her eyes back to his. "I think she's got a crush on you."

Calhoun smiled. "Really."

June nodded. "She's a vulnerable child. Her daddy was a

commercial fisherman, and he went overboard three winters ago. They never found his body."

"I didn't know that," he said. "That's rough."

"Yes, it is," June said. "I think Robin sees you as a father figure."

"You saying there's some kind of Freudian thing going on with her?"

"I'm just saying watch out, that's all," she said. "It wouldn't be hard to hurt her, and I don't think you want to do that."

"I generally go for more grown-up women anyway," Calhoun said, "but thank you for the warning."

June brought out the breakfast food on Sunday, too. Calhoun guessed Robin's day off went from after breakfast on Saturday until Sunday evening dinner.

It was around seven thirty in the morning, and Curtis Swenson wasn't at the table. Calhoun supposed he'd already eaten and was down at the dock getting the Cessna ready for their flight to Houlton to pick up Franklin Redbird.

After he and Ralph finished their breakfasts, they started down the pathway that led back to the cabin. About halfway there, a snowshoe hare popped out of the bushes right in front of them. It stopped for a moment with its long ears perked up and its nose twitching, then scooted down the path.

Ralph let out a yelp and bolted after the hare. Calhoun yelled, "No!" Yet he knew it was futile. In an instant both hare and dog were out of sight.

Calhoun yelled at Ralph to come back, but he knew that was futile, too. Ralph was normally obedient, but his training and discipline couldn't compete with his hunting instincts.

The dog's barking sounded like the baying of a hound as it faded into the distance.

"Well, damn," Calhoun muttered. He knew there was no sense in continuing to call to the dog. Even if Ralph heard his yells, he'd ignore them. This was not the first time he'd taken off after a rabbit or a squirrel or a fox. When he realized he couldn't outrun a snowshoe hare, he'd come trotting back with his tongue lolling and a big shit-eating grin on his face. Based on past history, that would probably take ten or fifteen minutes.

Calhoun continued on to his cabin, then sat on the steps and glanced at his watch. It was a little after eight fifteen. He hoped Ralph would be back in time for Calhoun to meet Curtis Swenson at the dock at eight thirty. In any case, Calhoun would wait for Ralph. He wouldn't go flying off to Houlton without knowing that the dog was back from his hare-chasing adventure safe and sound.

He'd been sitting there for a little while when he heard the unmistakable roar of a float plane's engine starting. Just one engine. The Cessna. He glanced at his watch. It was just about eight thirty. He assumed Swenson was getting the plane warmed up and checking his various gauges and lights and dials and buttons. Then the pitch of the engine changed, and Calhoun realized the plane was taxiing out onto the lake.

Son of a bitch. Curtis was leaving without him.

Calhoun got up and ran down to the dock. The Cessna was already a couple of hundred yards away, heading out to the middle of the lake.

Calhoun stood there with his fists clenched. "God *damn* it," he muttered.

Kim, the big lady guide, was there. She went over to Calhoun, touched his shoulder, and said, "I reminded him you were planning to go along. He said it was time to go and he'd be damned if he was going to wait, mumbled something about the weather." She glanced up at the sky, where some puffy white clouds hardly looked ominous.

"Well," said Calhoun, "maybe I am a couple minutes late. Ralph ran off, and I was waiting for him to come back. That's no damn excuse. Curtis could've waited. I really wanted to be there for when they let Franklin out of jail." He shook his head and blew out a breath. "It's no big deal, I suppose. Damn inconsiderate of Curtis, though."

Actually, it was kind of a big deal. Not because it might be nice for Franklin Redbird to have Calhoun there to greet him when he walked out of the jail in Houlton, although there was that. His main agenda had been to engage Curtis Swenson in conversation and see if he could get his guard down and elicit a contradiction or an ill-considered response out of him, something that might further convince Calhoun that Swenson was the key to what McNulty had been investigating, that the pilot was the one who'd tried to make McNulty's and Millie Gautier's deaths look like a murder-suicide, and that he was the one who'd shot Elaine Hoffman with Calhoun's Colt Woodsman .22 pistol— and, of course, why he did those things.

It wasn't a particularly clever or well-thought-out plan, he realized. It wasn't even a plan, really, but it was something, and now it wouldn't happen. At least, not today.

He stood there with Kim, shading his eyes with his hand against the glare that bounced off the wind-chopped surface of the lake, and watched the Cessna taxi toward the middle of the lake.

"I tried to talk him into waiting for you," said Kim.

"Thanks," Calhoun said.

When the plane got to the middle, it turned left and taxied

about half a mile down the lake. Then it turned, putting its nose into the wind, which was blowing hard down the lake from the north, and began its takeoff run. The pitch of the Cessna's engine increased as the plane gained speed, and pretty soon it appeared to be skipping like a flat stone over the tops of the little whitecaps out there in the middle of the lake.

Suddenly a great blossom of orange burst from the underside of the plane, and all at the same time, the plane's nose dipped and its tail lifted. The muffled *whoompf* of the explosion came echoing across the water to Calhoun's ears an instant later—the difference between the speed of light and the speed of sound. As if in slow motion, the Cessna flipped and landed on its side, so that one wing was in the water and the other was pointing at the sky.

Then came a second, bigger orange bloom, and a great cloud of black smoke, and a delayed *whoompf,* this one louder than the first explosion, and then, suddenly, the plane was gone. Whether it had exploded into a million parts or had sunk, Calhoun couldn't tell, but it had entirely disappeared from the surface of the lake, and the wind had blown away the black smoke, and it was suddenly eerily silent. It was as if the Cessna had never been there.

Calhoun hesitated for just an instant. Then he slid down into one of the Grand Lake canoes that was tied up to the dock. "Cast me off," he said to Kim. "Quick."

"Okay," she said, "but I'm coming with you."

She hastily untied the lines that held the bow and stern of the canoe to the steel rings on the dock while Calhoun got the motor started.

Kim climbed into the bow seat, and he gunned it, heading for the middle of the lake where he'd last seen the plane. The big broad-beamed canoe and the little outboard motor were designed for slow salmon trolling, not lifesaving speed, and it was frustrating how long it took them to get to the area in the middle of the lake. An oil slick marked the place where the plane had exploded. Calhoun cut back on the throttle, and they putted around the area for a few minutes. They did not see Curtis Swenson. Or his body.

Calhoun shucked off his shoes. "Grab a paddle and hold her steady," he said to Kim, and then he slithered over the side.

The frigid lake water momentarily paralyzed him. He gulped a lungful of air, then dove under. In the gin-clear water he saw that the lake was about twenty feet deep here. The bottom was sprinkled with airplane pieces. He spotted some engine parts, a hunk of upholstered seat, a piece of the tail section, half a wing. The gasoline and burnt oil in the water stung his eyes, and the smell of it seeped into his nose and mouth even though he was holding his breath.

He came up for air and dove again and again. He swam in increasingly large circles around the area where the plane had gone down. He did not find Curtis Swenson.

After a while he surfaced and waved at Kim, and she paddled the canoe over to where he was treading water, thoroughly exhausted. She grabbed the back of his shirt and helped him haul his belly onto the gunwale and then slide into the boat.

"Nothing?" she said.

He shook his head. "There's pieces of the blown-up airplane," he said, "but I couldn't find Curtis."

"Well, damn," said Kim.

He started the outboard, and they widened their search, looking for anything that might be floating. Aside from a hunk of stuffing from one of the airplane seats and a curved piece of tail section with air trapped under it, they found nothing.

After a while, Calhoun said, "We might as well go in."

"Might as well, I guess," said Kim.

He turned the canoe and headed back. As they got nearer, he saw that the dock was crowded with people, and he realized that just about everybody—guests, guides, and all three Dunlaps—was there, watching.

He turned off the motor and glided up to the dock. Kim steered with the paddle and nosed the canoe alongside the dock, then tossed up a line. One of the guests grabbed it and tied it onto a ring.

Marty Dunlap held down a hand to Calhoun. He took it and hefted himself onto the dock.

"You're okay?" said Marty.

Calhoun nodded. "Cold is all." He hugged himself against the shivers that seized his body.

Ralph came over with his stubby little tail all awag.

Calhoun knelt down. "You're back," he said. "Did you catch that damn hare?"

Ralph poked his nose at Calhoun's face and gave it a thorough lapping.

Calhoun hugged his dog. He was glad to have him back.

"I heard the explosion," Marty said. "Came running down. Curtis . . . ?"

Calhoun stood up. "Couldn't find him." He shook his head.

"So what happened?"

Calhoun shrugged. "I guess the plane hit a log or something out there when he was taxiing for takeoff. It flipped and blew up and just disappeared."

Marty shook his head. "Good Lord."

"A terrible thing," said Calhoun.

"Thank God you're all right, anyway."

"Huh?"

Marty said, "You were planning to go with him to pick up Franklin, weren't you?"

"I guess I wasn't thinking about that."

"You could've been in that plane."

"Would've been, too," Calhoun said, "if Ralph hadn't taken off after a hare. Made me late, and Curtis didn't wait for me." He gave Ralph's head a pat.

"So Ralph saved your life," said Marty.

"I guess he did," said Calhoun, "though I'll be damned if I'm going to give him credit for it. All he wanted to do was catch that hare."

CHAPTER NINETEEN

The guests and the guides and other staff continued to hang around the dock, talking in subdued voices as if they were comparing perceptions and trying to make sense of what had happened.

Marty Dunlap had jogged up to the lodge. He was back ten or fifteen minutes later. "Listen up," he said.

Everybody fell silent and turned to look at Marty.

"I just talked to the sheriff," he said. "He's on his way with some divers. He wants everybody to stick around and be available. He'll probably want to talk to all of us. So no fishing today, I guess. Or at least not till they finish their job. You can go to your rooms or hang around in the great room, have a swim, play horseshoes, whatever. Go back to bed if you want. We'll rustle up something for lunch at noon."

Calhoun, who'd been standing around with everybody else, felt a tug on his sleeve. He turned. Robin was standing there looking at him. "Can I talk to you?" she said.

He nodded. "I've got to go back to my cabin. I need to get into some dry clothes." He snapped his fingers at Ralph, who'd been sitting at his side, and they left the dock and started down the path.

"I heard you were supposed to be on that plane," Robin said. "Is that true?"

He nodded.

"That is very scary," she said.

"It is," he said. "I agree."

"I don't know what I'd do," she said. "I mean, first Elaine, then you?"

"Well, I'm fine," Calhoun said.

"Did you see what happened?"

He nodded. "It happened very fast. The plane just exploded. Looked like it hit something when it was taxiing."

"I'm glad you weren't on it."

"Thanks to Ralph," he said. "He took off after a hare. I waited for him to come back. Made me late. Curtis, being Curtis, I guess, he couldn't wait for me."

They came to the cabin. Robin sat in one of the rockers on the porch.

"Want a Coke or something?" Calhoun said.

"Sure," she said. "A Coke would be fine."

Calhoun got a can of Coke for her, then went inside and changed into some dry clothes. He got a Coke for himself and took it out to the porch and sat in the rocker next to Robin. "So," he said. "How old are you, anyway?"

She cocked her head and looked at him. "Wow. Where'd that come from?"

He shrugged. "I was just wondering."

"Worried I'm not of age, are you?"

"June told me what happened to your father."

She blinked. "What's that got to do with how old I am?"

"Nothing, I guess," Calhoun said. "I was just thinking how hard it must be for you, losing your daddy that way."

"You sound like a shrink," she said.

"Sorry," he said.

"I'm twenty-two," she said. "How about you?"

"Twenty-nine."

"Tell me the truth," she said.

"You first."

She peered at him for a moment, then smiled. "Okay. I'm nineteen."

"Why'd you lie to me?"

"Why did you?"

"Because you did," he said.

"I lied a little," said Robin, "because I wanted you to take me seriously."

"Don't I take you seriously?"

"You think I'm a kid," she said.

He shrugged. "The truth is, if you're nineteen, I'm exactly twice as old as you. What do you think?"

"I guess that makes me a kid to you."

"Doesn't mean we can't be friends."

"Sure." She nodded. "We're friends. I hope we are. I just don't need a shrink, okay?"

Calhoun and Robin made sandwiches from the fixin's that June Dunlap laid out in the guides' dining room—ham and cheese with mustard on rye for him, sliced turkey breast with mayo on wheat for her. They loaded their paper plates with potato chips and pickles, picked up Cokes, and took their lunches down to the dock.

They took off their shoes and socks and sat out at the end dangling their feet and eating, with Ralph eyeing them closely for handouts and dropped crumbs. Robin shared her chips with him.

Calhoun had just finished his sandwich when he heard the drone of an airplane engine coming their way from the east. He recognized the voice of the engine. He stood up and shaded his eyes, and a minute later he spotted the plane as it cleared the treetops. It was the sheriff's Twin Otter. It circled the lake and then began its descent.

Calhoun held his breath. A log or something floating on or just under the water had caused Curtis Swenson's Cessna to explode.

The sheriff's plane landed without incident. As it began to taxi in, the guides and some of the guests, along with Marty and Robert Dunlap, emerged from the lodge and gathered on the dock.

The Twin Otter turboprop with the Aroostook County Sheriff's Department logo on the side pulled up to the dock and shut off its engines. Ben and Peter, the young guides, held it steady while the sheriff's deputy—Henry was his name, Calhoun recalled—hopped out of the plane and tied it down.

Then the sheriff emerged. Right behind him was Franklin Redbird. Calhoun went over and held up a hand to Franklin, who took it and allowed Calhoun to help him climb down onto the dock.

"I'm glad you're back," said Calhoun.

Franklin nodded. "Me, too."

"Did they treat you okay?"

"Fine," he said. "No complaints."

"Your lawyer did a good job, then."

"Guess so. I'm here." Ralph was sniffing Franklin's cuffs.

The guide reached down and scratched the dogs's ears. "Nobody talks to me," he said, "but I gather there was an accident here this morning."

Calhoun nodded. "Curtis Swenson's Cessna exploded out there in the middle of the lake. He was taxiing for takeoff, on his way to get you and bring you back. Hit something, looked like."

"The sheriff brought a team of scuba divers," said Franklin. "To recover his body, I guess. Damn shame. Not that Curtis Swenson was any great friend of mine, but still . . ."

"It was hard to watch," Calhoun said.

The sheriff and Marty Dunlap were conferring. Three other men had emerged from the plane. They unloaded some diving gear—wet suits, air tanks, swim fins, face masks—and organized it on the dock.

After a few minutes, Marty yelled, "Listen up, please."

The crowd on the dock quieted down.

"I need some guides to take these divers out. Ben, Peter, Mush. Step up here, please."

The three guides went up to Marty and the sheriff, who proceeded to give them their instructions.

Pretty soon the divers had donned their gear. Each of them then climbed down into the front of one of the lodge's Grand Lake canoes. The three guides lowered themselves onto the stern seats and started up the outboard motors, and then the three canoes were heading for the middle of the lake.

Everybody on the dock stood there watching the canoes until they were dark blurs against the midday glitter off the water. Calhoun noticed that the canoes turned toward the foot of the lake rather than stopping at the area where the plane had exploded, where he and Kim had searched in vain for Curtis Swenson.

It took him a minute to understand why the divers were ignoring the site of the explosion. Loon and Big and Little Hairy, and the entire string of connected lakes, all were links in a great riverway that moved toward the sea. Subtle currents ran through them all. In the several hours since the Cessna blew apart in that sudden orange bloom, Curtis's body could have drifted quite a distance down the lake. Even if the lake currents only moved half a mile per hour, it had been over four hours since the explosion. Curtis might be down in the narrows—or already into the next lake in the long chain of lakes.

After the canoes disappeared around a point of land, Marty yelled, "Everybody listen up. The sheriff wants to say something."

The crowd quieted down and turned to the sheriff.

"Me and Henry, here, my deputy," he said, "we're gonna need to talk to each and every one of you. I guess it's probably too late to ask you not to talk with each other about what happened this morning, but I am asking you not to share with each other what me and Henry ask you or what your answers to our questions are. We'll be up at the lodge. I'm asking you all to make yourselves available to us for the next few hours."

There were a few grumbles from the crowd, but they all began shambling off the dock onto the path that led back to the lodge.

Calhoun waited until everybody else had left. Then he and Ralph fell in behind them.

The sheriff came up beside him. "Mr. Calhoun," he said.

Calhoun stopped. "Hello, Sheriff."

"I understand you were an actual witness."

"That's right. I was standing on the dock when the plane blew up. Saw it happen. Kim was there, too. She's also a guide."

"Just the two of you?"

Calhoun nodded.

"Before I start with all the guests and other guides," said the sheriff, "I'd like to get your story."

"You got questions," Calhoun said, "fire away."

"I need a place to sit down, take notes. Someplace where we can be private."

"My cabin, if you want."

"That'll do," said the sheriff.

Calhoun and the sheriff, with Ralph trotting ahead, followed the path to his cabin. Since no hare jumped out of the bushes, they made it without incident.

"We can talk out here on the porch," Calhoun said. "Want a Coke?"

"Wouldn't mind," said the sheriff. He sat in one of the chairs at the table. He took off his hat, put it on the table beside his elbow, and wiped his forehead with the back of his wrist.

Calhoun was back a minute later with two cans of Coke.

The sheriff took a long swig. Then he plunked the can down on the table, took a pen and a notebook from his pocket, and said, "All right, Mr. Calhoun. Why don't you just tell me what you saw this morning."

Calhoun told his story, beginning when he asked Curtis Swenson if he could accompany him to fetch Franklin Redbird, and ending with his futile efforts to find Swenson's body.

The sheriff listened without interruption, jotting an occasional note, nodding now and then, and arching his eyebrows a few times.

When he was finished, Calhoun said, "That's about it. That's how I remember it."

The sheriff frowned at his notebook for a moment, then

looked up at Calhoun. "Let's go back to when the plane exploded," he said. "Tell me again exactly what you saw, step by step. Go slow. Don't leave anything out."

"Actually," said Calhoun, "it all happened so fast, it seemed like everything happened all at the same time."

"Things hardly ever really happen all at the same time," said the sheriff. "Mostly they happen one after the other. Cause and effect. Try to remember, will you?"

Calhoun leaned back in his chair and closed his eyes. He summoned up the moving pictures of the minute or so before Curtis Swenson's Cessna blew up. This was a peculiar gift of his, the ability to remember something as if it were a movie he could slow down and replay in his head. He'd done it before, and he suspected he'd been trained to do it back before lightning obliterated his memory, back when he worked full-time for Mr. Brescia.

So he flicked on the projector in his head, and the images began to play behind his eyes in slow motion—the plane taxiing up the lake, bouncing on the riffled surface, slowly elevating until the pontoons seemed barely to be skimming the tops of the wavelets, and then the sudden mushroom burst of dark orange flame under the nose of the plane. The muffled *whoompf* of the explosion came to his ears a measurable instant later. Then the plane's tail lifted, and the nose dipped, and the Cessna did a flip, ending up on its side with one wing pointing up at the sky. Then came the second burst of orange flame, and again the delayed sound of the explosion traveling across the water to his ears.

Calhoun opened his eyes and looked at the sheriff. "The explosion came before the plane flipped," he said.

"Before," said the sheriff.

"Yes."

"You sure of that?"

"That's how I saw it."

The sheriff nodded.

"That what you suspected?" said Calhoun.

"I wondered," said the sheriff.

"It means the explosion caused the accident," Calhoun said, "not the other way around."

The sheriff shrugged.

"Meaning," said Calhoun, "it wasn't an accident at all. Somebody booby-trapped the plane."

"Well," said the sheriff, "not necessarily. Lots of things can cause an engine to explode."

"Somebody rigged the plane to blow up," Calhoun said. "Somebody set out to murder Curtis Swenson."

"Murder Swenson?" The sheriff shrugged. "Maybe."

"What do you mean, *maybe*? What else could explain it?"

"Didn't you say you had planned to be on the plane with Swenson?"

Calhoun frowned. "Sure, but . . ."

"Everybody knew that, right? You spoke to him about it at dinner last night."

Calhoun nodded. "I see what you're getting at—but why?"

"You tell me," said the sheriff. "Don't forget, whoever killed Elaine Hoffman—assuming it wasn't you—used your gun and planted it in Redbird's cabin."

Calhoun considered telling the sheriff about his quest to find out what McNulty had been investigating at Loon Lake, and his assumption that Elaine's murder, and now, apparently, Curtis Swenson's, were all connected.

So maybe the sheriff was right. Maybe the plane's explosion was aimed at Calhoun, not Swenson. Or maybe it was a convenient way to get rid of both of them.

He decided to keep these thoughts to himself for now. He wasn't sure how much he could trust this sheriff. He trusted himself more.

So he shook his head. "I don't know why anybody would want to kill me," he said. "I haven't been here long enough to make enemies. I'm just a fishing guide. I don't know anything or anybody."

The sheriff gazed up at the ceiling. "Well," he said, "it's mighty odd, if you ask me. You been here at Loon Lake—what, all of four days?—and in that short amount of time we got two deaths. One definitely a murder, the other might be. Don't that strike you odd, Mr. Calhoun?"

"How do you expect me to answer that question, Sheriff?"

"Oh, it wasn't a question, I suppose." He turned and looked hard at Calhoun. "An observation, I guess you'd call it."

"Well," said Calhoun, "I agree with you. It is mighty odd."

"You can understand how it would make me think twice about you."

Calhoun shrugged.

"I took the liberty of giving my colleague Sheriff Dickman down there in Cumberland County a call," said the sheriff. "He speaks well of you, said as far as he knew you were up here guiding. Doing no business for him, he said."

Calhoun spread his hands. "Well, there you are, then."

"Makes me wonder," said the sheriff. "That's all."

"The deputy thing is just now and then," Calhoun said. "When the sheriff thinks he needs some help. He doesn't pay me or anything."

"Sheriff Dickman tells me you're damn good at it."

"He doesn't need me," said Calhoun. "He just likes my company sometimes."

The sheriff closed his little notebook and stuck it in his

shirt pocket. "One of these days," he said, "I'm gonna figure out what you're up to, Mr. Calhoun."

"I'm just a fishing guide."

"If you're just a guide," said the sheriff, "then I'm just a short-order cook because I make breakfast for me and my wife every morning." He stood up and put his hat on. "We'll no doubt be talking again, Mr. Calhoun. Thanks for sharing your recollections. You've been a big help. Now I guess I better get up to the lodge, see what the other folks have to say."

He stepped over the sleeping Ralph, pushed open the screen door, left the cabin, and started up the path to the lodge.

CHAPTER TWENTY

After the sheriff left, Calhoun lay down on his bed, laced his fingers behind his neck, and stared up at the ceiling. He was thinking about the possibility that what happened to Curtis Swenson was not an accident, that somebody had booby-trapped the Cessna so it would explode on the water. The way the movie of it played out in his head, that's what it looked like.

He also considered the idea that he, Calhoun, and not Swenson—or maybe he along with Swenson—had been the booby-trapper's target.

He shut his eyes. He was suddenly very tired. Watching airplanes explode and diving into the water for survivors and evading the difficult questions of a suspicious sheriff was exhausting work.

Calhoun had plenty of questions of his own, such as: If not Swenson, then who shot McNulty and Millie Gautier, and who killed Elaine Hoffman, assuming it was the same person who blew up the Cessna with Curtis Swenson in it?

And especially, to all of those questions—why?

And whoever it was, did he now have Stoney Calhoun in his crosshairs?

He had no answers to these questions, and right now he didn't have enough energy to think about them.

He slept for a couple of hours and woke up feeling disoriented and fuzzy-brained and vaguely depressed, the hangover from another dream, this one instantly forgotten. A quick, steamy shower helped. He put on some clean clothes and grabbed a Coke from the refrigerator, and he and Ralph left the cabin and headed in the direction of the lodge.

As he approached the dock, he saw that Robert Dunlap was coming down the path from the lodge. The sheriff's Twin Otter was still tied up there. Calhoun went out onto the dock, and Robert came along beside him.

"The sheriff coming up with any answers?" Calhoun said.

"If he is," said Robert, "he's not confiding in me. I don't think anybody knows anything. We just had a horrible accident this morning. That's the only answer."

Calhoun nodded. "I guess you're right." He shaded his eyes and peered down toward the foot of the lake. "Those divers have been out there a long time."

"Don't know whether that's good or bad."

"I suppose if they found Curtis," Calhoun said, "they'd bring him right in."

As he was looking, a low, dark shape materialized on the water, coming from around the far point of land down toward the foot of the lake. Then two more shapes appeared, and as the shapes moved closer, they began to look like canoes. A minute later the drone of the three outboard motors crossed the water to Calhoun's ears.

"There they are," he said, pointing.

Robert tugged down the bill of his cap, squinted against the glare of the water, and said, "Yes. I see them."

About ten minutes later the three canoes pulled up along-side the dock. The guides—Ben, Peter, and Mush—climbed out and tied off the canoes. The three divers in their wet suits and swim fins hauled themselves awkwardly up onto the dock.

There were no dead bodies in any of the canoes.

"No luck, huh?" Calhoun said

"We went all the way down to the foot of the lake," Ben said, "and through the narrows, and into Muddy. Not a sign of Curtis. No scrap of clothing, no, um, no body parts. Nothing."

"He must've got blowed up in a million pieces," said Mush. "No other explanation."

"We just weren't looking in the right places," said one of the divers, a young guy with a red beard who was sitting on the dock peeling off his wet suit. "The visibility is real good in these lakes, and they ain't that deep. Lots of rocks on the bottom, but hardly any weeds. If the man had gone down where we were looking, we'd've spotted some sign of him."

A minute or so later the sheriff and his deputy, along with Marty Dunlap, came strolling down to the dock from the lodge. The deputy went over to talk to the divers, while the sheriff pulled Robert aside and engaged him in a private conversation.

Marty sidled up to Calhoun. "They didn't find Curtis, huh?"

Calhoun shook his head. "Nope."

After a few minutes, the sheriff went over and spoke to the divers, who then began to load their gear back onto their float plane.

Henry, the deputy who was also the pilot, climbed into the cockpit and got the two engines started.

The sheriff came over to where Marty and Calhoun were standing and leaned close to them. "You keep in touch," he said to Marty. He was yelling over the roar of the airplane engines. "I'll be back. Meanwhile, be sure to let me know, anything you learn, any thoughts you have." He turned and looked at Calhoun. "You, too, Mr. Calhoun. We ain't quite done with this, I don't think."

Calhoun nodded. "Always happy to help," he said.

The sheriff climbed into the cockpit and took the seat beside Henry. The divers piled in through the side cargo door and slid it shut. Ben and Peter cast off the plane's lines, and then it taxied out onto the middle of the lake, pivoted, and began to accelerate with its nose into the wind. A minute later it lifted off, tilted its wings, and disappeared over the treetops heading east to Houlton.

Calhoun realized he'd been holding his breath the whole time.

After dinner that night, Robert Dunlap took Calhoun and Ralph around to one of the many decks that jutted off the front of the lodge, giving an excellent view of the vista that Loon Lake and the surrounding hills and forests offered, especially toward sunset.

Two men were sitting at a small round table sipping after-dinner drinks. Robert introduced them as Jack and Harry Vandercamp from Chicago.

Calhoun shook hands with both of them and sat down with them. "This here's Ralph," he said, laying on the Maine accent. "He's a bird dog and a fish dog, and I hope you don't mind if he joins us in the canoe tomorrow."

"We like dogs," said Jack, who looked to be somewhere in

his forties, a lumbering bearlike man with a pleasant smile. Harry was considerably older—pushing eighty, Calhoun guessed—a wiry little guy with sharp blue eyes and wispy white hair.

"Anything special you like to eat, or don't like to eat, or are allergic to?" Calhoun said.

"We're meat and potatoes men," said Harry.

"Not fussy," said Jack.

Calhoun looked at them. "You're not brothers."

"Jack's my son," said Harry. "This is his treat. I grew up in the Midwest, spent a week in Maine when I was a boy. Stayed in a one-room log cabin on a lake with my brother and father. We fetched water from the lake, cooked on a woodstove, shat in the outhouse, and fished all day every day, and I've been dreaming about it and talking about it ever since. It's not bad when a son can make his old man's dream come true."

Jack was looking at his father with a softness in his eyes that Calhoun couldn't quite read. There was more going on here than just a man treating his elderly father to a father-son fishing trip.

"When'd you get in?" Calhoun said.

"Yesterday," said Jack. "Curtis Swenson flew us in from Greenville." He shook his head. "We liked Curtis. A real character."

"That was a terrible thing," said Harry. "What happened this morning."

"So who else up here flies?" said Jack. "Seems to me this place is dependent on its float planes."

Calhoun shook his head. "I don't know. I'm sure Marty's on top of the situation." He pushed himself to his feet. "We'll meet at the dock at eight thirty. That sound okay?"

"Sounds good," said Jack.

"Bring your foul-weather gear. I'll have everything else."

"Are we expecting rain?" said Harry.

"When you go fishing," said Calhoun, "it's always best to expect rain."

It was sometime in the middle of the night when Calhoun felt himself being dragged up from the depths of a black, dreamless sleep. It took him a moment to realize that Ralph was sitting on the floor beside him, growling softly in his chest. Calhoun put his hand on Ralph's head, and the dog quieted down.

He slipped out of bed just as the latch rattled and the door cracked open. Calhoun moved on silent bare feet to the wall next to the woodstove, where he lost himself in a shadow.

A moment later, somebody slipped in through the door, then shut it silently. Calhoun got just a glimpse of the figure—medium height, slender, athletic. He guessed he had many pounds and a few inches on his intruder, but he didn't know if the man had a weapon.

The shadow moved across the room to the bed.

Calhoun eased up behind him, and he was about to lever his forearm under the intruder's throat and ram his knee into the small of his back when he heard him whisper, "Stoney? Hey. It's me."

It wasn't a man.

It was Robin.

"Jesus H. Christ, woman," he said.

She whirled around and said, "Oh. Oh, wow. You scared the pee out of me."

"Ditto," said Calhoun. He reached over and switched on the light. "What the hell are you doing? I could've killed you, you know."

"I'm sorry." Robin looked at him and smiled. "You're pretty cute, you know that?"

Calhoun was wearing his usual bedtime attire, a T-shirt and a pair of boxer shorts. Robin had on a man-sized T-shirt and a pair of baggy sweatpants.

"Answer my question," he said. "What the hell are you doing here? It's the middle of the night. You should be asleep, not sneaking around in other people's cabins."

She looked at him with damp eyes. "I was scared," she said. "I don't know what's going on around here. I don't feel safe anymore. I tried to go to sleep, and I couldn't. I kept thinking about Elaine getting shot in her bed and Curtis getting blown up, and you, you were supposed to be on that plane, and . . . and I needed not to be alone." She gave him a little shrug. "I wanted to be with you."

"Feel safe with me, do you?" he said.

"Yes," she said. "Yes, I surely do."

"Some people think I'm the one causing all the problems around here."

"Who thinks that?"

He shrugged. "Me, for one."

"You saying you're feeling guilty about the things that have happened?"

"Not guilty, exactly," Calhoun said, "but you've got to admit, I've been here four days, and two people have died violent deaths in that time. I'd say that defies all odds, wouldn't you?"

"Something's going on, all right," said Robin, "but I don't see how you can say it's your fault."

He shrugged. "It's how I feel. Look, let me walk you back to your room."

"I don't feel safe there," she said. "I want to stay here with you."

"That ain't a good idea." He remembered what June Dunlap had told him. That Robin had lost her father at sea. That she might have a crush on Calhoun. He took Robin's hand. "Come on. I'll take you back."

"I'll behave myself," Robin said. "I promise. I can sleep on your sofa."

"No," he said. "It's a bad idea."

Robin narrowed her eyes at him. Then she nodded. "Fine. If that's how you want it. I'll go." She turned and headed for the door.

"Wait," said Calhoun. "I'll go with you."

"The hell with that," she said. "I came here all by myself. I guess I can find my way back okay." She opened the screen door, stepped out, and let it slam shut behind her.

Calhoun went out onto his screened-in porch. Already Robin had disappeared in the darkness. He waited there for as long as he guessed it would take for her to make it back to the lodge, and when he didn't hear anything unusual, like a woman screaming, he went back inside.

CHAPTER TWENTY-ONE

After breakfast the next morning, Calhoun picked up the cooler with the lunch fixin's that he'd asked for from the kitchen, lugged it down to the boathouse, and stowed it in the Grand Lake canoe he'd be using. In the corner of the boathouse he found some of the other gear he'd need for cooking a shore lunch, and he packed that away in the canoe, too. He started up the motor to see how it sounded. It started on the first yank of the cord and burbled smoothly. He turned it off, checked the gas can, and found it full.

Then he went back to his cabin, selected three fly rods, and got them set up—two for trolling streamers and one for casting dry flies. He sorted the rest of the gear—fly boxes, spools of leader material, pliers, insect repellent, dry-fly floatant, and so forth—into a single bag and hauled all the stuff back down to the boathouse.

Ralph was tagging along at Calhoun's heels with his ears perked up and his stubby tail wagging. Ralph knew a fishing trip when he saw one, and he'd be damned if he was going to be left behind.

Calhoun got all the fishing gear stowed neatly in the canoe where he could reach anything he needed from his seat in the stern. Then he smiled at Ralph, who was sitting on the dock inside the boathouse looking intently into the canoe.

"Okay," Calhoun said. "Let's go, then."

Ralph leaped lightly into the middle of the canoe, moved down to the thwart directly in front of the stern seat, curled up into what he probably thought was an inconspicuous ball against a bag of fishing gear, closed his eyes, and went to sleep, on the theory, Calhoun guessed, that nobody would be so cruel as to wake up a peacefully sleeping dog and kick him out of a canoe.

Calhoun climbed into the stern seat and paddled out of the boathouse and around to the dock, where Jack and Harry Vandercamp, his clients for the day, were waiting.

"Mornin'," he said.

"Good morning," said the Vandercamp men practically in unison.

"We got a nice soft day for it." Calhoun looked up at the sky, which was gray and still and smelled like rain. "Hope you remembered your foul-weather gear."

Both of them nodded.

"Well," said Calhoun, "climb in. There's fish out there waitin' to be caught."

Jack knelt on the dock and held the canoe while Harry, bracing himself on his son's shoulder, climbed into the bow seat. Then Jack got into the middle seat and pushed the canoe away from the dock.

Calhoun gave a couple of pulls with the paddle, then got the motor going. He steered them across the lake. The shoreline there was dark and fell off quickly into deep water. It was overhung with hemlock and alder and scattered with large boulders. He liked the looks of it. It looked fishy.

When they got there, he cut back the motor to trolling speed and handed rods to Jack and Harry. "Harry," he said, "you let your line out on this side here," indicating the side nearest the shoreline. "Jack, you fish the other side of the boat. You'll both be dragging your flies over the drop-off. We'll head downlake and see what might be inclined to take a bite out of those flies."

As they chugged slowly toward the foot of the lake, a misty rain began to fall, and the water lay as flat and glossy as a black mirror. They all pulled on rain gear, and pretty soon each of Calhoun's sports caught a nice salmon.

At the foot of the lake, he shut off the motor, stood up, and poled them down through the narrows, which was little more than a curved pinching of the lake and a boulder-strewn quickening of the water where Loon emptied into Muddy.

There was a small cove on the left right there at the head of Muddy Pond, and through the mist Calhoun spotted a couple of rings on the glassy surface. He pointed with his push-pole. "Look," he whispered, though there was no need to whisper. "See that?"

Harry and Jack shaded their eyes and looked where Calhoun was pointing at the widening rings.

"What are they?" said Harry.

"Maybe salmon," said Calhoun, "but if I had to guess, I'd say big squaretails on the hunt for mayflies."

"Squaretails," said Jack. "You mean brook trout?"

"We call 'em squaretails here in Maine," said Calhoun. "Lake trout are called togue, too, if anybody should mention it." He picked up the spare fly rod, which he'd rigged with a bushy dry fly—an Adams, his all-round favorite—and handed it up to old Harry. "Stand up and get some line out," he told Harry. "Let's catch one of 'em so we can tell for sure what species it is."

Calhoun put down the pole, picked up a paddle, and eased the canoe into the cove. Ralph, apparently sensing something was afoot, sat up to watch. Harry, up in the bow, was false casting, getting a good length of fly line in the air. He appeared to be a decent caster. A bit wristy, Calhoun thought, but certainly competent enough to get the job done.

"Okay," he said softly. "Strip it in, blow on your fly, and be ready. These fish are cruising, so when you see one boil on the surface, try to figure what direction he's heading and cast ahead of him. Don't put it in the middle of his ring. That's the one place we know he ain't gonna be."

Calhoun let the canoe drift on the flat surface, and a minute later a fish swirled ahead of them. He didn't need to say anything. Harry had his line in the air, and he laid his fly down about fifteen feet to the left of where the fish had come up.

"Yeah, good shot," Calhoun said softly. "Now just leave her set there. Don't twitch it or anything. If he's headed in that direction, he'll see it, and if he likes what he sees, he'll eat it."

Instead, the fish came up on the other side of the boat. This time Calhoun had a good look at the swirl it made. "Quick," he said. "That fish is heading left and a little toward us. About eight o'clock."

Harry dropped the Adams right where Calhoun hoped he would, and a moment later a large fish-shaped shadow cruised up to it, lifted its head, opened its mouth, and casually slurped in the fly. Harry raised his rod and set the hook.

"Oh, beautiful," said Jack. "Way to go, Dad."

The fish did not jump, leading Calhoun to conclude that it was a squaretail, not a salmon. Harry played it expertly, and after a good fight of a bit more than five minutes, Calhoun netted a gorgeous Maine brook trout. "A conservative four pounds," he said.

He extended the net down to Harry, who lifted out the fish, gently unhooked it, and held it up for Jack to photograph.

"You want to keep it?" said Calhoun. "Marty says they've got a great taxidermist in Pittsburgh who'll mount that fish for you."

Harry shook his head. "We got the photo. Anyway, that fish is mounted here." He tapped the side of his head with his forefinger. "I don't need to kill it to remember it."

Calhoun smiled. "Nice to know it'll keep swimming, isn't it?"

Harry nodded. He leaned over the side of the canoe and cradled the big fish in the water for a moment, letting it catch its breath, until it flicked its tail and was gone.

"That right there was worth the whole trip," said Jack. "Thanks, Stoney. Nice guidin'."

"Nice fishin', I'd say," said Calhoun. "Harry, you're a helluva man."

Harry grinned and jerked a thumb into the air.

They drifted there in the cove for another ten or fifteen minutes, but no more fish broke the surface, so Calhoun started up the motor and they resumed trolling along the drop-offs.

They were just approaching the point of land where Calhoun intended to stop for lunch when he noticed a flash of color on one of the bushes against the shore where it drooped down to touch the water. It was a shade of neon orange not usually found along a Maine shoreline. Perhaps it was some kind of wildflower, but Calhoun didn't think so.

"Reel up, men," he said. "We're gonna have lunch now."

After Harry and Jack got their lines in, Calhoun shut off the motor, picked up his paddle, and steered the canoe over to the bush. "Harry, grab that orange thing for me, would you?" he said.

Harry reached over and plucked the orange scrap from the bush. "Oh, shit," he muttered. "Do you know what this is?"

"I got a suspicion," Calhoun said.

Harry handed the orange scrap back to Jack, who looked at it for a moment, then passed it on to Calhoun.

It was a ragged strip of lightweight cloth—silk, maybe—and it was decorated with orange and yellow hibiscus flowers intertwined with pale green and blue vines. One edge of the cloth was black, apparently singed by flame.

"What do you think?" said Jack.

"I remember this design," said Calhoun. "It's a piece of Curtis's shirt, all right. I don't think the sheriff's divers got this far down Muddy yesterday."

"Just because we got a piece of his shirt doesn't mean his body's down here," said Harry.

"No, you're right," said Calhoun, "though I do think we've got to check it out. We'll have lunch first, but then I think we need to explore the rest of Muddy Pond all the way down to the outlet. We can fish for salmon and look for dead bodies all at the same time. Not many anglers get to do that."

"A unique experience indeed," said Harry, without any trace of cynicism that Calhoun could detect.

Calhoun had brought a bag of charcoal to speed up the preparation of the shore lunch. Quicker than building a fire from dead hardwood and waiting for it to burn down to coals. He scooped out a shallow bowl in the sandy ground, filled it with some birch bark and pine shavings and twigs, and got the kindling lit. Then he dumped in the hunks of charcoal. When they were glowing, he surrounded the firebowl with rocks, covered it with a grill, and put on the cast-iron pot of chili and the cof-

feepot. He waited for the chili to begin bubbling, then got out
the skillet and flopped down the three thick rib eyes.

Four minutes on each side and he figured the steaks would
be pinkish red inside. He put each slab of meat on a plate and
set them out, along with knives, forks, coffee mugs, the chili
pot, and a basket of corn muffins, on a big flat rock.

The rain had stopped, and the sun was threatening to
break through the clouds. Ralph was lying on the ground,
keeping an eye on the food. Harry and Jack were sitting on
boulders by the water's edge talking and gazing out at the
water and sipping from cans of Coke. "Come and get it,"
Calhoun called to them.

They came, and they got it, and they proclaimed it delicious, and all three of them tossed their meat scraps to Ralph,
who seemed to find it delicious, too.

After the food was gone, they sat around sipping mugs of
camp coffee, which Harry and Jack proclaimed the best coffee
they'd ever had.

Jack was sprawled on the ground with his head resting on a
log and his eyes closed against the glare of the sky. He might've
been sleeping.

Harry reached over and tapped Calhoun on the leg. "He
thinks this will be our last trip together," he said softly, jerking
his head at his son. "I've got this kidney problem. Jack doesn't
think I'm gonna make it till next summer."

Calhoun looked at him. "I'm damn sorry to hear that."

"I'm not going along with that thinking," Harry said. "I got
plenty more fishing in me."

"I hope you're right," said Calhoun. "Next summer you and
Jack have to come to Portland. I'll take you out for bluefish and
stripers."

Harry smiled. "We'd like that."

———

After they got their campsite cleaned up, they loaded the canoe and climbed back in. By now the clouds had blown away, and the sun was blazing from a clear blue sky, and the surface of Muddy Pond was corrugated with chop in the stiff afternoon breeze.

They trolled the entire eastern shoreline all the way to the foot of the pond without a single strike.

"These ain't very good conditions, I'm afraid," said Calhoun. "Bright sun puts down the fish. On the other hand, the salmon do like the riffled water. Maybe we'll do better along the other shoreline."

The west shore wasn't much better, though. At one point Harry's rod bounced, and its tip dipped, and a short length of line was yanked off his reel, but the fish failed to hook itself.

They didn't talk about it, but Calhoun could tell that both Harry and Jack were scanning the surface of the water, alert for something that might turn out to be Curtis Swenson's dead body.

They found the same number of dead bodies as the number of fish they caught from Muddy Pond that afternoon, which was zero.

Calhoun had just finished poling them up through the narrows into Loon Lake when he heard the drone of an airplane engine. He recognized the voice of the lodge's Twin Otter, and a moment later the big plane with the triple-L logo on its side cleared the treetops, circled around to the head of the lake, and dropped down until it was out of sight from their canoe. Then the pitch of the engine changed, indicating that it had begun to make its descent.

———

"That's the lodge's plane," said Jack Vandercamp. "I wonder who's flying her."

"One of the guides, I imagine," said Harry. "The tall young one. Forget his name."

"That'd be Ben," said Calhoun.

Harry nodded. "That's right. Ben. I heard him and Marty talking this morning. Ben's got his license. He was in Iraq, did you know that? I guess he flew planes or helicopters or something over there."

"I figured they'd have somebody to back up Curtis," said Calhoun. "This place is totally dependent on air transportation."

"Marty was saying they're hoping to hire a replacement as soon as possible," said Harry. "They need somebody full-time, and Ben was saying he had no heart for flying airplanes of any kind."

"After what happened to Curtis," said Jack, "it's hard to blame him."

"Never mind after Iraq," said Calhoun.

CHAPTER TWENTY-TWO

By the time Calhoun eased his canoe alongside the dock, the Twin Otter with the triple-*L* logo on its fuselage was already tied up there, and Ben and Robert Dunlap and the redheaded kid who drove the golf cart were unloading supplies from the plane and stacking them in the wagon that was hitched to the cart.

Robert held the gunwale of Calhoun's canoe against the dock, steadying it for Jack, who climbed out. "How was the fishing?" Robert said.

Harry grinned. "Excellent."

"My dad got a four-pound squaretail on a dry fly," said Jack.

Robert smiled. "That's great." He looked at Harry. "Did you keep it for the taxidermist?"

Harry shook his head. "Put him back for somebody else to catch. Like Lee Wulff said, a big fish is too precious to be caught only once."

"Well," said Robert, "that's admirable. You got photos, at least, I hope." He held down a hand to old Harry, who used it to help himself scramble out of the canoe.

"Thanks," said Harry. "Yes, we got some photos. We found a piece of Curtis Swenson's shirt down in Muddy Pond."

Robert's smile turned into a frown. "A piece of his shirt, huh?"

"One of his Hawaiian shirts, all bright colors and flowers. Hey, Stoney. Show that piece of shirt to Robert."

Calhoun had climbed out of the canoe. He went over to Robert and handed him the scrap of Curtis Swenson's aloha shirt.

Robert looked at it and nodded. "This is Curtis's, all right. It's the one he was wearing when . . ." He waved his hand in the air. "Look how the edge got burned. Where'd you say you found it?"

"Down in Muddy," Calhoun said. "It was stuck on a bush that was trailing in the water."

"Why don't you let me hang on to it," said Robert. "The sheriff might want it for evidence."

"Evidence of what?" said Calhoun.

"Of what happened yesterday," Robert said. "Of Curtis getting blown up in the Cessna. Of the fact that he's dead, I suppose."

"Keep it, then," Calhoun said. "We looked all over down there in Muddy but didn't see any dead bodies. I'm not sure you can call a man dead until you've got his body."

Robert shrugged. "We'll probably never find him. That doesn't make him alive." He folded up the ragged scrap of cloth and stuffed it into his shirt pocket. He glanced at Ben and the redheaded kid, then turned to Calhoun. "I better get back to unloading the plane."

"Need some help?" said Calhoun.

Robert shook his head "We got it. Thanks."

"I see we got ourselves a new pilot, huh?"

Ben looked up. "I hoped I'd never have to fly a plane again," he said. "Far as I'm concerned, the sooner we get someone to take Curtis's place the better. But, yeah, meanwhile, process of elimination, looks like it's me."

"You don't like to fly?"

"What's to like? A chance to die?"

"You were in Iraq, I heard."

Ben shook his head. "I don't feel like talking about that, if you don't mind." He turned and went over to the plane and stepped through the doorway into the cargo hold.

Jack Vandercamp came over and shook Calhoun's hand. "It was a great day," said Jack. "You available tomorrow?"

"I'm scheduled to be guiding," said Calhoun. "You want me again, tell Marty. I'd enjoy it."

Harry patted Calhoun on the shoulder, and the father and son turned and headed up to the lodge.

Calhoun lifted the cooler out of the canoe and lugged it up to the kitchen. Then he came back and paddled the canoe over to the boathouse, where he unloaded the fishing gear and the cooking equipment. He put the cooking stuff away, then hauled the canoe up on the dock, hosed it out, eased it back into the water, and refilled the gas can from the pump. All the chores that guides do that the sports don't see and probably never think about, although at least today he didn't have to clean any dead fish.

Fishing guides say eight hours on the water means twelve hours of work.

Calhoun liked guiding well enough, when he could take out companionable folks like Harry and Jack Vandercamp. But it was hard and often unrewarding work, and when you added the man-hours and expenses to the aggravation, the pay was piss-poor at best.

He was just finishing up his post-trip guide chores in the boathouse when another canoe glided in. Franklin Redbird was in the stern.

Calhoun held Franklin's canoe alongside while the Indian guide climbed out. "Thanks, Stoney," he said. He reached in, opened his cooler, and took out a big landlocked salmon. "My sports decided to get this fellow mounted."

"That's a five-pounder, I'd guess," said Calhoun. "Good fish."

"Five pounds four ounces, actually. A real nice fish." Franklin shook his head. "I'd rather know he was still swimming up there in Big Hairy Lake." He looked at Calhoun. "If one of your clients wanted to get a fish mounted, would you know what to do?"

Calhoun grinned. "I bet you're gonna show me."

Franklin shrugged. "If you want."

Calhoun nodded. "Sure."

Franklin took the fish over to a restaurant-sized freezer in the corner of the boathouse. Beside the freezer was a big carton box, from which he took a coffin-shaped foam container. It looked to be about three feet long, a foot wide, and maybe eight inches deep. He opened it and showed Calhoun that it was about half filled with foam packing peanuts. "You clean your fish soon as you kill it, of course," Franklin said. "Guts and gills. Then you just stick it in one of these. You put in a card with the sport's name and address, your name, and the dimensions of the fish—length, girth, weight—seal it with duct tape, and stick it in the freezer. Curtis Swenson"—Franklin hesitated—"*somebody* packs it in dry ice, flies it down to the UPS office in Greenville, and from there it goes to the taxidermist in Pittsburgh. Fellow down there does a good job, I understand."

"I've never been a big fan of stuffed fish," said Calhoun.

"Seems to me a good photograph does the job and lets a fish live."

Franklin shrugged. "I'm with you, Stoney."

Calhoun watched Franklin pack the salmon in the foam box. Then he said good-bye, whistled up Ralph, and picked up all his fishing gear, and the two of them headed back to his cabin. He still had a little more than an hour before dinner. Time for a Coke and maybe a quick nap.

When he opened the door to the screen porch, he saw that Robin was sitting there in one of the rocking chairs. She was wearing a pair of blue running shorts and a pink sleeveless tank top, and she was reading a paperback book.

She looked up, put the book on the table on its open pages, and gave him a big smile. "You're back," she said. "How was it?"

Calhoun stacked the fishing gear in the corner of the porch, then turned to Robin. "Am I supposed to yell, 'Honey, I'm home'?"

She frowned. "Huh?" She hesitated. "Oh, I get it. I guess I just assumed you wouldn't mind if I was here. It feels like a safe, comfortable place to me. Isn't that okay?"

"You don't live here," he said.

"I know. I'm sorry if I . . ."

He shook his head. "We ain't a couple."

"Sure," she said. "I understand. Sorry. My mistake. I should've got it when you kicked me out last night." She stood up. "Thanks for letting me hang out when you weren't here, anyway. Now I'll get out of your hair." She headed for the door.

"Hang on," Calhoun said. "Where are you going?"

She stopped. "What makes the difference? Somewhere else. Give you some privacy."

"Sit down," he said. "Have a Coke. Let's talk about it."

She looked at him for a minute, then came back and sat in

the rocker. "I'm sorry if I made stupid assumptions," she said. "I know we're not a couple, and I understand that you don't want me to spend the night, but we're friends. I felt like I could depend on you to be there for me. I didn't think you'd mind if I hid out down here in your cabin. I actually thought you'd be happy to see me when you got back from guiding." She shook her head. "I guess I don't know you very well."

"I don't know me very well, either," said Calhoun. "I apologize for myself. Maybe I overreacted. I tend to do that sometimes. It just felt a little . . . I don't know, *domestic*, you might say, having you waiting here for me to get home from work."

"That was you, not me."

"Yeah, I guess you're right," he said. "Let's start over, okay?"

Robin looked at him for a minute, then nodded. "Okay." She sat down, picked up her book, pretended to read for a minute, then looked up at him with a big fake smile of happy surprise on her face. "Oh, hi, Stoney," she said brightly. "Welcome home."

He went over to her and squeezed her shoulder. "Hi, honey. Did you have a nice day?"

"Oh, excellent," said Robin. "I vacuumed the whole house, and wait'll you see what I've got in the oven."

Calhoun laughed. "You've been watching way too much television. You want a Coke?"

"Sure. Thanks."

When Calhoun returned to the porch with a Coke for each of them, Robin said, "So are you gonna tell her about me?"

"Kate?" he said.

She nodded.

"Tell her what?"

Robin smiled. "How I've been chasing after you. Flirting with you. Coming to your cabin without being invited."

"June said she thought you had a crush on me," he said.

Robin rolled her eyes. "June would say something like that. I'm sorry, Stoney. I know you don't need this."

"She mentioned how you lost your father."

She nodded. "Right. I get it. She thinks I've got a daddy thing for you. Is that it?"

He shrugged. "I am twice your age."

"So, okay, I think you're pretty hot," she said, "and, yeah, I'd sleep with you in a heartbeat." She smiled. "You knew that, right?"

He shook his head. He knew he was naive about such things.

"Well," she said, "I said it out loud, in case you didn't. You gonna tell that to Kate?"

"I tell Kate everything."

"Everything? Really?"

"Yes."

Robin smiled. "How extraordinarily old-fashioned."

Calhoun shrugged. "I love Kate, and even if she's mad at me and not talking to me, and even though I'm here and she's there, it doesn't change anything. Do you understand?"

Robin was looking at him with a soft little smile playing around her mouth. She nodded. "Sure I understand," she said. "You're actually a man of principle. I've read about men like you, mostly in trashy novels. Never believed I'd run into a real one, though."

CHAPTER TWENTY-THREE

Calhoun was sitting in one of the comfortable rocking chairs on his screen porch that evening after dinner. The lights were turned off, and he held a mug of coffee in his hands. He was watching the sun descend behind the treeline across the lake, waiting for darkness to fill up the forest. A couple of loons were out there on the water laughing at each other, and from the woods behind the cabin came the hoot-hoot of a barred owl. Ralph was snoozing on the floor beside him. The poor dog had tuckered himself out with all that fishing.

Calhoun was thinking about McNulty and Millie Gautier, dead of botulism poisoning, then shot in the head, and Elaine Hoffman, murdered in her bed with Calhoun's own Colt Woodsman .22 pistol, and now Curtis Swenson, blown up in his Cessna in what was supposed to look like an accident but almost certainly was also a murder.

Too many dead bodies and not enough clues.

He'd been here for five days, and in that short amount of time, two people had been killed, and since Curtis Swenson turned out to be a victim rather than the villain, Calhoun hadn't come close to figuring out who was doing it or why. He guessed Mr. Brescia wouldn't be very happy with his progress.

Again he remembered what Sheriff Dickman liked to say about conducting an investigation. *Sometimes it's like partridge hunting*, he'd say. *You never know where a bird might be hiding, so you've got to go through the woods shaking every bush and kicking every clump of grass. You might shake a hundred bushes and kick a hundred clumps of grass and find nothing, but you can't lose faith. It almost always gets boring, but you've got to keep doing it. Just keep kicking and shaking, and eventually something will fly out.*

Time to get shaking and kicking, Calhoun thought.

When the sun had sunk all the way behind the trees across the lake, Calhoun went back inside. He put his mug in the sink, slipped on his dark blue windbreaker, and put a small flashlight in his pocket. Then he went out onto the porch. "I'll be back in a while," he told Ralph. "You guard the place. Bite intruders on the ass."

He opened the door and stepped outside. He stood there on the path in front of his cabin for a few minutes while his eyes adjusted to the darkness, and then the ambient light from the moonless sky showed the way along the pathway past the boathouse to the dock where the Twin Otter was parked.

He cut into the woods alongside the path and found a place where he could lean his back against a pine tree and obscure his silhouette. There was a screen of shrubbery between the tree and the path. It was thick enough to cover him in the darkness but sparse enough to give him an unobstructed view of the path from the lodge down to the dock, and he could see the float plane clearly.

He made a cushion of pine needles and sat on them with his back against the trunk of the pine, and almost instantly that old déjà vu feeling came over him again, and he knew he'd spent many nights sitting on outdoor stakeouts in his unremembered life. He felt his senses grow more acute, and the sensations were all familiar—the organic scent of darkness, the wet feel of the night air brushing his skin, the buzzing sounds of the forest, the flickering play of pale light and purple shadows in the underbrush.

Calhoun wore no watch, and almost instantly his sense of time became distorted. He understood that five minutes sitting quietly in the darkness could seem like an hour, and five hours could seem like fifteen minutes. He hadn't decided on a time limit for himself. He'd stay for as long as he could remain awake and alert, and he'd see what, if anything, happened.

He remembered the night when he and Ralph were sitting on the end of the dock and somebody sneaked into the Twin Otter, shone his flashlight around inside, and emerged a short time later carrying something. At the time he thought the man was Curtis Swenson. He had no idea what the man took from the plane. It looked like a small suitcase.

Now he wished he'd followed that man.

According to Millie Gautier's father, McNulty had been a man on a mission. He'd had something with him when he went to St. Cecelia, and he intended to take it to Augusta—so he could deliver it to Mr. Brescia, Calhoun guessed.

Now McNulty was dead.

So Calhoun was going to watch the float plane. This was the bush he was shaking, the clump of grass he was kicking.

Even though he was sitting on a cushion of pine needles, the ground under his butt was damp and chilly. The tree trunk was rough against his shoulder blades. His legs, stretched out in front of him, became stiff and achey. He wished he'd brought some coffee or a Coke with him.

The moon had risen over the lake, making wavy reflections on the water and illuminating the area around the dock. Calhoun was confident he'd be able to identify anybody who came to the plane.

He yawned. He had another day of guiding coming up. Harry and Jack Vandercamp again. Good guys. Undemanding. They loved fishing. Easy clients.

He thought about Kate, who wasn't talking to him. She'd told Adrian that she wouldn't speak with him on the telephone if he called.

Didn't matter. He loved her anyway. Couldn't help it.

Then there was Robin. He didn't know what to do about her. He felt bad for her, but she made him uncomfortable. She had a crush on him, June Dunlap said, and Calhoun supposed it was true.

Judging by the progress the moon had made in its arc across the sky since he'd been sitting there, he guessed it had been about three hours. He stretched out his legs, flexed his arms, rolled his head on his shoulders.

When he'd seen the shadowy figure go into the plane, it had been right after dark. That didn't mean that another time it wouldn't be much later. It could be anytime. Or it might never happen again. Calhoun didn't intend to spend the whole night sitting against the trunk of that pine tree.

His thoughts kept flipping back to Kate. He hoped things were all right with her. He wondered how Walter was doing, and how business was at the shop, and if Adrian was working out.

He was remembering the last time he'd slept with Kate, the slick feel of her skin against his, when the deer slipped past him in the darkness. It had been moving so quietly that Calhoun was unaware of it until it materialized out of the shadows right beside him—so close that he could've reached out and touched it. He could smell her musty wild scent. He held his breath. The deer—it was a small doe—paused and lifted her head and sniffed the air, then proceeded through the screen of shrubbery and onto the path. Calhoun watched her amble down to the lake, step into the water, bend her long neck, and drink. Then she turned and glided through the undergrowth back into the woods.

If the deer had been a person, Calhoun thought, she would've gotten the drop on him. She had moved silently and cautiously through the woods, and her superior sense of smell had alerted her to his presence, but that was no excuse for his being unaware of her. He'd been sloppy, and he had to do better.

He waited a while longer—an hour, he figured, gauging the passage of time by the movement of the moon across the sky. Nobody came down to the dock.

Calhoun stood up, brushed the pine needles off the seat of his pants, stretched, and followed the moonlit path back to his cabin.

He half expected to find Robin there, sitting on the porch waiting for him, or maybe curled up in his bed, and he was trying to figure out how he'd handle that.

But nobody was there except Ralph. When Calhoun walked in and turned on the light, the dog, who was curled up on the rug beside the bed, lifted his head and looked blearily at him.

"It's only me," said Calhoun.

Ralph sighed, tucked his nose under his stubby tail, and went back to sleep.

CHAPTER TWENTY-FOUR

Calhoun guided the Vandercamp men again on Tuesday. They fished both Big and Little Hairy lakes and caught a good number of salmon, though none as large as the one Franklin Redbird's sport had caught and killed the previous day.

That night after dark he again staked out the dock where the Twin Otter was parked, but nobody came to the float plane while Calhoun was watching.

He spent the next three days guiding a retired couple from Michigan. In the evenings he sat with his back against the same pine tree overlooking the dock. On Wednesday he watched a porcupine saunter up the moonlit path toward the lodge. Thursday evening a deer brushed close to him. He guessed it was the same one he'd seen his first night on stakeout, a small doe. He'd apparently set up his stakeout right next to a game trail.

Calhoun enjoyed his encounters with the wildlife, but he was getting frustrated. Nobody went near the Twin Otter while he was watching.

He couldn't come up with another way to shake the bushes and kick the grass, so he was back again on Friday, and around midnight, just as he'd begun to think about heading back to his cabin, his eye caught a movement on the path. Someone was coming down the slope from the lodge. By the shape of him and the way he moved, it appeared to be a man. He was hugging close to the shadowy edge of the pathway, moving slowly, and his body language said that he was trying not to be seen. He was wearing dark loose-fitting clothing and a cap with the visor pulled low. Calhoun couldn't see his face or the shape of his body. He couldn't tell how old the man was. He was just a dark amorphous shape easing through the night shadows.

Calhoun could see that the man was feeling alert and furtive, that he didn't want to be detected, that he was on a mission he didn't want anybody to know about.

The man had nearly reached the dock when he suddenly stopped on the path an easy cast with a fly rod from where Calhoun was hiding. The man swiveled his head around slowly, as if he were trying to locate somebody who he knew was watching him.

Calhoun held his breath and sat as still as a stump.

The man's eyes seemed to bore through the darkness and the shrubbery. His gaze hesitated, then passed over the spot where Calhoun was hiding. All the while, his face remained a black shadow under the visor of his cap.

After a long minute, the man turned and went out onto the dock. He moved directly to the Twin Otter. He flicked on a small flashlight with a narrow beam and used it to light his way as he climbed out onto a pontoon. Then he stepped up, opened the plane's door, slipped into the cockpit, and shut the door behind him. The light flickered through the side windows and then became dimmer, and Calhoun figured the man was moving into the bowels of the plane.

He realized he'd been digging his fingernails into his palms.

His heart was thudding in his chest. This was it. Finally. This was the reason he'd come to Loon Lake. This was why he'd been spending the past several evenings hiding in the woods. This, he figured, was what McNulty had seen. This man in the float plane.

It was, he guessed, what got McNulty killed. It was why Mr. Brescia had sent Calhoun here.

He forced himself to take a few slow, even breaths. He felt his adrenaline kicking in.

A few minutes later, the light inside the plane went out.

Then, as Calhoun watched, the figure seemed to materialize from the shadows. He was on the dock, heading back to the pathway, and he was carrying something by a handle down by his side. It looked like an attaché case.

When he got to the end of the dock, instead of following the path back toward the lodge, the figure turned the other way and headed in the direction of the boathouse.

Calhoun waited for a couple of minutes, then pushed himself to his feet. He slipped through the bushes to the path and followed along a safe distance behind the man with the attaché case.

When he got to the boathouse, the man stopped and looked around. Calhoun froze where he was standing in the shadows on the edge of the path. After a minute, the man turned to the building, flicked on his flashlight, shone its narrow beam on the door, opened it, and went inside.

Calhoun, moving soundlessly on the pine needles that blanketed the path, eased up to the window beside the boathouse door. The window was head high on the building's wall, and by bracing himself on the sill and going up on his tiptoes, Calhoun was able to see inside.

The figure was shining his light around in the back corner

beside the big freezer where Franklin Redbird had stowed his client's prize salmon for the taxidermist. As Calhoun watched, the man slid the big carton that held the foam fish crates away from the wall. He aimed his flashlight at the place on the floor where the carton had been. Then he knelt down, and Calhoun saw him lift and slide away a large square of plywood. It looked like a trapdoor in the boathouse floor. The man leaned over the hole in the floor and slid his attaché case into the opening under the floorboards. Then he wrestled the trapdoor back in place and pushed the big carton on top of it. He stood there with his flashlight pointed aimlessly at the floor and looked slowly all around.

Suddenly, his head stopped moving. The man seemed to be staring hard at Calhoun's window. To Calhoun it felt as if the man's eyes were drilling into his. He wondered if his head was silhouetted against the glass. He ducked quickly away, moved into the woods alongside the boathouse, and slid behind the trunk of a big pine tree.

A moment later the boathouse door opened, and the man stepped out. He panned his flashlight all around. When its beam approached the tree where Calhoun was hiding, he pulled his head back and flattened himself against the trunk.

The light seemed to stop moving when it came to Calhoun's tree, and he half expected to feel the beam of the man's flashlight center on his face, or to hear the man order him to step out where he could see him, or to see a gun materialize in his hand. Instead, after a long pause, the flashlight's beam resumed moving.

After what seemed like several minutes, the light went out. Calhoun peeked around the side of the tree trunk. He saw that the man had turned off his flashlight and had begun walking back along the pathway toward the lodge.

Calhoun still hadn't gotten a look at the man's face. The visor of his cap had kept it in shadow, and he'd never allowed his flashlight to illuminate his features. Judging by the general shape of his body and the way he moved in the darkness, Calhoun believed he could eliminate Ben, the tall, gangly young guide who was now the lodge's pilot pro tem, and Mush, who was short and rotund. Otherwise, this man could've been any of the guides or other employees—and most of the male guests—of the lodge. Calhoun was pretty sure it was a man, although, come to think of it, Kim, the female guide, moved and was shaped like a man.

He waited there behind the tree next to the boathouse until he guessed that the man had made it back to the lodge. Then he went to the door, pulled it open, slipped inside, and flicked on his flashlight.

Wood planking formed a U-shaped interior, with the open end of the U facing out to the lake. The boathouse was about the size of a six-car garage. There were three log walls with two windows and a door in each wall and a shallow-peaked roof. A rack against one wall held eight or ten Grand Lake canoes. About a dozen outboard motors hung from another rack. Paddles and life jackets and boat cushions hung on pegs. There was a long workbench with several big toolboxes, and in the corner stood the double-wide freezer and the carton of foam fish crates.

Calhoun moved quickly to the corner. He slid the carton away from the wall and shone his light on the floor. A two-foot square of plywood with a finger-sized hole drilled into it fit tightly into a cutout place in the plank floor. Calhoun used his forefinger to lift and slide the piece of plywood away, then shone his light down into the hole.

The hole was lined with fine-mesh wire, and water from the

lake came to within two feet of the floor planks. Calhoun guessed it had been built to serve as a live well for bait. He leaned in and shone his light around, and he saw that there was a wide wooden shelf built into the floor joists above the waterline. He reached into the shelf and felt around, and his fingers touched something hard and metallic. He slid it out and lifted it onto the floor.

The attaché case was made of brushed aluminum. Calhoun undid the two snaps, opened it up, and shone his light inside.

The interior of the case was padded with foam rubber. Twenty-four compartments were cut into the rubber, four rows of six, and each compartment held a glass vial the size of a small test tube with a rubber stopper. Calhoun took out one of the vials and shone his flashlight on it. It contained a yellowish powdery substance. When he shook it, he saw that the powder was as fine as talcum.

He had no idea what the stuff was. Some kind of drug, he supposed. Cocaine? Raw heroin?

Botulinum? He had no idea what the botulinum toxin looked like, or even if it was a powder.

He'd let Mr. Brescia figure it out.

He slipped the vial into his jacket pocket and zipped it shut. Then he closed the aluminum case, shoved it back into its compartment under the floor joists, returned the plywood trapdoor to its place, and slid the big carton back on top of it.

He guessed he'd been inside the boathouse for four or five minutes. Anybody looking at the building would've seen the flash of his light in the windows. He patted his pockets. He had no weapon, not even his filleting knife.

He had no excuse, either. What logical reason could he give for going into the boathouse with a flashlight at midnight?

Well, if he had to, he'd come up with something.

He turned off his flashlight, waited for a couple minutes

while his eyes adjusted, then felt his way along the back wall to the door. He hesitated there, and then, imagining a man with a gun waiting outside for him, he decided to use the door on the opposite wall for his exit.

It turned out to be a sensible but unnecessary precaution. When he sneaked around the outside of the boathouse and peeked at the area around the door he'd entered by, nobody was there.

He felt that rush you get when you've gotten away with something illegal or immoral—a combination of triumph and relief.

He walked quickly back to his cabin. Instead of going directly inside, he sat on one of the rocking chairs on the screen porch. He wanted to try to think this through.

The man who'd hidden the aluminum case in the boathouse would see that one of the vials was missing the first time he opened the case, so Calhoun figured he didn't have much time to decide what to do and then to do it.

His best move would be to deliver the vial to Mr. Brescia. It seemed pretty obvious that the contents of the aluminum case, whether it was botulinum toxin or not, was the key to what had gotten McNulty—and Millie Gautier and Elaine Hoffman and Curtis Swenson, too—killed. McNulty, he guessed, had found a vial of this stuff on the airplane. He'd taken it to St. Cecelia, where he'd met up with Millie. He'd intended to continue on to Augusta, but the two of them died from botulism poisoning. Whoever was responsible for the vials found their dead bodies, shot them in the head, and retrieved the vial that McNulty had taken. Calhoun figured that shooting McNulty and Millie was intended to confuse the police, to deflect their attention from who McNulty was and what he was really up to, and to prevent them from figuring out what really killed the two of them.

It could have worked. If the police had taken it at face value, and if the bodies hadn't been autopsied by the medical examiner, the two deaths might well have been chalked up to the murder-suicide of a pair of doomed lovers.

Calhoun guessed that Curtis Swenson had smuggled the cases containing the vials into Loon Lake on the float plane, most likely from some remote river or lake over the border in Quebec, which was only a few miles away. From there, he had flown them to Greenville or Houlton, and from there, they were shipped to the taxi dermist in Pittsburgh.

Before he got killed, Curtis Swenson appeared to be the villain, but now he was dead. Calhoun guessed that the shadowy figure who'd taken the case of vials off the float plane tonight was also the person who'd shot McNulty and Elaine Hoffman, and who'd booby-trapped the Cessna and killed Swenson.

Calhoun guessed he'd leave the *who* and the *why* questions to Mr. Brescia to figure out. Calhoun had discovered the *what*, and he had the evidence of it in his pocket. He thought that would be enough.

He pushed himself out of the rocker and went inside. There came a rustling noise from the direction of the bed, then the click of dog claws on the wood floor, and then Ralph was pushing his nose against Calhoun's leg and whining softly. Calhoun scooched down, rubbed the dog's ears, and let him outside.

When Ralph came back in, Calhoun took off his jacket with the glass vial in its zippered pocket and hung it carefully on a hanger. Then he slipped off his shoes and socks and pants and slid into his bed. Ralph curled up on the rug, sighed, and began snoring.

Calhoun lay there on his back with his fingers laced under his neck, staring up into the darkness, too pumped up to think about sleeping quite yet.

He was thinking that if he could just get this done, if he could deliver the vial to Mr. Brescia and tell him what he knew, it would be over, and he could go home. He'd resume his life. He'd patch things up with Kate, and things would be good again.

He lay awake for a long time, fine-tuning his plan, such as it was.

CHAPTER TWENTY-FIVE

On Saturday Calhoun guided a pair of brothers from Cleveland. One was a lawyer, and the other was a sports agent. Both were competent anglers, and Calhoun enjoyed their company, but all day he worried that whoever had hidden the aluminum attaché case under the floor in the boathouse would look into it and see that one of the vials was missing. He wished he could've left first thing in the morning, or even in the middle of the night, but he'd been scheduled for this guide trip today and didn't want to call attention to himself.

Sunday was his day off. He could be gone all day and nobody—except Robin, probably, and she couldn't be helped—would notice.

So Saturday evening after dinner, Calhoun went back to the cabin, snagged a Coke from his refrigerator, and took it out to the screen porch. He sat on one of the rockers to wait for the sun to go down. He'd make his move after it got dark.

Ralph knew something was up. Instead of sprawling on the floor and going to sleep, he sat beside Calhoun with his ears perked up.

Then Robin tapped on the door.

"Come on in," said Calhoun.

She came onto the porch, gave Ralph a quick pat, then took the rocker beside Calhoun. "So what's going on?" she said.

"Nothin' much."

"You're going somewhere," she said.

"What makes you think so?"

"A woman knows these things," she said. "You're leaving, aren't you?"

He shrugged.

"What's up, Stoney?"

"Tomorrow's my day off. Gotta take care of some business down in St. Cecelia. That's all."

"You coming back?"

"Sure," he said. "Why not?"

"Why don't I buy that?"

"I don't know," Calhoun said.

"Can't you tell me what you're up to?"

"I'm not up to anything," he said.

"Anything I can do to help?"

"Nope," he said. "I'm all set, thanks."

She folded her arms. "You're not going to tell me anything, are you?"

"Nothing to tell you."

"What I don't know can't hurt me, is that what you mean?"

"You're making something of nothing," Calhoun said.

"Ralph's going with you?"

He nodded. "Ralph goes everywhere with me. You know that."

Robin turned and looked at him. "You're not coming back, are you?"

"Sure I am. I told you that."

"Just my luck," she said. She stood up and went over to him where he was sitting in his rocker. She leaned down, put her arms around his neck, and pressed her forehead against his shoulder. Then she straightened up. "See you later, mister," she said softly.

"You going already?"

"I am, yes."

"What's your hurry?" he said. "You just got here."

"I hate saying good-bye," she said. "No sense of dragging it out." She stepped away from him. "Whatever you're up to, be careful, okay?"

"Okay," he said. "You, too."

Robin opened the screen door and stepped outside. Then she turned, looked back at Calhoun, and lifted her hand.

"See you later," he said.

"You think so?"

"Ayup."

"Promise?"

"Sure," said Calhoun. "I promise."

"Well, good." She smiled quickly, then turned and started down the path in the direction of the lodge.

Calhoun watched her go. He couldn't tell what she was thinking, but it was pretty clear that she didn't quite believe him. Somehow she sensed that he was up to something. Woman's intuition. Kate had it, and sometimes it was damned spooky.

Pretty soon Robin's shadow melted into the darkness, and he couldn't see her anymore. Night had fallen. It was time to get going.

He went into the cabin. He slipped on the dark windbreaker with the glass vial in its zippered pocket, strapped his sheathed hunting knife to his belt, and checked the batteries in his flashlight before shoving it into his pants pocket. He stuffed a handful of Milk-Bones into the other pants pocket along with his deputy badge, and he tucked his cell phone into his shirt pocket.

He'd worry about his fishing gear and his clothes another time.

Then he snapped his fingers at Ralph, who'd been following him around expectantly. "Let's go," he said, and the two of them went outside.

They followed the path toward the lodge but took the fork that led to the oversized garage behind it. When the building came into view in the gathering darkness, he stopped and studied the scene. No lights shone from the garage windows. No vehicles were parked outside. Nobody was standing around. The doors were shut. It appeared that the place was closed down for the night.

Calhoun told Ralph to heel, then he skirted along the edge of the dark woods until he stood next to the garage. He moved up to the outside wall and slid along until he came to a window. He peered inside. All was darkness.

He went around to the front. There were four double-sized doors, the kind that lifted up and slid back on steel runners. He bent over and tugged at one of the handles. The door creaked and groaned as if the moving parts needed oil, but he was able to raise it and slide it back on its tracks.

Parked right there facing the open doorway and ready to roll were two Loon Lake Range Rovers. Calhoun went into the garage. He flicked on his flashlight and shone it through the driver's-side window into the inside of one of the vehicles.

There were no keys dangling from the ignition.

What'd you expect? Calhoun thought. *How easy did you think it was gonna be?*

If he couldn't find the keys, he was out of luck. As far as he knew, with all of the training he'd had in his unremembered days as one of Mr. Brescia's resourceful operatives, he'd never been taught how to hot-wire a car.

He shone his flashlight around the inside walls of the garage, and its beam stopped on a rectangular metal lockbox mounted on the rear wall. He went to it and looked at it closely. It was locked, naturally.

So he panned his flashlight around some more until it stopped on a big steel toolbox standing open on the floor in the rear corner of the garage. He sifted through the jumble of automobile tools, found a sturdy foot-long screwdriver that he thought would do the job, and went back to the lockbox.

Jimmying it open with the screwdriver was easy.

Eight sets of keys hung from hooks inside the box. Each hook was numbered. Calhoun guessed that he'd opened the garage door on vehicles number one and two, so he plucked down the set of keys for vehicle one. When he went to the car and shoved the key into the Rover's door lock, it clicked open, and when he slid behind the wheel and tried the key in the ignition, the engine started without a sputter.

He held the door open and snapped his fingers at Ralph, who jumped in, climbed over Calhoun, and took his customary seat at shotgun.

Calhoun put the car into gear and pulled out of the garage. He left it running while he got out, went back, and closed the garage door. Whoever went into the garage first would notice the missing vehicle, of course, though depending on who it was, he might not realize the Rover had been stolen. Eventually, the scratched and dented lockbox would alert somebody to the fact that something had happened.

He hoped nobody noticed anything until tomorrow morning. By then he'd be long gone and hard to find.

In any case, there was no sense in advertising the larceny by leaving the garage door open.

He got back into the Rover, put it into gear, and followed the driveway by the pale light of the moonless night sky. He didn't know if headlights would be visible from the lodge, but he certainly wasn't going to take that chance.

The long driveway curved through the woods for about half a mile before it arrived at the lumber company road that led to St. Cecelia. Calhoun stopped there and got out of the car.

He moved all around the outside of the Rover, studying it in the beam of the flashlight. He shone the light around the back-seats and under the dashboard but didn't find what he was look-ing for. He opened the trunk, considered the spare tire well, and discarded it as too obvious.

Then he noticed how the taillight bulbs could be accessed from inside the trunk via snap-in plastic panels. He snapped one of them out. Perfect. There was just enough space behind the bulb. He unzipped his jacket pocket and took out the glass vial containing the yellowish powder. He wrapped it in his handker-chief to cushion it against bumps and stuffed it into the opening behind the driver's-side taillight. Then he snapped the plastic panel back into place.

A professional search of the car would eventually turn up the vial, he knew, but if you didn't know the vial was hidden in the car, would you look that carefully?

Maybe, maybe not. This was safer than keeping it in his pocket, at least.

He climbed back behind the wheel, turned on the head-lights, and went left onto the logging road, heading toward St. Cecelia and points south.

As he remembered from the day a week earlier when he drove down to St. Cecelia, the road was rutted and potholed and littered with big rocks. At night in the headlights it looked even more treacherous. Calhoun was bubbling with adrenaline, and he had to fight the urge to drive fast, to put distance between himself and the Loon Lake Lodge. The last thing he needed was a blown tire or a broken axle or a cracked oil pan.

So he crept along, picking his careful way around the sharp rocks and deep potholes, keeping his focus on the job of driving, and gradually he felt the tension begin to drain out of him. It left him relaxed but still keyed up and alert.

He reached into his pocket, found a Milk-Bone, and held it over to Ralph, who took it gently between his teeth.

"You're welcome," Calhoun said.

Ralph crunched the treat.

He guessed he'd put about five miles behind him, and he was feeling pretty good. His gas tank was full, and he aimed to drive all night. He wouldn't stop in St. Cecelia or Greenville or Skowhegan or Waterville, except maybe for a cup of coffee and to give Ralph a chance to pee on the bushes. He'd keep going for however long it took to get to Augusta. There he'd look up Ella Grimshaw. He knew he could trust her.

He slowed down when he came to a place where the narrow road dipped down to cross a brook. It was wet there, and he didn't want to get stuck. The road rose and curved to the left on the other side, and as he went up the grade and made the turn, Calhoun saw a red light shining in the darkness ahead of him. It took him a moment to realize that it was his headlights reflecting from the taillight of a vehicle that was stopped smack in the middle of the road in a place where the rutted old timber company road was barely one car width wide. This vehicle was blocking the way.

Calhoun pulled up behind the vehicle and saw that it was a heavy-duty GMC pickup truck. It appeared to be deserted. Most likely it had broken down and whoever was driving it had just left it there.

He stopped the Range Rover, put it in neutral, and pulled the hand brake, leaving the motor running and the headlights turned on. He sat there for a few minutes looking at the truck. He felt his adrenaline surging again. This was a problem.

When he opened the door and stepped outside, Ralph hopped out, too, and began exploring the roadside shrubbery.

Calhoun went up to the truck and shone his flashlight around the inside. Nobody was sleeping on the seat, and there were no keys in the ignition.

He walked all around the truck, trying to see if he could squeeze the Range Rover past it. A stand of thick-trunked pine trees barred the way on one side, but the other side, the left, looked passable. A screen of alder saplings mingled with some birch whips grew there. The ground looked kind of boggy, but it was flat. Calhoun guessed that the Range Rover could plow right over those saplings. If he put the Rover into four-wheel drive, he might avoid getting stuck in the mud.

Well, he didn't have many options. He had to get past the damn pickup truck.

He whistled to Ralph and went back to the Range Rover. Just as he put his hand on the door latch, something hard jammed into his kidneys.

CHAPTER TWENTY-SIX

"Put your hands on the roof of your vehicle," said a man's voice close to Calhoun's ear.

Calhoun obeyed. "You don't need to stick that gun into me," he said. "I wasn't aiming to steal your truck. I just want to get around it and continue on my way."

"Shut up," the man growled.

Calhoun recognized the voice. "Robert," he said. "Is that you? What the hell are you doing?"

Robert Dunlap was patting Calhoun down. He unsnapped the hunting knife out of its sheath and took the cell phone, the flashlight, the deputy badge, and the wallet from his pockets. "Hold on to these things, sweetheart, will you?" he said.

Then Calhoun realized that there was another person there. He recognized her clean, soapy smell. "Robin?" he said.

"I'm sorry, Stoney," she said.

"What've you got yourself into?"

"That's enough," said Robert. He jabbed his gun hard into Calhoun's lower back. "Where is it?"

"Where's what?"

"You know."

"Nope, I don't. You better tell me."

"It doesn't belong to you."

"You mean the Rover?" said Calhoun. "I was borrowing it. Didn't intend to keep it."

"Not the car, damn you."

"You better tell me what you want, then," Calhoun said. "Me, I was just hoping to visit one of the casinos in St. Cecelia tonight, play a few hands of Texas Hold 'Em, have a little fun. Tomorrow's my day off, you know."

"Don't bullshit me," said Robert. "If I have to shoot you, I will."

"Like you shot McNulty?"

"Give me that duct tape," Robert said to Robin. "Here, you hold the gun on him."

The gun barrel left Calhoun's kidneys, and then Robert Dunlap grabbed Calhoun's left wrist and pulled it around to his back, and that's when Ralph growled and Robert yelped and Calhoun spun around and smashed his right elbow into Robert's throat, an instinctive move, but one, Calhoun realized, that he'd been taught and had practiced until he could do it without thinking.

Robert was thrashing around on the ground gagging and gasping for breath. Ralph had his teeth sunk into the man's calf. Calhoun dropped onto Robert's chest with both knees and grabbed his throat. Blood pounded in Calhoun's brain. He felt Robert's fragile life fluttering in his hands.

Then the muzzle of a gun pressed against the back of his head.

"Get off him, Stoney," Robin said.

"I don't think so," he said. "This sonofabitch will kill me, and that's unacceptable."

"Then I'll do it," she said. "I'll kill you."

"Aw, come on," he said. "You won't do that."

"You don't know me," said Robin. "I'm not such a nice girl."

"I never accused you of being nice," he said, "but you ain't a killer."

"You might be surprised."

"You're not going to kill me," said Calhoun.

"Just let go of him. And tell Ralph to let go."

"Let him go," Calhoun said to Ralph. He lifted his hands away from Robert's throat.

"Get off him. He can hardly breathe."

"Ralph," said Calhoun quietly.

Ralph came flying through the darkness, a brown-and-white flash, and then Robin screamed.

Calhoun got off Robert's chest. Robin and Ralph looked like they were wrestling on the ground. Robin was grunting and cursing. Ralph was growling deep in his chest. Calhoun looked around, and in the indirect light from the Rover's headlights, he found the revolver where Robin had dropped it. He picked it up and pointed it at her. "Okay," he said to Ralph, who had latched on to Robin's forearm. "Let her go now."

Ralph released his hold on Robin and sat down. He seemed to be glaring at her.

"What kind of a dog *is* this?" she said. "He always seemed so . . ."

"Gentle?" said Calhoun.

"I guess so." She was holding her right wrist in her left hand. Calhoun saw some blood ooze through her fingers.

"Well, you seemed gentle, too," he said.

Robin laughed quickly. "You never know, huh?"

"I've trained him," Calhoun said. "Plus, unlike you, he's loyal as hell. You mess with me, you've got to deal with Ralph."

He spotted his flashlight on the ground. He picked it up, shone it around, and found his hunting knife and his cell phone, his wallet and his badge.

"Where's that duct tape?" he said to Robin.

"I gave it to him."

He shone the flashlight on Robert. He was holding his throat in one hand. His breath came in short raspy gasps. He was still clutching the roll of dut tape in his other hand.

Calhoun took the tape and handed it to Robin. "Tape his wrists together."

"Why should I?" she said. "You're not going to shoot me. Are you, Stoney?"

"Probably not," he said, "but I wouldn't mind shooting him. I figure he's the one who killed your friend Elaine and blew up Curtis Swenson in the Cessna. He doesn't deserve to live. You I've still got some hope for. If you can't tape him up, I guess I'll have to shoot him, and if I do, it'll be on you. That what you want?"

She smiled. "I don't believe you—but okay, I'll do it. I don't want you to be mad at me."

"I'd say it's a little late to think about that." To Robert he said, "Sit up and hold out your hands."

Calhoun held the gun on them while Robin taped Robert's wrists together halfway up to his elbows. Then he patted Robert's pockets, took out the keys to the truck, and slipped them into his own pocket.

He opened the passenger door of the truck and folded it forward. "Stick him in there," Calhoun said to Robin.

She helped Robert lurch to his feet, steered him around to the open door, and stuffed him into the cramped backseat.

"Now tape up his ankles," Calhoun said.

Robin wrapped duct tape around Robert's ankles all the way up to his knees.

"Give me the tape," Calhoun said. "Your turn." He taped Robin's wrists together. Her right forearm was bleeding a little from Ralph's teeth. It probably hurt, though she wasn't complaining. He didn't feel sorry for her. Ralph wasn't rabid. She'd live.

He told her to climb into the front seat, and after she did that, he taped her ankles together. He checked the tape jobs on both Robin and Robert. Neither of them was going anywhere.

Calhoun told Ralph to jump in back with Robert. "Don't hesitate to bite somebody," he told the dog.

He went back to the Range Rover. He opened the trunk, pried off the snap-on plastic cover over the taillight, and took out the vial wrapped in his handkerchief. He stuck it in his jacket pocket and zipped it up.

He left the keys in the Rover's ignition. Then he went back to the truck and climbed in behind the wheel. "Ready to go, kids?" he said.

Neither Robert nor Robin answered.

Calhoun started up the truck, turned on the headlights, and headed for St. Cecelia.

In the backseat behind him, Robert groaned every time they hit a bump in the road. Robin, riding shotgun beside Calhoun, kept her face turned away from him.

"I don't want to think about the possibility that you betrayed your friend Elaine like you betrayed me," Calhoun said to her.

"She wasn't really my friend," said Robin.

"So all that crying when she got killed . . . ?"

"Oh, I was sad," she said, "but I understood that it had to be done. I guess the tears were mostly for your sake, Stoney. Robert was suspicious of you right off, the way you kept asking about McNulty."

"So he told you to seduce me, huh?"

"I tried," she said.

"Yes, you did," he said. "Good try, too."

She laughed softly.

"I showed you my badge," he said. "I confided in you. I trusted you."

"Well, I'm sorry," she said. "How was I supposed to know I was going to like you?"

"Tell me about Curtis Swenson," he said.

"Just shut up," said Robert from the backseat. "Don't talk to him."

"Ah, he's gonna find out sooner or later." She turned to Calhoun. "Robert was over in Afghanistan," she said. "He learned how to make those roadside bombs. What do you call them?"

"IEDs," Calhoun said. "Improvised explosive devices."

"That's it," she said. "So he made one of them for the Cessna. You were supposed to be on that plane. Two birds with one stone."

"Me and Curtis," Calhoun said. "Why Curtis?"

"Robert stopped trusting him," she said.

"And me?"

"He thought you were too curious about things. He thought you had some other agenda besides guiding. He didn't trust you from the beginning. He knew you were a deputy sheriff. Robert thought—"

"Will you shut the hell up?" said Robert.

"He's right," Robin said. "Time for me to shut up."

"The more you tell me," Calhoun said, "the easier it'll go for you."

"No," she said, "Robert's right. I'm not going to say anything else. Robert can tell you whatever he wants, but I'm done."

"Suit yourself," Calhoun said. He hesitated. "There is one thing, though."

"What?" she said.

"Why?"

"Why what?"

"Why you? What do you get out of it?"

She shook her head. "You'd never understand."

He shrugged. "You might be surprised. I understand greed."

"It wasn't greed," she said. "I had to get away from Madrid, Maine. I deserve more than that."

"There are better ways," Calhoun said.

"There are plenty of slow ways," she said, "and there are hard ways, and none of them are dependable."

"And Robert showed you a fast, easy way."

Robin chuckled softly. "I thought so."

"Well," said Calhoun, "it looks like you're going to get your wish."

She laughed softly.

"So what about him?" he said.

"Robert?" Robin hesitated. "He's like me. He can't stand it around here. He wants more for himself. He feels like he's getting sucked into his family business. This was his way out of here."

"Smuggling illegal drugs?"

She said nothing.

"Working for terrorists, huh?"

"I'm not saying anything else," said Robin. "I'm just sorry it ended up like this."

"I bet you are," he said.

The rest of the slow drive to St. Cecelia passed in silence. As they approached the town, the casinos and cafés alongside the road shone bright neon lights, and their parking lots were crowded. Calhoun remembered that it was Saturday evening. He guessed folks came from all the nearby townships for Saturday night fun in good old St. Cecelia.

He drove through town and pulled into the lot beside the police station, which he expected would be a busy place on a Saturday evening. He told Ralph to stand guard over their two prisoners and went inside.

A female officer was sitting at the front desk inside the door. She had a phone tucked against her shoulder, and she was talking and typing on her computer at the same time. She had black hair, cut short and flecked with gray. Calhoun guessed she was somewhere in her forties. The nameplate on her shirt pocket said SGT. C. BROXTON. She looked up at him, narrowed her eyes at him for a moment as if she were memorizing his face, then returned her attention to her monitor.

After a couple of minutes, Sergeant Broxton said, "Okay, ayuh, thanks," and hung up the phone. She sighed and frowned at her computer screen, then looked up at Calhoun. "So what can I do for you?" she said.

He fished his deputy's badge from his pocket and showed it to her. "My name's Calhoun," he said. "Cumberland County. I got two prisoners outside I'd like to turn over to you."

"What'd they do?"

"Killed two people," he said. "Or one of them did, anyway. You probably heard about what's been going on up at Loon Lake."

Sergeant Broxton nodded. "Woman got shot in her bed," she said. She hesitated. "Oh, and that float plane that exploded, pilot killed. That was a murder, too?"

He nodded.

"Cumberland County, huh? You're a long ways from home."

"That's why I'm turning these people over to you," he said. "They both might need some medical attention. Oh, and there's an abandoned vehicle in the middle of the road fifteen or twenty miles north towards Loon Lake. Keys're in the ignition. It's blocking the way and needs to be moved. It belongs to the lodge."

Amusement sparked from her eyes. Calhoun noticed that they were dark brown, almost black. "You got any more instructions for me tonight, Deputy Calhoun?" she said.

"No," he said, "I guess that's about it for now."

"Well," she said, "I know Chief Baldwin will want to talk with you, so I'd appreciate it if you'd sit tight here while I radio him. Those prisoners of yours. Where are they?"

"In a GMC truck right outside there in your lot," he said. "They're trussed up quite thoroughly with duct tape. My dog's in there with them. I'm going to go let him out now. I'll stick around for the chief."

Calhoun went outside and opened the driver's door to the truck. "Come on," he said to Ralph, who hopped out and went looking for bushes. "You folks just sit tight," he said to Robert and Robin. "I wangled you an invitation for a night or two at this establishment. Free room and board."

He shut the truck door, looked around, and spotted a boulder that he could sit on. Ralph was sniffing around some shrubbery against the side of the building. Calhoun whistled, and when Ralph came over, Calhoun gave him a Milk-Bone.

He watched as two cops came out of the building. They went to the truck and opened both doors, and a few minutes later they were helping Robin and Robert hobble back inside.

Then he fished his cell phone from his pocket. From his wallet he took the card that Mr. Brescia had given him. He dialed one of the phone numbers.

It rang twice, and then Mr. Brescia's growly voice said, "Mr. Calhoun."

"Yes, sir," said Calhoun. "It's me."

"You have a report for me."

"Haven't got it all yet," Calhoun said, "but I've got the man who shot McNulty, name of Robert Dunlap, plus one of his accomplices, who may not have committed any actual crimes beyond stupidity. They're both here in the St. Cecelia jail. Dunlap killed two other people this past week, and he tried to kill me. He's been smuggling something in from Canada on a float plane. Don't know what it is for sure. My best guess is botulinum toxin. Turns out botulism's what killed McNulty. I've got a sample of it. Thought I'd hand it over to Dr. Grimshaw. She's the chief medical examiner for the state of Maine."

"I know who Grimshaw is," said Mr. Brescia. He was silent for a minute. Then he said, "No. You hang on to that vial. The fewer locals we involve in any of this, the better."

"How do I get it to you?"

"Don't worry about that," said Mr. Brescia. "I'll take care of it."

"The chief here, Chief Baldwin, he wants to interrogate me," Calhoun said. "How do you want me to handle him?"

"Tell him nothing."

"That might not be so easy," said Calhoun. "I mean, I'm turning over two murder suspects to him."

"Use your judgment," Mr. Brescia said. "Be creative. Improvise. You're a resourceful man, Mr. Calhoun, and you've been well and thoroughly trained. If you needed me to tell you what you should do, you wouldn't be working for me in the first place."

"Okay," Calhoun said.

"You know better than to tell those officers what you are and what you do."

"That's easy," said Calhoun, "inasmuch as I don't know what the hell I am."

"Sure you do," Mr. Brescia said.

Calhoun found himself nodding. "Yes," he said. "Now that you mention it, I suppose I do."

CHAPTER TWENTY-SEVEN

It took Calhoun about three and a half hours to drive the narrow winding roads through the middle of the night from St. Cecelia to the parking area beside Moosehead Lake in Greenville where he'd left his truck the day Curtis Swenson flew him to Loon Lake. He abandoned Robert Dunlap's truck there, unlocked with the keys on the floor, and he and Ralph climbed into Calhoun's own Ford pickup and continued on to his house in the woods in Dublin.

It was a few minutes after five in the morning when he turned onto his long rutted driveway. The stars had all winked out, and the black springtime sky was just beginning to fade to silver. Through the open truck windows, the woods smelled of dew and pine pitch, and they rocked with early-morning birdsong.

When he started down the long slope to the clearing in front of his house, he saw the Audi sedan parked there. He shook his head. He'd missed the signs—the bent-over grass, the tire treads in the soft dirt, the leaves knocked off the bushes that grew close to the driveway. He was tired after driving all night and eager to be home, but that was no excuse. He couldn't afford to get careless.

He parked beside the Man in the Suit's Audi, and he and Ralph got out and climbed the steps onto his deck.

The Man in the Suit was sitting there in one of the Adirondack chairs. It was the first time Calhoun could remember that the man wasn't dressed in a suit and tie. Now he was wearing blue jeans and work boots and a green flannel shirt with a gray hooded sweatshirt that looked too big for him, and he was holding a large foam cup in both hands. He looked cold.

"I'm gonna put on some coffee," Calhoun said. "Get you a refill."

"Thanks, Stoney."

"Then I'm gonna kick you to hell off my property. I've been driving all night, and I'm tired."

"What we've got to do won't take long," said the Man in the Suit.

Calhoun went inside, and when he went to pour the water for the electric coffeepot, he saw that his peace lily in its big clay pot was sitting in the sink, not in its regular place on the floor beside the sliding door that led out to the deck. Kate had given him the plant a couple of years earlier after they'd had an argument—her way of trying to put the issues, which now he couldn't even remember, into perspective. He'd repotted it twice since she gave it to him. Now it had a root-ball the size of a soccer ball, and it put out a flurry of those delicate white flowers every couple of months to remind him how much he cherished a peaceful relationship with Kate.

He felt a pang of guilt. When he was preparing to go to Loon Lake, it had never occurred to him that the lily surely would die if he left it unwatered for six weeks.

Kate had come while he was gone and watered the plant. It

couldn't have been anybody else. Maybe she wasn't speaking to him, but she'd kept the symbol of peace between them alive, and that made him happy.

He went into the bathroom, peed, washed his hands, splashed water on his face, combed his fingers through his hair. He hoped the Man in the Suit didn't intend to debrief him. If he did, Calhoun decided, he just wouldn't cooperate. Not tonight. He was too tired, and his mind was still too jumbled. Before he said anything, he had to decide what he was willing to share, and that would require some clear, careful thought.

When he got back to the kitchen, the coffee was ready. He poured two mugs full and took them out to the deck. He put one on the arm of the Man in the Suit's chair, then sat down and sipped from his own mug.

"Mr. Brescia sent you, huh?" said Calhoun.

"I came to retrieve what you brought with you," the Man in the Suit said. "I've been sitting out here for over an hour."

Calhoun nodded. "Good thing it wasn't raining."

"Well," the Man in the Suit said, "I got to see the sky grow light, and I heard the birds wake up, so it wasn't a total waste. Kind of chilly, though." He looked at Calhoun. "Let's have it, Stoney. I'm overdue for a hot shower and some sleep."

Calhoun unzipped the pocket of his windbreaker, took out the vial wrapped in his handkerchief, and handed it, including the handkerchief, to the Man in the Suit.

The man unfolded the handkerchief. He held the vial up to the brightening sky. "What's in it?" he said.

"It needs to be tested," said Calhoun, "but I'm going to suggest you keep it corked up tight. My guess is McNulty, or maybe the girl who was with him, got careless with this stuff."

The Man in the Suit turned and looked at Calhoun. "They

died from botulism poisoning. You think this is botulinum toxin?"

Calhoun shrugged.

"That is absolutely lethal stuff," said the man. "The most poisonous substance on earth."

"So I understand."

"Jesus." The man was shaking his head. "And you were carrying this little glass vial around in your pocket?"

"I didn't seem to have too many other options," Calhoun said. "Now you've got it, and that's a relief."

"Where'd it come from?"

Calhoun shook his head. "I don't feel like talking about any of that. Not now."

"You're going to have to talk about it," the Man in the Suit said.

"Not tonight."

The Man in the Suit shrugged. "I'm not going to push you." He drained his coffee mug, then stood up. He held the vial in his hand. "This is what I came for. Now I'll let you go to bed." He wrapped the vial up again in Calhoun's handkerchief and slipped it into his shirt pocket. Then he held out his hand. "This was good work, Stoney. Thanks for doing it."

Calhoun shook the man's hand. "It's not like I had much of a choice," he said.

The Man in the Suit started down the steps. He stopped halfway down and turned back to look at Calhoun. "I almost forgot," he said. "I've got a message for you."

"A message," said Calhoun.

"A message from Mr. Brescia," said the man. "He asked me to remind you of the importance of absolute secrecy. You must tell no one anything about where you've been, what you've been doing, and what you've learned." He hesitated. "The conse-

quences of disobedience would be dire, as I'm sure I don't need
to remind you."

"I get it," Calhoun said.

When he woke up, the sun was streaming in through his windows, and Ralph was sitting on the floor looking at him.

"What?" said Calhoun.

Ralph just kept staring at him.

"Oh," said Calhoun. "Breakfast."

He got up, dumped some dog food into Ralph's bowl, and
put the bowl on the floor. Then he dropped a handful of raisins
on a bowl of Wheaties, poured a glass of orange juice, and took
them out onto the deck. He sat in a chair with the late-spring
midday sun blasting down on him and ate his breakfast.

Loon Lake seemed far away. Robin and Robert and all the
others—Marty and June Dunlap, Harry and Jack Vandercamp,
Franklin Redbird and the other guides, Kim and Mush, Ben
and Peter, old Leon, and the dead people, Elaine Hoffman and
Curtis Swenson—they were abstractions to him now, realistic
but not quite real, like characters in a novel he'd been reading.

He'd done his job. Now it was all behind him.

When they finished their breakfasts, Calhoun and Ralph
climbed into his truck and headed for Portland.

He pulled into the lot beside the shop a little after one o'clock
on this pretty Sunday afternoon in the first week of June. Kate's
old Toyota truck sat in its usual spot in the far corner, and there
were half a dozen other vehicles parked there.

The bell dinged over the door when he pushed it open.
Ralph squeezed in ahead of Calhoun and trotted over to where
Kate had her elbows on the counter and her chin in her hands,
listening to two white-haired guys who appeared to be telling

her a long fish story by way of flirting with her. When she saw
Ralph coming toward her, she smiled and knelt down so he
could lick her face.

Then she looked over toward the door, where Calhoun was
standing. She gave him a quick half-smile that he didn't know
how to interpret, rubbed Ralph's ears, stood up, and returned
her attention to the two white-haired guys.

Calhoun wandered toward the back of the shop. Adrian
was at the fly bins talking with a bald man and a young blond
woman who might have been father and daughter. When he
saw Calhoun, Adrian jerked his chin at him.

He nodded to Adrian and went into his office. His desktop
had been cleaned off. He supposed Adrian had been using his
phone and computer while he was gone.

He sat in his chair and checked the phone for messages.

There were none.

Ralph came wandering in. He went over to his dog bed in
the corner, turned around three or four times, lay down on it,
sighed, and closed his eyes.

A minute later Kate came in. She sat on the wooden arm-
chair across from his desk and looked at him. She was neither
smiling nor frowning. Calhoun couldn't read her expression.

"You're back?" she said. She was, if anything, even prettier
than he'd remembered.

"Ayup."

"For good, I mean?"

"Yes, ma'am."

She nodded. "I'm glad."

"Thanks for taking care of my plant," Calhoun said. "I
guess it would've died of thirst otherwise."

"Your peace lily," she said. "I didn't want it to die."

Calhoun smiled. "You're talking to me. Did you notice?"

"I know," she said. "I hadn't decided whether I would or not. Then you showed up, and not talking to you didn't make sense anymore."

"Did it ever make sense?"

"When I figured you might never be coming back?" She nodded. "When I guessed you were off doing something dangerous that could get you killed?" She nodded again. "Bet your ass it made sense."

"Well," he said, "here I am. I didn't get killed."

"You gonna tell me about it?"

He shook his head.

She blew out a quick, exasperated breath. "Well, Jesus Christ, anyway."

"I can't, honey."

"You can't tell me where you've been, even?"

"No. I can't tell you anything."

"I don't get it. How come?"

"Well," he said, "I can't tell you that, either."

"But I'm supposed to smile and welcome you home, right?"

"Sure," he said.

Kate rolled her eyes.

"Come on, honey," said Calhoun. "Don't do this. Let's not do this anymore."

She glared at him for a long moment. Then she shrugged. "Yeah, I guess you're right. If it's something you can't talk about, the hell with it." She smiled. "I'm happy to see you, Stoney. I am. I'm glad you're back. I missed you."

"I missed you, too."

She stood up, went around the desk, pushed his chair back on its rollers, and sat sideways on Calhoun's lap. She draped her left arm around his neck and slid her right hand under his shirt. She rubbed his chest and kissed the side of his throat and pressed her breast against his arm. "We've got to get caught up," she murmured. "Tonight, steaks and bourbon, your place?"

"I'll have to check my schedule," Calhoun said, "but I think I can squeeze you in."

Calhoun met Mr. Brescia at the coffee shop near the Stroudwater Inn on a Saturday morning three weeks after he'd come home from Loon Lake. Mr. Brescia was sitting at an outside table sipping from a mug of coffee and reading a newspaper. An attaché case sat on the brick patio floor beside his chair.

When Calhoun sat down across from him, Mr. Brescia looked up, nodded, folded his newspaper, and put it on the table by his elbow. Then he held his hand across the table. "Mr. Calhoun," he said. "Thanks for coming."

Calhoun took his hand. "I don't figure I had much choice."

"Well, of course you didn't." Mr. Brescia didn't smile. Calhoun guessed he didn't smile very much. "I thought you deserved to hear the epilogue to your story," Mr. Brescia said.

Calhoun shrugged. "I don't care. It's ancient history."

A waitress appeared. Calhoun asked for coffee. Mr. Brescia said he was all set, thank you.

After the waitress left, Mr. Brescia said, "I thought you might like to know that we decided to give the girl, Robin, immunity in exchange for her testimony."

Calhoun shrugged.

"She said she tried to seduce you," said Mr. Brescia. "She said she was unsuccessful."

Calhoun said nothing.

"Robert Dunlap was paying Curtis Swenson, the lodge's float plane pilot, to smuggle cases containing vials of botulinum toxin over the border from Canada. As you know, we've managed to button up the highway crossings between our two countries pretty tight. But there are thousands of miles of unprotected border where you can swim a river or drive an ATV or a snowmobile or, in this case, fly a float plane back and forth across the border without being detected. Enemies of our country have begun to exploit this for their purposes. McNulty was onto it before he died."

"You saying Robert Dunlap was some kind of terrorist?" said Calhoun.

"Not him," said Mr. Brescia. "He was just an entrepreneur making what must've seemed like easy money, as were the pilot and the girl and a taxidermist named Soria in Pittsburgh. Dunlap hid those vials in the containers of dead fish packed in ice that they flew down to the UPS office in Greenville, and from there were shipped to Mr. Soria in Pittsburgh. At the end of the line, though, yes, there were terrorists who aimed to kill thousands—maybe millions—of Americans with that poison."

"Did you catch the terrorists?"

Mr. Brescia shrugged. "We got some of them. We've got others in our sights. Once we convinced Dunlap and Soria of how serious we were, they were most cooperative. Your girl, Robin, of course, was a big help."

"She ain't my girl."

Mr. Brescia almost smiled.

Calhoun said, "Robert Dunlap murdered Elaine Hoffman and Curtis Swenson, too, don't forget."

Mr. Brescia waved the back of his hand at Calhoun as if he were brushing away a couple of murders.

"I figure Swenson got greedy," said Calhoun. "Did Robert tell you why he had to kill Elaine?"

"He guessed she had figured out what he was up to," Brescia said, "and he was worried that she'd tell you."

"Dunlap killed her right after I got there," Calhoun said. "He saw through me that quick?"

"He didn't exactly see through you," Brescia said. "But the McNulty thing rattled him, and he was uneasy about you. He prowled through your room first chance he had, and he saw your sheriff's badge and your .22 pistol. So he took the pistol, killed the Hoffman woman with it, and planted it in the Indian's room."

"Franklin Redbird is his name," Calhoun said.

"Sure," said Brescia. "Redbird."

"You're going to prosecute Dunlap for those murders, aren't you?" Calhoun said. "I mean, it ain't just about smuggling that poison."

"Our job is to prevent terrorist events, Mr. Calhoun. You do understand that."

"I don't know what your job is."

Mr. Brescia shrugged as if it was of no importance what Calhoun knew.

"You saying you bargained away the murders?" Calhoun said.

"I'm saying," Mr. Brescia said slowly, "that it's none of your business what we do. You did your job, and you did it competently, and that enabled us, in turn, to do our jobs, and you should trust me when I tell you, we are very good at our jobs."

The waitress came with Calhoun's coffee. He waited for her to leave, then said, "A couple things still bother me."

Mr. Brescia lifted his hand, turned up his palm, and let if fall, which Calhoun took to mean, *You can ask, but I might not answer.*

"McNulty and the girl," Calhoun said. "They died of botulism poisoning. They must've inhaled it, to die so fast. Right?"

Brescia nodded. "That's right."

"How'd it happen?"

"We surmise," said Mr. Brescia, "that McNulty or the girl, Millie Gautier, one of them—most likely the girl, because McNulty would've known better—uncapped the vial that he'd taken. Robert Dunlap told us that when he found the vial missing and McNulty gone, he tracked down McNulty, and when he caught up with him, he and the girl were parked in their car, already dead."

"So Dunlap retrieved the vial," Calhoun said, "and put bullets into their dead bodies."

Brescia nodded. "To make it look like a suicide and a murder. To make it obvious. Because he didn't want anyone to know they died from botulism poisoning."

"The ME solved that one."

"Yes," said Mr. Brescia. "To Dunlap's credit, though, it did confuse things. Until you went up there and got it all figured out."

"I didn't figure everything out, by a long shot."

"Speaking of a long shot . . ." Mr. Brescia reached down and took something from his attaché case. It was wrapped in a soft chamois cloth. He put it on the table and pushed it at Calhoun.

Calhoun unfolded the cloth. It was his Colt Woodsman .22 pistol. It looked like it had been cleaned and oiled. "Thank you," he said to Mr. Brescia.

"It's from the sheriff up there. He said to tell you hello."

Calhoun nodded. "So now it's over."

"Oh," said Mr. Brescia, "It's never over."

"But you're done with me, right?"

For the first time, Calhoun thought he saw the flicker of a smile in the man's dark eyes. "We're done with you for now, Mr. Calhoun," Mr. Brescia said. "For now, anyway."